The Love of Gods

Tarrant Smith

This book, and all the books within the Legends of the Pale Series, are a work of fiction. The characters, incidents, and dialogue are drawn from the author's imagination and are not to be construed as real. Any resemblance to actual events or persons, living or dead, is entirely coincidental.

Please do not participate in or encourage piracy of copyrighted materials in violation of the author's rights. Purchase only authorized material.

Copy Editor: April Wells-Hayes
Cover Design: Tarrant Smith

Copyright © 2019 Tarrant Smith
All rights reserved. ISBN 978109612786
www.tarrantsmith.com

For my husband

Cast of Characters

Lugos is a god who over the centuries has been known by many names. In Ireland, he is known as Llew or Lugh (pronounced Lou). In the Mediterranean, he is Apollo. In the far North, he is Thor. To his young employee, **Griffin**, he is Agent Lugh Hart. His most used titles include Light Bringer and God Killer.

Keely Ann Lee is a sassy Southern bartender who works at the Witches Whistle in Salem, Georgia. Everyone agrees she has the worst taste in men, and that probably should include her nearest neighbor Lugh Grant.

Rhiannon is a goddess of sovereignty and the horse. She is the acknowledged leader for a supernatural community known as the Pale. Lugos owes her a debt and so he finds himself occasionally aiding her in settling problems within the Pale.

Angus is a god of beauty; known sarcastically as Angus the Pretty. His current occupation is that of model. He and Bride are siblings.

Bride is a goddess of home and hearth; known sarcastically as the Saint because she was the only pagan god canonized by the new faith. Her newest obsession is all things Martha Stewart.

Murmur is a demon of the clan Abraxas, bound in serves to Lugos for all eternity.

Zee is an aging demigoddess who owns far too many cats and likes to bake.

Seraphine is also known as Elizabeth Dunbar. She is both a high-ranking witch and a shifter. It is her death that Rhiannon instructs Lugos to investigate.

Talon is Seraphine's brother and is the new leader of the United Shifter League. Like his sister, he is also a witch and a shifter.

Ken Larkin is a close friend of Talon and Seraphine. He works for Talon at Triton Security Corporation which is a front for the United Shifter League.

Cutter Fleming is an aging shifter who has given up his rambling ways to run a bar in Salem, Georgia, named the Witches Whistle.

Alex Blaylock is a shifter who was Seraphine's familiar and probably her lover as well.

Bo Prideaux is a cocky shifter who works for Ken Larkin.

Shea is a shifter and analyst for Triton Security Corporation.

Cassie is a middle-aged priestess for the Sacred Grove Coven of witches located just outside Murray Kentucky.

Jewel and Josie are twins and witches in training who recently joined the Sacred Grove Coven despite Seraphine's objections.

Harmony, Fawn, and **Cygnet** are young witches with various talents who are current members of the Sacred Grove Coven.

Officer Carson Pratt is a Murray police officer and a shifter whose small farm and family border the Sacred Grove Coven's land.

Blye Pratt is a shifter and Carson's wife.

Blake Pratt is a shifter and Carson's younger brother.

Old Man Grady is a shifter and Carson and Blake's surly father.

The Pale is a collection of supernatural communities that live on the fringes of modern society. The few earthbound gods who have remained in this realm acknowledge Rhiannon as its leader. The communities include the scheming witches who adored Lugos's estranged mother, the power-struggling shifters, the temperamental dragonkin, the elusive but decidedly dangerous fae, the deeply misunderstood demon clans, the cursed werewolf packs, and the occasional pissed off demi-god with parent issues all their own.

Prologue

The truth can be hidden. It can be denied and never spoken of again. But just as belief has never needed truth in order to inspire, truth has never required belief in order to exist. It is this very chasm that protects an ancient race of cosmic beings we once called gods.

Wednesday

Chapter 1

Dismissed as a traitor to his race, Lugos preferred the company of modern man to that of his own kind. His reluctance to remain in contact with his kin was why he had ignored Rhiannon's call the previous evening, but the Celtic goddess was persistent when she wanted something. So when he received two texts the following morning within fifteen minutes of each other, Lugos reached for his cell phone before she had a chance to send him another. Or worse yet, pop in on him unannounced.

He scanned the stark messages on the illuminated screen, and his stomach knotted. His jaw clenched as he thumbed a terse reply.

"Is everythin' all right, Lugh?"

He shoved the device back into his jeans pocket and forced a smile for the woman beside him.

"Bad news. Family, I'd wager." Her tone was just the right balance of sympathy without pity.

Keely's guess was dangerously close to the mark. She was entirely too intuitive for his own good. Lugos opted for a very male, noncommittal grunt.

"Lugh."

Lugos easily registered the impatience she infused into the

one word. He leaned back under the hood to feel along the seals and hoses leading to and from the radiator. "I'm fairly sure you're going to have to do more to the radiator than a cheap patch this time," he told her, hoping against hope that the car's problems would be enough to distract her from any more questions about Rhiannon's text.

It had never mattered what physical form her soul took or what circumstances had thrown them together; he unfailingly found her, recognized her. His soul simply craved her soul. He would always be drawn to her light. It was that very light that anchored him, bound him to all humanity. That was her role. Without her influence, without her warm light, Lugos would have long since become numb to all but his own selfish needs, like the rest of his kin. Even after all this time, after being the cause of her death and suffering her loss time and time again, Lugos had yet to find the strength of will or discipline to stay away from her.

He had, however, managed—at least so far, this time—to allow Keely the freedom to live a relatively normal mortal existence free of knowledge of the Pale and the dangers that being in his world entailed. It had not been easy on him. Currently she was between bad boyfriends, and because of that situation, Lugos found that he could breathe again. Each morning was a gift, to wake up knowing that no man had hurt her or used her. None of them had the need to love her, cherish her as Lugos did. None ever would. But Lugos had hoped that if he gave it enough time, if he stood by long enough, that someone mortal might come along who was worthy of her.

In this lifetime, she was a brunette and, as fate would have it, his nearest neighbor. Five years ago, they'd met by happenstance over a car and her ongoing boyfriend troubles. Her soul had been apart from his for nearly two centuries, and Lugos had begun to fear that the apathy of his kind had finally taken root in his soul. But while driving home one night, Lugos had spotted the '69 Mustang parked in Keely's drive. "Best Offer" had been angrily drawn in soap across the Boss 302's back windshield. Intrigued for the first time in a long while, he had stomped on the Audi's brakes. After introducing himself as Lugh Hart to the twenty-something brunette who'd answered the door of the rundown double-wide, he'd inquired about the price of the car.

With her hands planted firmly on her hips, Keely had surprised him by saying, "I'll take whatever you've got in your wallet."

He was amused and asked the determined Keely, "Is it yours to sell?"

"Sure as hell is! Smartest damn thing I done since hookin' up with Carlos was puttin' that raggedy car in my name and not his lazy ass's." Keely's eyes had glittered with both laughter and satisfaction, a wicked smile teasing the corners of her lips.

Lugos's heart had slammed painfully inside his chest as recognition struck him hard. And just that quickly, the world, his world, seemed to suddenly right itself.

With little prompting, Keely had gone on to confess that she'd kicked Carlos, her most recent mistake, out of the rented trailer for cheatin' on her. It was then that Carlos had made the fatal error of hitting Keely—not once but twice, leaving behind a bruised eye and a split upper lip before storming out. Keely had prudently filed a restraining order against Carlos and was now selling all of the man's possessions. This included his pride and joy, to which she did indeed hold title.

"It needs tunin' a mite. But it runs," she'd told him, pointing at the car and waving the pink slip in her hand like a bullfighter's red cape.

When he'd least expected it, she'd come back into his life. Lugos had grinned to himself while running his palm over the faded, Acapulco Blue fender to disguise the joy and relief that had set his heart racing. The car was an excuse; he'd known it at the time. It would take money to rebuild it, and judging by the boyfriend's attempts at restoring the car's interior, it was money Carlos didn't have. What was also clear to Lugos was that the fist-wielding Carlos loved this automobile and would greatly suffer its loss. After glancing up at Keely's battered face again, Lugos had also decided it was the first of many punishments he'd inflict on the mortal.

"I'm good with my hands. Tuning the engine won't be a problem," he'd told her. Reaching for his wallet, he'd then fished out what money he had and counted it before handing her $1,573.00. Lugos knew that it was more cash than she was used to seeing. The discrepancy between his financial circumstances and hers had given him a twinge of guilt. Had her existence in this world been the real reason he'd relocated from Europe to tiny Salem, Georgia? Was he so far gone that he'd felt her need and yet not known it for what it was?

Ignoring her stunned expression, he'd then told her, "Make out a bill of sale with the car's VIN number for that amount. That should piss off your ex. If you'll follow me to my house and park the car in the garage, I'll give you another ten thousand in cash for your trouble."

A tremendous grin had appeared on Keely's face before suspicion had crept in. "You're not messin' with me, are ya?"

"No, Keely. The car will be worth much more once I've restored it. We're doing each other a favor."

She'd liked that idea. Fairness and justice had always been important to her. It was the one scale by which she measured everything, no matter the lifetime he'd found her in. Thrusting her hand out toward him, palm open, she'd declared, "Deal!"

Lugos had then clasped her hand to seal the bargain and perhaps both their fates. It had been in that moment, in that touch of flesh on flesh, that he'd known it wasn't just wishful thinking on his part. She had come to him again when he had been ready to quit his fight, to withdraw completely from the world, from all he'd worked toward. He was tired of the emptiness of time, tired of fighting for the betterment of humanity, and exhausted by the never-ending feud with his kin.

But because her bright spirit was in his life once more, everything felt new again.

Thus far, Lugos had been careful to keep her at arm's length, satisfied for now that her soul was near. But fate and his own heart were a hard combination to fight. She would be drawn to him as well but would not understand the reasons why. Though he'd tried hard over the last five years not to encourage Keely, she tended to stop by his cabin on a regular basis these days, usually with something for him to fix. Today the problem was with her late-model Land Rover. It was overheating, something it often did in the Georgia summer heat.

"How much is it gonna cost me this time, Lugh?"

Lugos didn't have to see Keely's face to read the worry behind the inquiry. "Not much," he boldly lied while inspecting the engine. Rover parts were expensive, and his Keely had an independent streak that wasn't always in her best interests. He'd quote her an amount she could afford and then pay the majority of the cost without her knowing. That way he could satisfy the needs of both of them: his need to take care of her, and her need to believe that she was self-sufficient.

"I'll see if I can get a used part. Until it comes in, you can drive the Mustang," he said, stepping back from under the Rover's hood once more. He wiped his hands on the rag he'd used to check the oil level, before brushing the back of his hand across his sweaty brow. It was that time of year again, when even Georgia mornings were hot, and the humidity made you feel like you were breathing underwater.

"You sure? 'Cause I don't want to put you out."

Lugos grinned. It had always been so easy to please her. "Not a problem, Keely. I have to go out of town for a few days. When I get back, the part should be in. In the meantime, you've got a set of wheels to get you to and from work."

"Thanks, Lugh. Damn generous of you." She gave him a playful slap on the arm. "Tell me again why you don't have a girl?"

"I'm too old for that kind of thing," he replied, closing the Rover's hood with a bang.

"Bullshit. You're what? Thirty-five?"

If only, Lugos wearily thought. Lugos reached into his pocket and produced the keys that had brought Keely into his life. "As old as the universe," he told her flippantly, averting his gaze as quickly as he dared.

"Ha!" Keely scoffed as she lifted the keys from his hand. "The problem with you is, you're all closed up. Tight as a damn clamshell, you are. No woman wants a mystery all the damn time."

"Says the woman with the absolute worst taste in men," he teased her.

"Now, Lugh, that's just plain mean," Keely accused. "Why'd ya have to go an' say that?" She tried to pout, but Lugos had heard the humor wrapped around the complaint.

"It's true. So, so sad but true," he teased.

In a dramatic huff, she turned on her flip-flopped heel and sashayed around the Rover in shorts that were a little too short. Reaching through the passenger-side window, she hooked her arm through the pocketbook's leather strap and slung the bag over a shoulder. "Well, at least I haven't given up on findin' me a good man," she called over her unburdened shoulder. She then opened the Mustang's driver-side door and slid in, tossing the purse onto the passenger seat in one fluid motion.

"Not once have I seen you with a girl," she added. The last word had been muffled by the slamming of the door, but Lugos understood it easily enough. After the engine roared to life, she cranked the driver-side window down and gave him a coquettish glance out of the corner of her eye.

He didn't mind her frankness. As a matter of fact, it was one of the things Lugos liked best about her. He could always count on his Keely saying exactly what was on her mind. "Is that your way of fishing for a date, Keely?" he joked.

She pursed her lips and rolled her eyes at him, a gesture he'd seen countless times in multiple lifetimes.

"Hardly. If I wanted a date invitation out of you, I'd've already got one." She put on a pair of overly large sunglasses, adjusted the review mirror, and then fluffed her hair.

Watching her, Lugos chuckled. Despite the current hardships of her mortal existence, despite the superficial package, the essence of the woman he loved always managed to shine through.

Once satisfied with her appearance, Keely put the car in reverse and then slowly backed to where he stood. She pulled the sunglasses down on her nose so he could see her eyes clearly before adding, "Besides, for all I know, Lugh, you're married or secretly gay."

He raised one blond eyebrow and tried to hide his grin behind an expression of complete shock. "Does it have to be one or the other?"

"Rich, good-looking man with a Christian heart as generous as the day is long, but no girl in the picture? Yeah, Lugh. I'm thinkin' those are the only choices left, cause you sure as hell ain't Jesus."

He leaned forward, his hands resting on the Acapulco Blue roof. "Keely, tell you what. When I get back from this business trip, I'll take a chance on you breaking my heart for good by asking you out on that date you seem to want so bad." The two of them had been slowly inching their way toward this moment. Lugh had known it the instant he'd touched her hand five years ago.

Now it was her turn to laugh, a nervous little titter of unease. "All right. Will this date include a tour of where all the bodies are buried?" she asked, accepting his dare.

The soul remembers. The soul endures because it is not bound by the laws of time. The thought came to him unbidden, along with a hope he had no business nurturing.

Lugos grinned. "No, Keely. That's second date material."

She slid her sunglasses back up on her nose and put the Mustang in gear. "Have a nice trip, Lugh. See ya when ya get back."

He stepped away just as Keely pressed down on the gas pedal, his eyes and heart following her down the long blacktop driveway until the trees finally obscured his view.

Long after the roar of the Mustang's engine had faded from

his hearing, Lugos stood there.

What had he done? The familiar path lay before him yet again, and so did the yearning to set his feet upon it. He had revealed his true identity to her many times. In each lifetime, there had been difficulties; but in the end, the truth of who and what he was had been something she had found a way to accept.

He'd been called by many names throughout his long life. Lugos absently massaged the back of his neck and tried to tamp down the wave of frustration and longing her company always seemed to stir in him. How could he explain to a lifelong church-attending, hell-fearing Baptist like Keely that the word *god* was just another honor, a title that had nothing to do with the concept of divinity she had been taught? None of his kin had ever been divine or all-knowing. The title had been attributed to them because of the extraordinary things they could do. Quite frankly, he had more in common with dark matter and stardust than he did with the mortal her spirit inhabited.

Unlike so many of his kin who had fled this realm, Lugos had chosen to remain behind because of her. He'd chosen to nurture mankind while he waited for her spirit to return to him. Not long after he'd made that commitment, Lugos had set about hiding his true nature, his very existence. It was the only way to protect himself and her.

No, her life would be safer not knowing this time. And as much as he wanted her, craved her, he needed to find the strength to protect them both. He'd have to avoid that date. Because if he didn't, the alternative would set them on a path that was simply too dangerous for both of them.

Chapter 2

Still standing under the increasing heat of the Georgia summer sun, and with the thought of Keely snugly cocooned in a protective place in his mind, Lugos pulled the cell phone from his pocket and reread Rhiannon's text. It had been direct and brief, just like the goddess:
Problem. Call me. KY

If it had been any other kin, Lugos would have ignored the summons altogether, but he genuinely liked the red-headed goddess. She was the ultimate authority where the Pale was concerned, and unfortunately he still owed her a favor. After a brief debate with himself, he scrolled through his contacts and then dialed her cell number. She let the phone ring twice before answering.

"Llew. I'm so glad you called."

The relief in her greeting was palpable. "It's been Lugos for a few years, now," he gently corrected.

"Well, aren't we being obscure," she replied, her voice smiling in his ear. "Call yourself whatever you please. I'll try to remember, but you know that you'll always be Llew to me."

"Thanks. And yes, I know."

"Don't mention it. So, can you come? We need to talk," she

continued cheerfully, her question no question at all.

"Can't we do this over the phone?" he pressed.

"No."

Lugos sighed. That meant only one thing: there would be others at this meeting. Best to know beforehand, so he asked, "Who else is there?"

Rhiannon filled Lugos's ear with her breathing.

"That bad, is it?" His gut cramped with dread.

"Angus is here," she said brightly. "He's between shoots. Bride's here also." Her voice had gone flat at the mention of Angus's half-sister.

"I saw Angus on the cover of a tabloid." According to the caption, Angus, a god of beauty, had been having an affair with a Hollywood starlet, but the couple had broken up, leaving said starlet heartbroken. "Is he the problem again?" Lugos hadn't been able to tell whether the faint bronze glow emanating from Angus's skin had been a product of Photoshop or the god's power showing itself.

"No, Lugos. And Angus has assured me that this silly escapade of his will only last for a few more years. He's promised me a spectacularly tragic death."

Lugos couldn't help but notice that she'd once again come to Angus's defense. She had defended the god so often that he was starting to think Rhiannon had a thing for the boy. Lugos would never have asked her outright; he and Rhiannon might share a history, but in truth they just weren't that tight anymore. Instead of pursuing the topic, he absently nodded his head.

"Caution him, Rhiannon. He'll listen to you. It shouldn't be too memorable. He can't go all Elvis on us. Nothing for the conspiracy theorists to sink their teeth into," he warned. The Internet was proving to be both a blessing and a curse to his kind. Databases and security cameras seemed to be everywhere these days. It had gotten harder, for the few who had chosen to remain earthbound, to hide among the masses. The occasional staged death had become a necessity. And the trick to any effective con was in the details—details Lugos wasn't confident Angus could be bothered with, and that was a potential problem.

Leaving that conundrum alone for the moment, he asked, "And the saint, what's she been up to?" Not that he cared. He only asked because he knew it would let Rhiannon vent a little.

Of all the Celtic deities, Bride had somehow managed to make the transition from pagan god to Christian saint. She'd been repackaged as Saint Brigid. But Bride's canonization had caused a rift between Rhiannon and the goddess of home and hearth. And Bride had only made matters worse by continually reminding her fellow gods of their inability to achieve the same. She was their Cinderella rags-to-riches story. But Bride's constant glow of power both infuriated and frightened his kin.

"To be honest, I haven't asked her. Right now, Susie Homemaker is playing hostess with the mostest in my house. My house! Of course, my entire staff loves her because she won't stop baking for them. It's pissing me off. I may stoop to breaking a dish over her head soon, Lugos."

He chuckled into the phone. "Where are you right now?" Rhiannon had been walking during their conversation, and her breathing told him that the goddess was now moving at a pretty good clip.

"On my way to the barns. I just couldn't stay in the house with her any longer. She's driving me fuckin' crazy!" Rhiannon was never happier than when she was with her horses. Goddess of sovereignty and the horse, she had often taken the guise of Epona, the Celtic horse goddess, when living among the Gauls. Rhiannon now ran two racing stables, one in Kentucky, the other in Pennsylvania.

Circling their conversation back around to the reason for her call, Lugos tried once more to coax some answers out of the goddess. "Are you sure you can't tell me over the phone? You know how the others feel about me."

Rhiannon stopped walking. "I wouldn't have contacted you if it weren't important," she replied curtly. "And weren't you the one who warned me about using my cell phone to discuss sensitive subjects? *You* said there was always someone listening these days."

Lugos knew this to be true, so despite all his misgivings, and there were many, he caved as gracefully as he could manage. "Give me an hour to pack a change of clothes and button the place up. I'll meet you in the stable yard."

"Thank you, Lugos. It will be good to see you again," she said, relief so evident in her voice that it worried him. Then the connection went dead. Having obtained exactly what she desired, Rhiannon had hung up on him.

Chapter 3

He'd lied to Rhiannon. His cabin wasn't what he needed to button up; he could always leave at a moment's notice. Clutching the phone, Lugos stalked into the shade of his well-ordered garage and slapped his palm against the garage-door button. With his other hand, he snatched the oil-stained rag from his back pocket and tossed it at the cleared workbench, not caring if it reached its intended destination.

He strode past the sleek black Audi and into the house, pausing only long enough to lock the door behind him before he activated the security system for the main floor. "Damn it," he muttered, deliberately jamming his index finger against the mounted security pad. When the indicator light turned red, Lugos felt a small twinge of satisfaction. It could be argued that of all the earthbound gods, he was the most dependent on technology; but he was also the most forward thinking. And why not? Hadn't he been the one to fund Nikola Tesla's early experiments? And it had all led to this, the red security light, the Internet, and so much more that was still to come.

They blamed him, of course—the others, his kin, and various members of the Pale. They knew what he knew. They recognized that the ever-growing accomplishments of humanity could lead only to the further decline of the Pale. If Lugos understood nothing else, it was that the balance of power never remained static. If one group rose, then another fell, and he and those like him were in a death spiral, whether or not certain factions of the Pale still refused to admit it. One day, if Lugos had his way, mankind would understand and wield all the secrets of the universe. And on that day, his flawed kin would finally be forced to abandon the practice of stealing energy from those who would call themselves believers, the faithful, followers, or disciples. His race was like a bunch of drug-addicted junkies. But instead of cocaine, meth, or crack, it was power they craved.

Lugos turned away from the steady red light and his dark thoughts to evaluate the simplicity of his latest sanctuary. Outwardly it was a single-story cabin, a wealthy man's hunting retreat, a modern log house that was more a prefab kit than a real log home. Lugos had prepared the site himself, on land that—at least on paper—had been bequeathed to him upon a distant relative's death. That had been a lie, of course. Two hundred years ago, another cabin had stood here. That one he had built himself, but nature and fire had long since claimed it.

Lugos crossed through the kitchen with its marble countertops, custom-built cabinets, and carved moldings. His other residences were much older and lay in Wales and Ireland, but those lands he had quit in order to get away from his mother.

Bitch was always the first word that came to his mind whenever Arianrhod's name manifested in his memory. *Cold* would be next, followed by *calculating, manipulative,* and *irrational*. Yeah, he had his fair share of parent issues, he mused—and wife issues, too, he admitted as suppressed memories of Blodeuwedd resurfaced. Technically he'd lied to Keely. He was married, though not in a way a mortal would understand. His mother had tied him to the spring goddess eons ago. And now the two spiteful goddesses were forever intertwined inside his mind.

Of course, he understood that all this ancient history had bubbled to the surface like a boil in need of lancing because of

Rhiannon's call. With a great deal of effort, he relaxed the tension in his jaw and made his way to the great room.

Resigned to the impending ordeal, Lugos dragged the glass-and-wrought-iron coffee table to the side and folded the area rug back to reveal the trap door. Within moments, gears lurched into motion and the heavy metal yielded, sliding back to reveal a gaping black hole.

Rhiannon was the Pale's reigning leader, and because she'd done him a favor century ago, Lugos was (for lack of a better descriptor) her much-disliked lawman. He was her inquiry agent, her problem solver. Rhiannon's private dick, if you wanted to get all noir with it. Standing there and staring down into the opening, Lugos made a noise that was something between a moan and a grunt of disgust. He climbed down the metal staircase and unerringly found the light switch. When the pad of his hand skimmed over it, the final shadows evaporated, but the fluorescent lights did little to alleviate the oppressive feel of the vault. "There had better be a damn good reason for having to do this," he muttered to himself.

This particular hole in the ground was filled with secrets: his history, his battles, his obsessions. It was where he stored his spear, the magickal weapon he'd once wielded against the monstrous Balor. There were swords, battle-axes, and bows of various sizes and ages packed away in dusty crates, each with its own tangled story. There were the more personal artifacts, mementos that had been given to him in various lifetimes by her. He treasured each one of them, though they held no value to anyone but him. He'd kept them because he could do nothing else.

"Enough!" The command to himself was as loud as it was harsh. Only harm would come from reliving the past. There was simply too much of it. To wallow in the past was to be lost to it. The debilitating malaise of remembering was called the Last Slumber by his kind. They were all susceptible to it. Vigilance and discipline were the only way to keep it at bay. The Last Slumber could render a god like himself irrelevant—or worse, nonexistent.

He had seen it happen to others; Dylan, his brother, for one. Having witnessed how quickly his brother had slipped into the void, Lugos had vowed to keep his mind trained on the present. In many ways, it was the destructive nature of time that kept his mind and heart reaching for her. She'd come to him so many times, with so many faces, so many names. All different, yet all the same.

Lugos moved farther into the vault, thoughts of his love for her sitting warm inside his chest. Beyond the weaponry stood a charcoal-gray safe approximately half the height of a man and just as wide. Its contents held various items needed to ensure a certain amount of freedom in this modern world: aliases, passports, and money, all bundled according to need and intended destination.

Lugos pressed his left thumb against a pad while he punched in a six-digit code with his right. As soon as he heard the click, he pulled on the door and plucked out a bundle of U.S. bills along with the topmost passport. Cracking open the blue cover, he checked to be sure the passport read "Lugh Hart," the same name printed on the driver's license sitting snugly inside his wallet. Satisfied, he then pushed the heavy safe door closed and reactivated the lock. Stuffing the money and the passport into a black gym bag he kept at the ready, he straightened and shouldered the innocuous luggage. The bag also contained a change of clothing and his two weapon choices: a hunting knife with a nine-inch blade and an unregistered handgun whose serial number had been filed smooth. Lugos preferred the knife to the Glock, mainly because the gun's noise tended to attract attention. He knew neither weapon would stop one of his kind for long, but if used precisely it would do enough damage to buy him the time he'd need to retrieve a weapon that could finish the job.

Frankly, he wasn't worried that Rhiannon would betray him, but Angus and Bride's allegiance had shifted wildly over the centuries. And then there were the other members of the Pale to consider: the scheming witches who adored his mother, the power-struggling shifters, the temperamental dragonkin, the cursed werewolves, the elusive but decidedly dangerous fae, the deeply misunderstood demon clans, and the occasional pissed-off demigod with parent issues all his own. Rhiannon only chose to reach out to him when disaster was imminent. It was for this reason and this reason alone that he'd tried to make peace with her summons.

Lugos paused at the base of the stairs, his eye catching the gleam of light that should not have reflected off the spear's dark tip. Should he? Would it be wise? But before he was aware of moving, his hand had already risen to hover inches from the warm wooden shaft. Lugos flexed his hand in anticipation. Then, taking a preparatory deep breath, he closed his outstretched hand around the hard surface.

A tangled bolt of pleasure and pain shot up the length of his arm. As always, the pain quickly subsided, though his arm still tingled as if he'd taken hold of a live wire. Lugos had always been credited with slaying Balor using this weapon, but the truth was much worse. With great care, he lifted the spear from the hooks that mounted it to the wall. Yes, he had plunged the spear into the god's one eye—a terrible injury, to be sure, but not a death blow. It had been she, the entity trapped inside the spear, who had defeated Balor. The goddess was so ancient that her name had been lost to time. Balor was now trapped in the spear as well, having been sucked into the shaft with her—trapped, as she was, for all eternity.

Lugos could feel both of them now, Balor's burning rage and her insatiable hunger. While her voice was that of a lover's whisper in his ear, Balor's rage set Lugos's blood on fire. Two wills at odds with each other and his own. To be the guardian of this spear was as much a curse as it was a blessing. None of his kin could defeat him as long as he carried it. As a precaution, Lugos decided to take it to the meeting with his kin.

His index finger felt for the node along the wood's smooth surface and pressed it. The tingling in his arm eased a bit as both of the spear's ends silently retracted into its center. What was left was no more than a length of polished wood the size of a gentleman's cane, complete with silver cap. It had been the height of fashion a few hundred years ago for gentlemen to carry canes, but not so much these days.

Lugos plunged the basement into darkness and climbed the staircase before he could reconsider the wisdom of taking the staff. He glanced at his watch. It was almost noon and he had one more thing to do before meeting Rhiannon.

Chapter 4

The cabin wasn't Lugos' only holding in America, there was the building in Atlanta, not too far from Little Five Points. The unassuming warehouse-styled brick building was occupied by retail establishments at street level. Office space dominated the second floor. The third and final floor had been split into three handsome lofts, all of which were leased. The first two lofts were home to members of the Pale; a demon named Murmur, and the other was occupied by an elderly demi-god named Zee who had once requested his services. Lugos had begrudgingly aided Zee, but only after striking a deal with her. As part of her payment, Zee had been charged with keeping an eye on Murmur, but otherwise Lugos left the demi-god alone so she might live out her last few years in relative peace. Zee's loft smelled perpetually of cats and strange baked goods so Lugh didn't feel the urge to visit her often.

The west end, and final loft, was where Lugos had stashed Griffin. The young man was an Internet savant. Lugos had given Griffin the impression that he'd dropped out of Georgia Tech to accept a position with a clandestine security agency linked with the CIA, and that Special Agent Lugh Hart had recruited him specifically for his bad-ass hacking skills. It was those same skills that had gotten the young man in trouble with the real FBI and given Lugh the opportunity he'd needed to acquire the soon to be expelled Griffin. It was Special Agent Lugh Hart who had been able to make the FBI and federal prison problem go away. Luckily the Georgia Tech student had been smart enough to see the writing on the wall and accepted Lugh's offer of employment. Thus far the salary, accommodations, travel, and the secretive nature of Griffin's duties had lived up to the twenty-two-year old's idea of what a spy's life entailed. Lugos had intentionally kept Griffin in the dark about his true identity. In the age of Goggle and Bing, Lugos had needed someone to monitor the web and facilitate information transactions so he could keep his secrets and remain invisible. He also needed time for Griffin to trust him before risking the truth with the kid.

***

"Miss me?"

Griffin jump from his computer chair. "What the fuck man?" The sudden appearance of Agent Hart was always a shock that guaranteed to send a bolt of adrenaline through his veins. The guy seemed to get a kick out of slipping past all of the security efforts Griffin had installed in order to scare the shit out of him. It was like a sadistic game with the man.

Agent Hart chuckled. "Missed my approach yet again?"

Griffin glared at his boss before scrolling through the various camera views on the array of monitors before him. He'd updated the building's tech as soon as he'd moved in. It was the latest in spyware, small and almost impossible to see unless you knew where to look. There was a camera on every corner of the building. Two views of the foyer, one in the only public elevator which serviced all three floors. Five cameras had been installed in the all but the unused stairwell, and two in the hallway leading to and from the loft. There shouldn't have been anyway for Hart to sneak past them. That is, not unless his boss was actually Ethan Hunt of Mission Impossible and had climbed through the too small air vent or traversed the disgusting sewer system that ran under the building. Griffin made a mental note to check the buildings schematics to see if such a thing were even possible.

"You should rethink the roof, Griffin. You have a blind spot behind one of the large air conditioner units."

Eyes still glued to his monitors, Griffin nodded, his thoughts on the problem, a puzzle yet to be unraveled. "Right. The roof. I'll do that." Hart was definitely Ethan Hunt, super-spy and he, Griffin, was just as obviously some bumbling analyst who was expected not to ask questions or think beyond the parameters set for him by the agent in charge. Wasn't that always the case in the movies? Griffin swiveled around in his chair. "What do you need today?" He'd been working on his observation skills, yet another one of Hart's suggestions.

The bag, the way Hart was poised lightly on the balls of his feet suggested that his boss was in a hurry. They had a new mission. The cane was an odd touch, but Griffin didn't think it was his place to say so. *Probably some prop or gadget*, Griffin figured. His boss was built like one of those statues of the gods you found in Rome or Greece, but Hart dressed like a banker, as if trying too hard to hide the muscle just under the pressed white shirts and slacks. Today he was sporting the beginnings of a beard which only added to the he-man vibe his boss tended to give off without even trying.

Unlike Agent Hart, Griffin was not exactly super spy material. He was tall and wiry. Never once had he entertained the idea of putting in the time or effort to build the kind of muscle Hart carried as if it were a birthright. Nor did Griffin have any desire to be in the field alongside Hart. He enjoyed the safety of his job, as well as the money. The money was really good, almost too good. Mostly he just monitored persons of interest, or transferred top secret packets of code to whomever Hart designated. It was also Griffin's job to scrub the web of any signs of Hart's comings and goings. But the simplest of all his assigned tasks was the gathering of intelligence via the web and dark-net so Hart could do whatever it was he needed to do. Hart had often told him that a life might just depend on the information Griffin unearthed, so he took this job seriously and it worried him that the security measures he'd installed still could not, on most days, catch sight of his boss's arrival. He really didn't want to get fired. Perhaps he should think about thermal imaging.

"I'm going out of town for a few days; a meet-up in Kentucky. I'll call you with instructions when I know more, so don't wander too far from your desk."

The announcement snapped Griffin back from his musings. "Will do." Griffin had to keep himself from saluting Hart. It wouldn't have been meant as a mocking gesture on Griffin's part. His boss just kind of made one feel like he'd received orders from a four-star general. Perhaps it was his tone, or the way Hart exuded a sense of command, but either way, Griffin wished some of that super-hero shit would rub off onto him. "You expecting trouble?"

"No, but stay close anyway."

Griffin nodded while another part of his mind worked on the earlier problem. He should have seen Hart walk through the door of the loft, even if his boss had quietly picked the lock instead of using his key. It was an open floor plan, except for the two bedrooms, and bath. Perhaps he should install the motion sensors Hart didn't want installed.

Hart strolled away from Griffin's array of computers and into the kitchen in search of his usual espresso. Because of the openness of the loft, Griffin had a clear view of the copper monstrosity at all times. It was expensive and slightly frightening. Hart had installed the Italian espresso machine himself. Griffin had thought initially that the contraption was an elaborate DIY bomb before Hart had explained its purpose. Despite Hart's enthusiasm over the thing, Griffin much preferred the corner Starbucks to the steaming, sputtering, temperamental copper work of art. He'd never admit to Hart that the thing made him nervous, but Griffin had been avoiding the kitchen ever since it had been erected. Thank God for takeout.

Griffin sat at his computer, hopefully far enough away from the fuming machine to avoid getting killed should the damn thing explode, and waited for Hart to explain the particulars of their new mission. Hart was not someone you could rush. And in all fairness, Griffin was still getting used to the 'need to know aspect' of his support roll. His boss barely told him enough to do his job. And Hart hated follow up questions. Griffin quickly learned that he'd have to dig on his own if he wanted to know more. His boss, as far as Griffin could discover, had existed only since 1993, before that there was no such person as Lugh Hart. To make matters worse, Griffin had begun to question just who Agent Hart worked for, and by extension himself. Their missions were definitely off the books, black opts, so secretive that Griffin had begun to wonder if he should figure out a way to part ways with Hart. Or even if that was possible. But after Hart had provided Griffin with clearance for both the CIA and FBI databases Griffin had begun to sleep a little easier. Hart was legit, but legit with which agency Griffin still wasn't sure. At least the work he did was safe, and if not always satisfying at least it was interesting. Without fail a weekly check had been directly deposited into an account for him. Griffin even had a 401K, something he had not thought of establishing for himself until Hart had insisted on it. And, although Hart was not exactly his best bud, he was easy to work for. Well, Griffin thought, most of the time.

Signature espresso in hand, Hart launched into the details. "The meet is at Bonner Farm in Kentucky. It's billed as an information exchange only. It should be a clean in and out. I don't necessarily expect any trouble. The information I receive will decide what happens next. I may need you to do your internet magic. I'll contact you as soon as I know more and we'll go from there." Hart tossed the shot back in a single swallow.

"Sounds clear enough. Taking the jet today?"

"No, I have other travel arrangements." Hart set the now empty espresso mug on the kitchen's black marbled counter top. "Keep one eye on the cabin. I've loaned my Mustang to a neighbor to help her out. She might stop by my place while I'm gone, but I doubt it.

"Her?" Griffin's eyebrows lifted. This was the first time Hart had ever mentioned a her. And the casual way in which he'd done it almost made Hart seem like a normal guy. "What her?"

"A neighbor, that's all."

Griffin couldn't help the grin that spread across his face. "Do I get to meet this mysterious her?"

"No."

Griffin stopped grinning. Just like that Hart's voice had turned cold and hard. Seems Hart thought his neighbor fell into that need to know category. Griffin held up his hands in surrender. "Okay, okay."

Hart cleared his throat. "Right, I'm off."

Griffin tried to shrug it off, but it was just scary how quickly Hart could go from buddy-buddy to chilly. "I'll wait to hear from you," Griffin replied. He'd do an Internet search, take a look at Google Earth again. Discovering Hart's *her* would be child's play.

Hart collected his black bag and cane and strolled toward the door. Pausing in the doorway, Hart said, "Don't forget to deliver the packet on time."

"Have I ever?"

"There's always a first time for everything." Then he was gone.

Cycling through a series of cameras Griffin watched his boss depart the building and stroll unhurriedly down the street. And then, and instant later Griffin lost track of him. None of the street cameras he'd hacked into gave him a view of Hart. The man had simply disappeared like the super spy he was.

Chapter 5

Teleporting through time and space in order to cover large distances was the one indulgence Lugos still allowed himself. It wasn't a particularly difficult skill to master, nor did it require him to expend much power. Transporting more than just himself was a little more complicated.

The paddock grounds of Rhiannon's Kentucky farm were as pristine as they were deserted. It was just as hot here as it had been in Atlanta. Lugos instantly regretted the sport coat he'd worn. He stepped into the shade of the nearest barn, set his bag at his feet, leaned his cane against a stall door, and stripped off the coat. He could have just as easily thought the coat away, but Lugos had long ago made it a habit to live as human a life as possible.

Although he didn't immediately spot Rhiannon among the long rows of stalls, Lugos knew the goddess would have felt his arrival, as would the others. He hoped she was the only one coming to greet him. As he methodically rolled up the sleeves of his pressed but now damp shirt, he began to feel her presence like an itch between his shoulder blades. Taking a deep breath, he listened, using a technique that had nothing to do with his hearing. Dismissing the earthy smell of dung and horseflesh, he let his mind travel down the neatly swept aisles. Like a sudden radar ping in his mind, Lugos located her easily. She was to his left and moving fast. He snatched up the bag and cane and draped the discarded coat over his arm. Turning ninety degrees, he pushed Keely from his mind and waited for the goddess to appear.

A mortal would describe Rhiannon as well rounded. The goddess was a big woman, but a casual onlooker would not know that muscle, not fat, lay beneath the tailored fawn shirt and pressed blue jeans. She was truly a force of nature, and quite deadly for those who made the mistake of underestimating her. Today her signature red hair was barely contained inside a pink baseball cap, the excess spilling out the back like a fox's tail. She looked reassuringly human, mainly because sunlight obscured the faint glow of power that always surrounded her like a red halo. But what Lugos couldn't see with the naked eye, he had no problem feeling.

"Welcome to Bonner Farms and thank you for coming," she said, stepping close to him. She glanced briefly at the cane he carried before leaning forward to kiss the air beside his cheek, judiciously avoiding his two-day-old stubble.

"It's nice to see you, too, Rhiannon," Lugos replied, a smile tugging at the corner of his mouth.

"You look pale under that tan, Lugos."

"I'm fine." The reply was a little too quickly given. He'd long since given up his Apollonian glow of power to better hide himself among the mortals he championed.

She leveled her startling green eyes on him. "Are you ready for this?"

His smile faded. Lugos gave her a shrug and gripped the cane a little tighter. The knots in his stomach that he'd been trying to ignore rolled like dice on a craps table. He kept his reply carefully neutral. "We'll see."

"The spear is a little much, don't you think?"

"Sometimes family squabbles can get out of hand. This," he said, raising the collapsed spear, "is only meant to keep everyone cordial."

"Just don't point that thing at me, love. Remember, I've been on your side more often than not."

"Of course."

Her eyes narrowed, catlike, the only sign that she might doubt his assurances.

Without preamble, she announced, "Seraphine is dead." She then looped her arm through his free one and set off, her heeled steps surprisingly light beside his heavier footfalls.

He thought the name sounded familiar, if only vaguely. "Seraphine?"

"She...," Rhiannon drew out the word for clarity. "is...was..." She hesitated, correcting herself. "Both witch and shifter. A respected elder within the Sacred Grove Coven." Rhiannon waited a moment for him to absorb that bit before continuing. "She also held the post of ambassador elect in the Shifter community. Seraphine often helped negotiate rather difficult issues between the Greater North American Witch Collective and the more militant wing of the United Shifter League."

Lugos made a noise, something between a groan and a grunt. "No wonder she's dead."

Rhiannon narrowed her eyes in that same judgmental cat's stare. "Reason enough, I know, but there is something going on that isn't exactly kosher. There's been a recent regime change within the USL. Seraphine's brother, Talon, who happens to be both witch and shifter as well, has made a clean sweep of the old guard. It was a quiet takeover, but I didn't think twice about it until Angus arrived with his news. It has given the whole affair a rather nefarious feeling."

Lugos remained silent, merely inclining his head at hearing her news. There were regime changes among the shifters all the time. It was in their nature to want to be top dog—or wolf, tiger, bear, whatever. But pointing out such facts to Rhiannon wasn't going to get him back home any faster. He'd just have to hear the whole story before he carefully told her that she was overreacting. By the time they'd reached the other end of the barn aisle, he could almost feel her teeth grind with frustration at his clear lack of interest.

"I know when the mighty fall and why," she went on. "What's happening now is different. I just don't understand the why of it yet. Something is in motion. I can feel it."

"And you want me to find out the why?" he asked incredulously.

There was a golf cart parked at the edge of the barn area. When they reached it, she released his arm.

"Please tell me that you haven't come to the conclusion that all is not right in Oz because of what Angus told you."

"Yes, I have," she spat back.

"Not an altogether reliable source."

Rhiannon glared at him and then pointed one perfectly painted turquoise fingernail at the golf cart. "Don't lecture me about Angus. Get in."

His and Rhiannon's alliance had always been unusual for his kind. He didn't exactly need her, nor did she exactly need him. But a happy Rhiannon did make his life easier. She had the power to keep members of the Pale out of his affairs; in turn, he occasionally offered up his unique set of skills. And then there was that favor she'd done for him when he'd needed it most.

To avoid a larger argument, he wordlessly took his position on the golf cart's white-upholstered seat. As soon as he'd settled himself and his gear, she pressed the pedal to the floor and sent them careening down a paved path. Their destination was a two-story white house that sat a good distance away nestled within a ring of very old oak trees.

"I'm not chasing ghosts, Lugos. Something's off. Now I've got Angus and his annoying sister on my doorstep crying wolf. They're beside themselves."

By *them,* Lugos knew she meant that Angus the Pretty was the one he'd find upset. Very little ever ruffled Bride's feathers.

Rhiannon didn't slow when the asphalt path veered abruptly to the left. Lugos was forced to brace a hand against the cart's side to prevent being ejected.

"If I didn't know better, I'd say he was scared." She didn't alter their speed for the next turn to the right. This time Lugos could feel the outside wheels briefly leave the pavement. "He's demanding to see you. Won't say anymore until he does."

"That's got to piss you off," Lugos replied, his hand still firmly gripping the cart's frame. They were much closer to the main house now.

Instead of watching where they were going, Rhiannon turned to stare at him. Despite her lack of attention, the cart never strayed off the path. "See, you know me so well. I'm incensed. Who do they think they are? No one comes on my turf and makes demands of me!"

"You couldn't you romance it out of him?"

"As if," she replied dismissively, her lovely lips thinning. The cart abruptly slowed to a crawl a few hundred yards away from the house. "He's pretty, I'll give you that. But, you can't walk a dog that won't get off the porch." She turned her attention back to the path, stomped on the pedal, and laughed. It wasn't a pleasant sound.

Lugos had stayed for a time at Rhiannon's Pennsylvania farm, but this was the first time he'd been summoned to Kentucky. He found her taste in homes to be consistent, a curious combination of brick fortress and early American federal. The brick had been painted white, which gave the eye nothing to focus on except the neo-Grecian touches within the moldings that encased the long rectangular windows, of which there were eight. Two large stone horse's heads flanked the central front door, their only adornment the healthy ferns erupting from their necks like manes. There was no welcome mat or door knocker, a telling sign in Lugos's mind.

Lugos followed Rhiannon up the steps, past the horse planters, and through a heavily paneled front door. Once inside, he was greeted by a welcome blast of cold from the air conditioner. The expansive foyer was austere, bordering on minimalist. A soothing blue had been applied to the walls; white marble floors lay under his feet. The sparse equestrian theme was continued by the placement of a well-crafted bronze Thoroughbred in mid-gallop upon a central marble table. There was no sound save the echoing of their own footfalls as Rhiannon and he proceeded without pause toward a room that lay ahead and to their left.

The fact that he had yet to see a soul was not out of the ordinary. He could feel them moving about in other areas of the house. As a rule, Rhiannon employed only members of the Pale. As a favor to him, she had always taken the extra precaution of clearing out her staff before his arrival. Lugos hadn't exactly been kidding about his reason for bringing along the spear; past meetings between him and those of his kin had tended to get out of hand. All it took for chaos to erupt was a perceived slight. Ego and self-importance were family traits few of his kin even tried to overcome.

Rhiannon slid open a set of enormous wooden doors, which parted smoothly and swiftly as if they weighed no more than drapes. As the panels rolled back into their wall casements, Lugos caught his first glimpse of Angus just as the bronze god turned from a window.

Angus smiled indulgently at his hostess, the warmth of the practiced smile never quite reaching the god's eyes. Lugos's first impression was that Angus had changed very little from the last time they'd been forced to endure one another. The god's boy-band beauty had only ever altered according to the dictates of fashion. In the 1950s Angus could very well have passed for Fabian. In the '90s it had been 'NSync. Now, he probably found himself mistaken for some teen heartthrob Lugos had never heard of or cared to.

After giving Lugos a nod of recognition and receiving one in return, Angus said, "So, fucking glad you showed." A wrinkle of worry appeared on the god's face the moment he registered the cane in Lugos's grip. Angus had seemed clearly relieved before spying the spear; now he tried for hurt, but the emotion, like the smile, never actually reached his eyes.

Sauntering away from the window, Angus flopped his lanky body onto the cushions of a green leather sofa. "Looking tired, bro." He cocked his head to the side. "Should have hit the Beltane celebrations with me. Nothing like getting a little bit of god-honoring to refuel the juice packs—if you get my meaning. Perhaps you should drop in at Burning Man with me." He grinned up at Lugos. Even in the bright light of the sun-filled room, Angus's skin glowed with newly acquired power.

Lugos kept his expression neutral. Being a god of youth had definite drawbacks, the worst of which had to be that Angus would never mature physically or mentally beyond the sheer hell of adolescence. It was his nature to be flippant, impulsive, and generally a pain in everyone's ass. Lugos typically found himself slipping into the role of older brother when he was forced to deal with the superficial god. And as far as Burning Man or any other witch's celebration was concerned, Lugos would continue to stay as far away from his mother's followers as possible, even if it meant that his own god-powers had to run on empty.

He skipped the niceties. "Rhiannon says you have a problem."

As she sank into a chair nearest Angus, Rhiannon gave him an encouraging nod. If Lugos found himself playing the role of older brother, Rhiannon was the doting sister whose reassuring touch came across as a little incestuous. Angus shook off his host's petting with a wave and an impatient frown. His ice-pale blue eyes missed Rhiannon's anger at being so openly rebuffed.

Lugos took a firmer grip on the cane in his hand.

Just as Angus began to speak, Rhiannon cursed. "The damn bitch is crafting again! Look at this!" She swept the diminutive votive off the glass coffee table and held it aloft for Lugos's inspection. It sparkled in the sunlight. "She put goddamn glitter on my Lenox vase!" The goddess's cheeks and nose had turned an unflattering shade of red.

As if cued, Bride glided into the room and announced the arrival of tea and cakes. Lugos watched her float by in her long skirts, a blurred stream of reddish-gold light trailing behind her like a ghost. The color of Bride's power had always reminded Lugos of dying coals. When she stopped moving, the comet effect ended, but the goddess's power made her skin appear a bit unworldly, as if tiny flecks of dancing flame lay just under the surface. Even more unsettling, Angus's twin sister had never made the effort to move much past the restrictions of Victorian fashion or social decorum. Not until Martha Stewart came to the petite goddess's notice had the all-consuming passion for crafting unsettled an otherwise predictable mind. None of Lugos's kin truly looked forward to Bride landing on their doorstep—at first, because they didn't want the constant reminder of her canonization, but now because things like Rhiannon's vase happened. And because it was difficult to get the goddess of home and hearth to leave before she'd re-purposed every possession you ever held dear.

Completely ignoring Rhiannon's mounting anger, Bride set the burdened silver tea tray on the coffee table, the defined edges of her exposed skin blurring disconcertingly as she moved.

Rhiannon inserted the twinkling vase between Bride's face and a tilted teapot.

Bride ignored the object and busied herself with the task of pouring tea for everyone.

"Didn't I tell you not to mess with my things? When in bloody hell did you manage to do this?"

Bride looked past the vase into Rhiannon's flushed face and smiled. It was a rather sweet smile, one Lugos imagined a mother might give a beloved child. "It's pretty now, don't you think? It only needed a bit of help, a pop of color. You take cream and two sugars, as I recall." She then righted the teapot and set it aside, not having spilled a drop.

Rhiannon's mouth snapped shut. She turned and glowered at Lugos. The silent plea in her gaze seemed to suggest he use his spear to rid them all of Bride's presence.

Lugos gave her the slightest of nods. Satisfied, Rhiannon lowered her ample hips back into the cushions of the chair, the glittery vase still clutched in her hands, while she grumbled a few more curses under her breath. Angus continued to mutely stare at his sister, a genuinely pained expression fixed upon the glowing face of beauty.

Lugos held his tongue through all this. There was no winning an argument with the saint. Rhiannon's only option for surviving Bride's stay was to pack away her possessions and keep them under lock and key until the saint left, hopefully with her brother in tow.

Completely unruffled by Rhiannon's outburst, Bride passed around the porcelain teacups. Lugos took his, giving Bride a nod of thanks, absently wondering if somewhere within the folds of those thick skirts lay the defiling glue gun. Choosing the chair closest to the doorway, he settled himself, his bag, jacket, and cane within easy reach.

"You were saying," Lugos prompted. He waited for Angus to accept his sister's proffered refreshment. It took a few more seconds for the sibling to tear his eyes away from her, but when he did, Lugos clearly read the disgust residing there. Rhiannon flatly refused the saint's offer of tea with a glare that would have turned any mortal to stone.

Bride, in turn, gave a delicate shrug before resuming her seat nearest her brother. She had discreetly eyed the cane while serving the tea. Lugos was fairly certain that everyone would go to great lengths to remain civil as long as it was in the room. In truth, he didn't really plan to use the spear's terrible power on any of them. He'd only do so if he had no other option. But they didn't know that.

"I believe Llew asked you a question, Brother?" Bride prompted.

Lugos didn't bother to correct Bride as he had Rhiannon about his choice of names. She would no doubt refuse to hear him, and after today he was unlikely to see either her or Angus again for another century or so. He hoped.

Angus set his teacup down, the brown liquid untasted.

Lugos followed suit, unwilling to be the first to drink, just in case Bride's concoction turned out to be laced with something altogether unpleasant.

"'Kay. Like I was saying, I'm chillin' at this Beltane party. Lots of hot babes wanting a piece of this, and I'm accommodating, making everyone happy. Everything is fucking fabulous." Angus grinned, having traded the distress his sister had caused for the memory of young witches vying for his godly attentions.

Lugos briefly wondered if Angus had been as Pan-like as he wanted them all to believe but, despite his doubts, leaned forward in his chair to feign interest in the boy-god's exploits.

Warming to his own storytelling, Angus reclined further into the cushions and stretched an arm along the back of the sofa. "So…it's getting near dawn, and the party's mellowing out. I got bodies draped all over me, some sleeping, some still touching me, some chatting among themselves because they think I'm sleepin' too. And as relaxed as I am, I find myself keyin' in on this particular conversation between Josey and Jewel. They're twins," he explained, grinning broadly.

Rhiannon looked to be grinding her molars. Bride was nurturing an often-worn expression of disappointment. She'd never exactly approved of her brother's rampant lasciviousness. But neither goddess attempted to interrupt Angus.

"Jewel's telling Josey about the day before. Seraphine and them are all coven mates, see."

"Get to the point. What happened?" Lugos prompted, his patience wearing thin.

"Talon, Seraphine's brother, had paid the witch a visit earlier, and they argued. Jewel tells Josey that Talon wants to lead the shifters out, like the witches did in the '70s and again in the '90s. Seraphine, of course, was tellin' him it wasn't time yet, that they had to wait a mite longer, but he wasn't having any of it, according to Jewel. Said he didn't care anymore, he was doing it his way from now on. Then Jewel told Josey that the two got all quiet-like, and that she couldn't make out what they were sayin'. It's just that Rhiannon says Seraphine turned up dead soon after. Local police called it suicide, but I'm thinking Seraphine's brother killed her to have his way. Jewel hinted to Josey that Seraphine had something on her brother because of the way the witch talked to him, bossing him around and such, even though he's a big fuckin' bear and a hell of a lot more powerful than Seraphine ever dreamed of bein'. Now I hear Talon's taken control of the USL." Angus paused a moment before adding, "He's gonna do it, bro. He's gonna lead the shifters out into the light of day and scare a hell of a lot of people in the process."

"And once the shifters break rank, the rest will follow," Bride chimed in. "We can't allow this, Rhiannon. My followers won't know how to handle it, not even the radical ones who broke with the church."

"You mean during the Reformation," Rhiannon supplied.

Bride still smarted from that break, having lost quite a few followers because of it. Rhiannon knew it as well and always enjoyed reminding the saint of the event.

Lugos ignored the two goddesses, his thoughts inevitably turning to Keely. In other lifetimes, she'd learned of such things and had dealt with it—but, then, her spirit was accepting and generous by nature. And she was cosmically tied to him. If this was the great danger in this lifetime, he would find a way to protect her from it. This time he wouldn't fail her.

"Modern-day media would label the entire shifter community monsters, abnormal, perhaps even mutants," said Lugos. "The governments of the world would act to eliminate the threat but not before capturing and studying as many as they could." He was stating the obvious, but sometimes his kin needed to be reminded that humans weren't benign creatures. The witches had been discredited. Most of them were human to begin with, which had made the task an easy one at the time, but Lugos was getting ahead of himself. Nothing had happened yet. So far, this was just speculation on Angus's part.

"Other than the gossip between these two women, what proof is there? Seraphine's death could very well have been a suicide and unrelated to her brother. This witch, Jewel, could be making shit up to impress her sister. Talon might want to come out, but that's no guarantee that he can lead a band of shifters out with him." Lugos knew that one shifter in the media would be a bad tabloid story, easily dismissed as freakish, a prank, a Ripley's *Believe it or Not!* item. But a hundred or more shifters coming forward would cause a media frenzy.

Angus shrugged. "Isn't that what a god of light does, bro? Illuminate the truth?"

Lugos couldn't help recognizing the implied insult. He tried to relax his jaw before answering the irritating god-dude. "Aye, that's what I do," he replied. Lugos was the bringer of light. Usually that meant knowledge, but sometimes the description had been quite literal—Apollo and his chariot and golden horses, Thor and his thunder and lightning. But that was a long time ago.

"The witch's death is not the problem," Bride cut in. "The problem is Talon. You have to put a stop to it, Llew."

Lugos held up a hand to silence Bride before she could lecture him on his duty. He knew keeping the Pale a secret was paramount. He turned to Rhiannon. "What, if anything, do you want me to do?" He secretly agreed with Bride that Talon's agenda was a hell of a lot more pressing than one witch's death, but he took his mandates from Rhiannon, not Bride.

Drawing her shoulders back, Rhiannon glanced at Angus. "Investigate Seraphine's death first. That will put you in contact with Talon in a way that won't raise his suspicions. I'll use some of my people to test the waters. If Talon actually intends to reveal the shifters to the general populace—" Bride opened her mouth to argue, but Rhiannon silenced her with a stormy glare, then rushed on, "and if he does have a working plan in place, and you feel he has a good chance of convincing enough shifters to participate, we will act together to stop it."

This last bit seemed to mollify Bride. The saint settled herself into the cushions of the sofa, drawing a hand over her skirts to smooth them. "When you do smite him, Llew, use a thunderbolt. We can't let them think we've gone soft."

Angus laughed at the unexpected bloodthirstiness of his sister's request. "There's my sis. So glad to see you're still one of us."

Lugos exchanged a silent eye roll with Rhiannon. He tried not to think about how low his god-powers were in comparison to those of the others in the room. To be sure, there had been opportunity, a few in the pagan community who actively sought him out. At all costs, he'd tried to avoid those meetings. He knew how addictive freely given power was and how counterproductive in achieving his larger aims and goals for all humanity. Yet, despite his best intentions, Lugos had occasionally succumbed to the gnawing desire. Sometimes it had been because circumstances demanded it of him, and other times it was because he'd simply been unable to deny himself. It was partially this failing in himself and his kin, along with their seeming immortality, that had spawned the vampire myths. The only difference between the myth and the reality was that they fed on energy, not blood. Blood was a demon's need. And even that had been designed by the gods for their own selfish purposes.

"If you will excuse me for one moment," Rhiannon announced. Abruptly the goddess rose to her feet, the Lenox vase still clutched in her hands. "I'll be back." She strolled out of the room, leaving Lugos to manage the two siblings.

He regarded them both in determined silence. After a short time, it was apparent that they were just as uncomfortable alone with him as he was with them. Bride kept her eyes averted and her hands busy by worrying the edges of her cake slice until it was mere crumbs on her plate. Angus had reverted to his practiced expression of boredom, focusing his attention on everything but Lugos. For all his "bro" this and "bro" that, Angus considered Lugos no more a brother than any passing mortal.

Still studying Angus's perfect profile, Lugos asked, "What's Jewel's last name?" The simple question upset the fragile china teacup resting in Bride's lap. She hastily set the teacup on the silver tray and wiped at the damage done to her skirt with a napkin instead of just wishing the spill away.

Angus shrugged. "Nobody at those things has a last name. I'm not even sure Jewel is the woman's real name."

"Well, that's less than helpful. Which coven?" Lugos pressed. He had already assumed it was the Sacred Grove Coven, since that was the one in which Seraphine had been an elder, and Angus had said that the two gossiping sisters were Seraphine's coven mates.

Angus gave Lugos another shrug. "Man, I don't know. It was an open invitation. I get dozens of them this time of year."

Lugos's patience had reached its limits. The tension in his shoulders and jaw was surely going to end in a spectacular headache before the day was done. "Do you know what city you were in? Can you at least give me a state?"

Angus's limited repertoire of expressions shifted to affronted. "Here. It was here in Kentucky. It was in a field, no fuckin' city for miles around."

Chapter 6

"Outside Murray," Rhiannon announced. She had quietly reentered the room, a young woman close on her heels. The woman was hastily but discreetly tucking a gray cotton t-shirt into the back of her jeans.

"Lugos, this is Alex," Rhiannon explained. "She can take you to where Seraphine's body was found."

Lugos studied the slender young woman standing nervously before the four gods as Rhiannon resumed her seat. Alex was athletically proportioned. Her hazel eyes were slightly slanted, set in a perfect, heart-shaped face framed by straight, cropped black hair. "You're a shifter." His remark was not a question.

She glanced around at the assembled gods before answering. "I was Seraphine's familiar."

Lugos thought Alex's deep-blue eyes had grown a mite brighter at the mention of Seraphine's name. Perhaps with tears, Lugos thought. Nerves? Grief? He had seen the shifter's nostrils flare ever so slightly when her eyes traveled over Angus. Had she recognized him? Did she dislike the god? Had Seraphine honored him that night as well, along with her coven mates?

"Not many witches have a shifter as their familiar."

"We were close for several years before she accepted me as

her familiar," Alex replied, finally settling her gaze back on him alone.

"You were lovers," Lugos gently offered. His statement startled her, but to her credit the young woman did not deny the extent of the relationship. She gave him a nod, confirming his guess.

"I'm sorry for your loss." Unlike his kin, Lugos understood loss and grief better than most because of his link with Keely.

"It wasn't a suicide like the police said. I wasn't there." Alex paused a moment, then rushed on. "But Seraphine had no reason to——." She paused again.

It was clear that the shifter's emotions for her lover ran deep. What exactly the emotions were and precisely how they were layered, Lugos had yet to determine: guilt, grief, anger, fear. Rising from his chair, he beckoned Alex forward and offered up his own seat so their interview would feel less like an interrogation. It hadn't occurred to any of the others to do such a thing, Lugos noticed with a touch of irritation. And why would it? They were gods, after all. They were immortal; Alex was not. Her life was but a flicker, here for just a moment and then gone, only to be replaced by another mortal. It was an endless parade for them.

He settled himself in another chair. If he was going to use Alex to get information about Talon, he needed to make his investigation into Seraphine's death appear convincing. Lugos leaned forward. "Who are Jewel and Josey?"

If this question surprised the shifter, it didn't show, which led Lugos to briefly wonder if Rhiannon had prepared Alex beforehand.

"They're sisters, and they joined the coven about two months ago. They told Cassie, the high priestess, that they'd had a bad experience with a coven in Alabama and that after moving to Kentucky they'd been cautious about joining another. That's why they didn't have any letters of recommendation or introduction from their last mentor. Cassie took them on as apprentices, since they were sisters. But Seraphine didn't like that, or the fact that

Cassie didn't follow up to find out if anything questionable had actually occurred in Alabama. At the very least, Seraphine wanted the two to be taught separately until their strengths and weaknesses could be properly assessed. She and Cassie fought over that, but Seraphine had more pressing demands on her time, so she let Cassie have her way. The matter was dropped, but Jewel never warmed up to Seraphine after that, though Josey didn't seem to hold a grudge."

"Any other coven member have a problem with Seraphine?"

Alex flinched as if Lugos had slapped her. "No. We all loved her."

"Jewel didn't," Lugos quickly reminded her. Alex had just revealed a potential power struggle between the high priestess and Seraphine. But Lugos didn't mention that. He could see that Bride was about to say something. Lugos cut his eyes in her direction and fingered his cane. Bride snapped her mouth shut.

Turning back to Alex, he said, "If I can prove Seraphine didn't end her own life, then it's murder, Alex, which means someone didn't love her." Lugos let that idea sink in for a moment before asking, "Who would that be, Alex?" He leaned back in his chair. "You knew her best of all. You were lovers, her familiar." Lugos didn't know what animal Alex turned into, but from the way the woman moved and sat, he guessed it was a cat of some kind.

After a long silence, Alex just shook her head, her black locks swaying slowly from side to side. "I really don't know who would hurt her. I just know that I would have known if she was going to hurt herself."

Lugos believed the shifter. A lover might miss the signs that preceded suicide, but a familiar would not. Unless Alex was lying to them—and for now he doubted it—then Seraphine was murdered, and there might be something to Rhiannon's suspicions. Murder also gave him the perfect reason he needed to delve into Talon's plans.

After a few more questions, Lugos had the basic details leading up to Seraphine's last days. The timeline was fairly straightforward and predictable. The Sacred Grove Coven's headquarters was located in Murray, Kentucky, but the coven had a long-standing lease on a piece of property not too far outside the city limits, which is where the May Day celebration that Angus attended had been held. On the morning before Beltane, an early-arriving Jewel had overheard the argument in question between Seraphine and Talon. Alex had arrived at the farmhouse next and found Jewel eavesdropping on the porch. The shifter continued to claim that she'd only caught the last of Talon's threats against his sister, though Lugos repeatedly pressed her on that point. With Alex's arrival, Seraphine had realized they had been overheard. Talon had stormed out, knocking Jewel to the ground. According to Alex, Seraphine flatly refused to discuss the episode with her. In Jewel's case, Seraphine had threatened expulsion from the coven if the witchlet breathed a word to anyone. In front of Alex, Jewel had given her word to the elder never to speak of the episode.

The day following Beltane, Seraphine had gone to Louisville alone, refusing to allow Alex to accompany her. Twenty-four hours later, Seraphine had been found dead. Forty-eight hours after that, the police had officially declared Seraphine's death a suicide, and her body was released to her brother. The very next day, Talon had buried Seraphine in Lexington. The funeral had been attended by all Seraphine's coven mates, Alex, Talon, various high-ranking USL members, and a handful of witch elders from across the eastern seaboard.

Less than a week had passed since the funeral when Alex had shown up on Rhiannon's doorstep. Apparently, the coven had thrown her out. Lugos did a quick count. If Seraphine died on the night of the second, then the trail was already eight days old. Why Angus had chosen to sit on the Talon issue for that long was anyone's guess.

"Well, first things first. I need to go to Louisville." Lugos stood, snatching up his things in the process.

"Now?" Alex asked, surprise causing her voice to rise an octave.

"How cold do you want the trail to get? We could wait a few

more weeks if leaving right now is too inconvenient for you." Lugos hadn't meant to sound angry, but he was past ready to quit the company of his kin. The sooner he got this charade of an investigation started, the sooner he could get home. It was going to be hard to prove anything without a body. He'd have to rely on the reports of local law enforcement, who had no fucking idea what to look for when investigating a shifter's murder.

"No. No. I'm ready," Alex replied, popping up from her seat.

Lugos gave the shifter a curt nod before turning to Rhiannon. She, too, had risen from her perch beside a determinedly distracted Angus. He had spent the better part of Lugos's questioning with his head bent, posting tweets on his cell phone, while Bride worried the folds of her skirt. With a grimace, Lugos also noted that none of them had touched Bride's tea. With a profound sense of relief, Lugos followed Rhiannon from the room. Alex trailed behind.

Once they were in the foyer, the goddess put a set of keys in Lugos's open palm. "I had the car brought around front for you. Nothing flashy—it's Kentucky, after all." The smile was a little too wide, the twinkle in her eyes a little too bright.

Lugos grinned. "You know me too well, I think."

Without warning, Rhiannon then leaned forward and placed a lingering kiss on his left cheek. It startled him, both the intimacy of her action and the selfless gift of energy she so ruthlessly pushed into him. An old, familiar strength and tingling spread through his limbs, and for a moment her halo of power extended outward to embrace him like a lover. Even as his mind rebelled at the act, his body recognized and absorbed her power greedily. And then the blessing was over. Without explanation, Rhiannon stepped back, smiled and walked away.

Chapter 7

"Car?"

Lugos ignored the surprise in Alex's voice. His mind was reeling from what had just happened. Only once before had Rhiannon done such a thing for him. And he'd been just as much at a loss then as he was now as to why she'd shared her power with him.

With the keys clutched tightly in his hand, Lugos hastened toward the door. With Rhiannon's gift, Lugos knew he was perfectly capable of teleporting himself and the shifter to the scene of Seraphine's death. But the drive would give him an opportunity to discover what Alex was hiding. And why waste his newly acquired power unnecessarily?

Rhiannon's "car" turned out to be a white Ford F150 dually truck. Lugos swore under his breath the moment he laid eyes on it. Stowing his bag, cane, and jacket in the space behind the driver's seat, he barked over the bed of the truck, "Coming?"

Alex scurried down the front steps and bounded up and onto the passenger seat like a scalded cat. Lugos cringed inwardly at his tone. He'd need to try, once they were on the road, to manage his frustrations and set Alex at ease.

Lugos dialed Griffin. The phone rang once before the young

man's voice came on the line.

"Yeah. I was just about to text you. It was delivered."

"Good. Now do something for me. Scan the Net for Seraphine." Lugos paused and looked pointedly at Alex through the truck's window.

"Dunbar. Elizabeth Dunbar."

"Elizabeth Dunbar," Lugos amended. "Seraphine may only be what her...friends call her. She's a resident of Murray, Kentucky, and died sometime between the evening of May second and the morning of May third. Check Louisville PD for a case file, and get me a copy of the autopsy report. It was ruled a suicide fairly quickly, so there may not have been one." As an afterthought, Lugos added, "Also, get me everything you can on the Sacred Grove Coven, also located in Murray: leases, deeds, assets, the works." When Lugos was done with his demands, there was a long silence on the other end of the line.

"What is it, Griffin?"

"Uhhh..."

This was the first time Lugos had asked Griffin to search into anything remotely resembling the Pale. The kid was about to get a crash course in weird. Lugos almost felt sorry for him. Careful to keep the impatience out of his voice, he cautioned, "No questions why, Griffin. Just do it. I've got a few hours before I get there."

"Uhhh...all right. I'm on it. I'll send you what I find."

"Thanks." Lugos then ended the call and punched in Louisville, Kentucky, letting Google Maps find their current location. It wasn't until he saw the little blue dot blinking back at him that he realized Rhiannon's farm was just east of Lexington. Perhaps he should have known that, but he hadn't. According to Google, Griffin had an hour and a half to find out everything he could about Alex and the coven before they reached Louisville.

Lugos slid behind the wheel and started the dually's engine. When it roared to life, he found himself briefly wishing he were back in Georgia. The only problem he faced there was not claiming what was his.

Despite Lugos's initial intentions, it wasn't until they were halfway to Louisville that he started questioning Alex again. To be honest, it was because she started talking first. His mind had been centered on Keely before tackling the Talon dilemma should Angus's information prove accurate.

"You're not like the others."

Lugos glanced at her before checking to see if the silver sedan that seemed to be following them was in fact still there. He had spotted the Pontiac a mile or two before the interstate. If the driver was trailing them, he wasn't doing a very good job of it. At no point had the Pontiac attempted to pass, even though Lugos had taken the precaution of varying his speed.

"No, I'm not like the others," he replied, his attention once more on the road that lay before them. "Did you know about Talon's plans to take the shifters public?"

Alex sat in silence far too long. "Yes. He and Seraphine talked about it often."

"And she thought it was a good idea?" Lugos sped up and overtook another car.

"When she and I first met, yes, she did."

"What changed?" Lugos glanced over at her. She was staring out the passenger window at the interstate landscape, so he could not read as much of her expression as he would have liked.

"I did, I think. She and Talon had this idea that once average people realized how much the shifter community had sacrificed to protect them, that would remove the fear. And maybe for some, it would. Does it really matter if the guy down the street who did four tours in Afghanistan with Special Forces is a wolf on the weekends?" Alex gave a little shrug as if to say it shouldn't. "But neither Talon nor Seraphine ever gave any thought to those of us who can't change into badass predators or who don't have a military career to point to, or even the poor souls whose control is sketchy and are forced to live far from people. Coming out into the open as Talon wants is simply impossible. The plan was, is, a recipe for shifter genocide. I don't know why he can't see that."

True, Lugos thought. Most shifters tended to choose some form of military service as a sanctioned way of channeling their innate aggression. When that part of their life ends, they typically retire to all-shifter communities so control can then be maintained by the strict discipline of a single leader. But not all shifters are made equal, nor equally moral. A stellar career dedicated to country and flag would never offset the sheer terror people would feel once they discovered the world they thought they knew never actually existed.

"So…by the time Talon and Seraphine argued on the eve of Beltane, you had changed her mind on the subject." Lugos felt Alex's cat eyes on him.

"Yes."

"Did Seraphine ever fear her brother?" he asked, with a quick glance in the rear-view mirror. The car was still there.

Alex gave a snort of derision and turned away again. "No. She adored him. No matter how much he railed, I never felt any fear in her where he was concerned."

It was rude to ask a shifter what their dual form was, but he pressed anyway. "Because she was a bear as well?"

"No!" Alex replied. "She and Talon grew up together, but they weren't blood siblings."

Lugos took his eyes off the road to glance at Alex, who had turned away from watching the monotonous landscape.

"Seraphine was a cougar."

He could tell that she was surprised he hadn't already known this. "Was there anything in their past that might make you think they were once something more than the brother and sister everyone thought them to be?" Lugos checked on the silver sedan again. He made plans to exit, see if the driver was stupid enough to follow.

Alex shrugged. "Not that I ever saw. We didn't talk about the past much, kind of a rule with us. But she was completely loyal to me. I never got the impression she liked men in that way."

The basic dynamics of a relationship, whether human or not, tended to be fairly predictable. In Alex and Seraphine's relationship, it was clear to Lugos that Seraphine had been the teacher and Alex the student. Seraphine had been more mature, an elder, an ambassador between two very different communities. Somehow, she'd figured out how to balance the two sides of her nature, witch and shifter. Her relationship with Talon was obviously more complicated than Alex was willing to admit.

Lugos guided the dually onto the expressway off-ramp. "I'm going to put some gas in this thing and let you grab a bite to eat while I make a call or two." He watched the silver Pontiac fly past their exit, and the tension in his shoulders eased a bit.

Chapter 8

"You mark my words, Keely Ann Lee, you're gonna end up as the devil's own bride if you don't get yourself to church, and soon!" her mother's voice railed. "The whoredom of a woman may be known in her haughty looks and eyelids. If thy daughter be shameless, keep her in straightly, lest she abuse herself through overmuch liberty. Ecclesiastes 26:9–10."

Clutching the phone tighter than was strictly necessary, Keely rolled her eyes. In the process, she couldn't help but take in the empty, slightly depressing interior of the only bar in Salem, Georgia, the Witch's Whistle. "Yes, Mama," she responded. It wasn't the first time her mama had all but called her a whore. And it wouldn't be the last. "I'll be there Sunday, just like every Sunday, sittin' right up front next to you. I just ain't coming tonight. Got to work to pay bills." She hesitated only a moment before hastily adding, "and the Lord's ten percent." In the silence that followed, Keely could feel her mother's disapproval seep through the telephone line. "Mama—" she began, trying to find a way out of the conversation.

"You shouldn't be workin' in that devil's den. Naught but sin and wickedness to be got from a place like that."

Before her mother could sling another Bible verse at her,

Keely replied, "Ain't nothin' evil to be had on a Wednesday afternoon, Mama. I'll see you Sunday, bright and early. Gotta go now." Keely abruptly ended the call.

As she slipped her cell phone into her shorts pocket, Keely sighed. Mama didn't like the Witch's Whistle, nor its owner, an aging Hell's Angel who went by the name of Cutter Fleming. And she never would. No need to keep fighting a battle that was unwinnable.

"Mama says hi." Keely forced a grin for Cutter's benefit.

With a shrug and a grunt, Cutter continued to stock the beer case. He was a big man whose once-bulldozer-like build had long since begun to carry more marshmallow than steel. That's not to say that Cutter couldn't put a hurt on you if he caught you stealing from him. Or smash a customer's face with a single, meaty fist if Keely was being hassled by a drunk. But Keely suspected that all in all, the sixty-four-year-old Cutter had mellowed since his arrival in Salem some five years back. Cutter's sudden appearance and his plans for opening a bar had indirectly helped Keely. It had all but stopped the small-town speculation about Keely's father's death, which had occurred just the previous year.

Keely suspected that her father had shot himself to get away from her mama's constant nagging and Bible thumping. Or it had been his way of escaping the boredom of Salem. A small place, hardly more than a wide spot in the road, Salem was home to some three hundred and sixty-six souls. Most of those souls were old either because of age or because they'd been born that way. The town itself didn't have much going for it other than the fact that it bore the same name as the wicked one in Massachusetts. The town had no bowling alley, no movie theater. Nearly all the books a body would want to read had been banned by one of the dozen churches populating Salem's outskirts. From the tongue-speaking Pentecostals to the somber Methodists, the biggest choice left to those living in Salem was in which church they might gain salvation.

Cutter had once commented that any place with that much

religion needed a bar. And so, soon after his arrival, he'd parked his Harley, effectively ending his gypsy ways, and opened the Witch's Whistle—to the horror and the secret delight of more than just a few of Salem's repressed residents.

Keely smiled when the skull-shaped chime over the bar's door jingled brightly. Burk took his usual seat at the end of the bar, just in time for his 3:15 pick-me-up. Keely eyed her tip jar and sighed again. Burk was no tipper.

She set an amber-filled glass on the polished wood in front of him, the ice in the tumbler tinkling invitingly. "Good afternoon, Mr. Jasper. Heard anythin' new?"

He accepted his afternoon libation from her with a salute of his glass. "Not much happens at the shop, 'cept for changing Mrs. Dawson's oil and rotating a set of tires that didn't really need it." Burk had been strictly a shade-tree, cash-only mechanic until Mr. Sallie retired from the gas station on Grayson Street. He was still a cash-only businessman when it came to those he didn't know.

After a sip, he set his glass down on the bar and looked beyond her to Cutter, who'd yet to say "boo" to the only customer who'd come in since noon. "I thought you weren't gonna let this pretty thing back again, Cutter. Thought we'd finally got this girl a real job with Doc Bennett."

"Doc Bennett is a nearsighted old goat," Cutter grumbled, his voice rising from inside the beer cooler.

Doc Bennett was by all appearances the perfect southern gentleman. Keely's mama thought him the most respectable man in Salem, or at least equal to Pastor Franklin. It was a common thought held among the ranks of the blue-hairs of the church, regardless of denomination or marital standing. He'd even courted Keely's mama back in the day. In truth, Doc was a horny son of a bitch who regularly cheated on his wife of nearly forty-three years.

"He got handsy one night in the office. Not that you heard that from me," Keely butted in. She'd been so stunned that it had taken her a full five seconds for her mind to reconcile that the man groping her breast without so much as a please or thank you was the same grandfatherly figure her Mama had held up to her Daddy as the ultimate in refined male charm.

Burk took another sip of his drink. "Hope you put him in his place."

"She did," Cutter replied, raising his head out of the depths of the cooler to put an end to the topic.

Keely tried to shake off the sudden rush of shame that colored her cheeks. After all, it hadn't been her fault. She'd done her best to be professional, had dressed each day like she was going to church and not to the Witch's Whistle. She'd told Cutter straight away what had happened, but not Mama. Keely had known that no sympathy would be forthcoming from that quarter. She'd been told often enough that men saw the sin in her, smelled it on her like some lustful perfume. Keely didn't rightly believe that, but then hadn't Lugh pretty well summed up her entire dating life just this morning? He was convinced that she had a stunning talent for attracting the worst type of men. Whether they looked like Carlos, all leather and tats, or Lugh in his rich and tailored clothes, Keely knew herself well enough to realize that she always fell the hardest for the forbidden.

To stop herself from thinking too much more on her many character flaws, Keely busied herself with the task of cleaning a line of wine glasses that no one ever used. The repetitive, mindlessness of the work helped ease the sudden flutter of butterfly wings that tickled her stomach. It happened each and every time she thought of Lugh. Keely tried not to speculate on what it would be like to step out with him. Or about him smiling at her like he'd done this morning. It had been like looking at the sun, warming her so that she felt like chocolate in the summer heat.

The skull chime rang out again.

Keely glanced up in time to see the door swing shut behind a young man about her age. He was tall and lean, in a red t-shirt and blue jeans. Dark-haired, he moved to the bar with a cocky grace that warned Keely that he knew just how hot he was. Despite hearing Cutter's low growl of annoyance, she smiled prettily at the new arrival. When Mr. Red T-shirt smiled back, it was not at all like Lugh; more like a wolf who'd spotted his next meal, all hungry-like.

"Warm out, isn't it? How's about a cold one?" Mr. Red T-shirt slid onto a stool at the bar two spots down from Burk.

Cutter pulled a beer at random from the cooler, popped the top, and slammed it down in front of the stranger. Beer foam splashed onto the counter. Mr. Red T-shirt's gaze shifted from her to Cutter.

"Keely, go finish counting the inventory in the back."

Not once did Cutter take his eyes off the new arrival, not even when he shoved the clipboard toward her. None of Cutter's gruff behavior seemed to ruffle the guy's cool swagger, though Burk looked a little out of sorts. She watched as Mr. Red T-shirt took a slow sip of his beer, amusement clearly written on his face. The guy shrugged off Cutter's snarling attitude as if he hadn't a care in the world. He then deliberately smiled at her again.

Keely set the bar rag down to take the clipboard from Cutter's outstretched arm. Thinking of her empty tip jar, Keely returned the stranger's flirtatious smile. "His bark is worse than his bite," she told him, nodding her head in Cutter's direction.

The statement made Mr. Red T-shirt's smile widen, white teeth in the dim glow of the neon lights.

"I wouldn't count on it," Cutter growled.

Satisfied that she'd made an impression, Keely left Cutter alone with the stranger and sashayed to the storeroom. Any other day, she would have ignored Cutter's interference and stayed to flirt with Mr. Red-and-Sexy, but Lugh had finally lowered the barrier that up till today he'd seemed bound and determined to keep. Sure, he'd always been friendly, always helpful, right there if she needed him. He'd even flirted a bit, but always he'd stayed just shy of some line he'd drawn. It had taken her five long years to get him to ask her out, and not even Mr. Red T-shirt in all his hot and dangerous badness was going to mess up her chance to see what might lie behind the cool exterior that was her neighbor.

In passing, Keely stole a cigarette from the open pack resting on Cutter's desk and walked out the back door to have a quiet smoke. But no sooner had she taken that first, glorious drag than Mr. Red T-shirt himself appeared, striding toward the only other car in the lot besides Lugh's Mustang and Cutter's Harley. Shading her eyes from the glare of the gravel, Keely called, "Hey, he throw you out?"

Pivoting smoothly, Red T-shirt changed directions and ambled toward her as if he'd just been waiting for her to call out. "Nah. It would take more than threats from your boss to send me packing with my tail between my legs, sweetheart," he boasted, smiling back like he knew more about what Cutter was capable of than she did. Pointing at the cigarette in her hand, he added, "You know, those things'll kill ya."

She shrugged, then smoothed her blue-jean shorts unnecessarily with her free hand. Now that they were outside, she thought, perhaps he wasn't all that handsome.

He glanced at the Mustang and then back at her. "You own that?"

Keely shook her head. "No. Belongs to a friend."

"Must be a mighty good friend to lend you a classic like that baby."

Keely shrugged again. Dropping the cigarette on the ground, she extinguished it under the sole of her cowboy boot. She then took a minute to gather her hair and wind it into a knot so what little breeze there was could get to the back of her neck. Fixing it in place with a pen from her back pocket, she said, "Perhaps." She wasn't sure why, but she didn't like him quite as much now. It happened that way with some guys. The more they talked, the less interested she became.

Mr. Red T-shirt smiled, once again giving her the impression of a wolf. "I didn't know Lugos had many friends, at least none as cute as you."

Keely's polite smile faltered. "Don't know no Lugos. I think you mean Lugh."

"Smart, blond, rich guy, likes his privacy. Yeah, I know him. Matter of fact I was hoping to run into him, seein' that Salem is such a small place, but before I could get around to asking, seems your boss took an irrational dislike to me."

Suddenly protective of Lugh's privacy, Keely took a step back and said, "He left on a business trip this morning. You got a card or somethin'? I'll let him know you were lookin' for him."

Mr. Red T-shirt grinned knowingly. "Yeah, think I do, over in my car. It'll take me just a minute." He turned and started walking away fast. "Found a car I think he'd be interested in. A classic like his 'Stang over there."

Relief washed through her. Mr. Red T-shirt was just another car buff like Lugh. Feeling remorseful for her earlier reaction, Keely trailed him across the lot, slowly at first, but feeling a little silly for being paranoid, she hurried to catch up. She stood by as he reached through the open window of his orange-and-black muscle car.

Still digging for the card inside the car, he said, "I know him fairly well, sweetheart. If he's letting you drive that ride over there, then he must think you're pretty special."

Despite the heat of the sun, Keely felt the blush rise to her cheeks. "Maybe," she replied. She leaned a hip against the side of the car. Maybe Red T-shirt was right. Perhaps Lugh would come back from his business trip and tell her that he'd always liked her. Maybe he'd been trying to show her all along, but she'd been too preoccupied with guys like Mr. Red T-shirt, here, to realize it.

Rising from his crouch through the car's window, Mr. Red T-shirt straightened, turned, and smiled.

A flutter of unease quickened Keely's pulse.

In a blur of motion, his hand abruptly clamped around her throat. Squeezing, he pushed her up against the car. It was at that point he showed her the pistol he'd been hiding.

Keely tried to scream. When that didn't work, she desperately tried to pry his hand off.

With only the single grip on her neck, he swiftly jerked her forward, slammed her back against the car, and then pinned her there using his body.

Unable to breathe, she clawed at the hand cutting off her airway. He had left her no room in which to fight.

"Now, sweetheart, you're going to get into the car without giving me any trouble," he said, his hot breath against her ear.

Dizzy, Keely blindly pushed against a chest as hard as stone. She blinked. She could feel her limbs turning to mush, her legs to water.

"Nod once for me. No, no, no… you ain't gonna pass out." He patted her cheek, once, twice, and then Keely felt the grip around her neck ease. She coughed and gulped air like a fish stranded on shore. She would have collapsed in a heap except for his body and the car holding her in place.

"Let me know you heard me, sweetheart."

Staring up into his calm face, she nodded, because no other option was left open to her. Her Mama was right. The devil had come for her.

His lips then brushed her cheek like he had all the time in the world. "That's a good girl."

Keely heard the car's door creak open, and her heart, which had started racing the moment he attacked, now nearly leaped out of her chest. He herded her toward the opening, hand still viselike around her neck. The edges of her vision darkened as he pushed her down into the passenger seat. When he finally released his grip, Keely rocked forward to ease the dizziness and accidentally banged her forehead on the dash, just as the door slammed shut beside her. Seconds later, he was in the car with her, the barrel of his gun jabbed into her ribs. Keely tried to clear the spots from her vision, still gulping air through her bruised windpipe like a dying fish. Instinctively she reached for the door handle as the engine roared to life.

Beside her, Red T-shirt bellowed over the engine noise, "Fuck!"

Keely looked up past the spots in her vision to see Cutter standing in the path of the orange car. He looked like some dark avenging angel, a double-barreled shotgun aimed at Mr. Red T-shirt's face.

"Get out of the goddamn car, Keely."

For a moment she just sat there. She couldn't move. Her mind seemed stuck in slow motion. Keely glanced down at the gun pointed at her side, then back up at Cutter through the windshield. Her right hand still on the door handle, she gently applied pressure, enough to release the lock. When Red T-shirt didn't shoot her dead, she pushed the door open a crack.

"Go on, he's gonna let you out!" Cutter bellowed over the roar of the engine.

As a kind of confirmation, Mr. Red T-shirt removed the metal barrel from her ribs, laid the handgun in his lap, and revved the car's engine. Not once did he take his eyes from Cutter or the end of the barrel aimed at his face.

Quick as she could make her limbs obey, Keely stumbled out of the car. As soon as she cleared the seat, a spray of gravel pelted her. Keely ducked her head behind her hands and turned away to protect her face. When the boom from Cutter's shotgun exploded beside her, she nearly wet herself.

The tires squealed when rubber found asphalt. Only then did Keely managed to look up. Cutter's shot had been well over the top of the car. His way of saying, "Get the fuck out of here."

Cutter cracked open the shotgun, plucked out the expended shell, and dropped it before turning toward her. "Thought I told you to see to the inventory."

Raising a shaky hand to her abused throat, Keely croaked, "Fuck you." Then her knees buckled. Cutter dashed forward and caught her, barely sparing her the added humiliation of slicing her knees open on the sharp gravel.

"Easy, girl. You're going to be all right. Let's just get you back inside and out of this heat."

Keely let him guide her across the parking lot and into the

coolness of the bar's back storage area. Glancing toward the front, Keely vaguely found herself wondering if Cutter had left Burk in charge of the bar before coming out to play Dirty Harry, redneck style.

As if hearing her thought, Cutter said, "Wednesdays are slow. It's just us. Have a seat while I go fetch a bag of ice for that neck of yours." He awkwardly helped lower her down onto the swivel chair before disappearing into the bar area.

Once he was gone, Keely closed her eyes and leaned her throbbing head against the chair's high back. Her throat hurt with each swallow. Without warning, tears sprang up behind her eyelids. She wiped at the few that managed to leak down her cheek. She didn't want Cutter to see just how humiliated she felt. God, she was an idiot. Keely didn't reopen her eyes, not even when she felt Cutter's bag of ice press gently against the side of her neck. She could feel him there, waiting. Probably worrying a little, too. Thankfully, Cutter said nothing. He just let her sit and hide as long as she needed to.

When Keely did find the courage to face him, her avenging angel appeared more than worried; he looked downright apprehensive. It was not an expression she'd ever seen his craggy face wear before.

"What did y'all talk about before he asked you to take a ride with him?"

Keely didn't offer up a sassy retort. Instead, she told him the truth. "Lugh." Her voice sounded raw and huskier than usual. She swallowed and tried again. "Said he knew him. Said I must be more than a friend because he loaned me the Mustang."

"Didn't I tell you to stay away from that guy?"

Keely's temper flared. "I don't need no lectures from you," she croaked back. Mr. Red T-shirt had scared the shit out of her. The last thing she wanted was to be told by Cutter that she deserved it all for not listening.

"Have you and him…?" Cutter's brow pinched.

"His name is Lugh."

"Yeah, you know who I mean. Have you two...?"

Guessing at the direction of his thoughts, Keely's mouth fell open.

"Well?" Cutter pressed.

"It's none of your damn business."

Cutter's nostrils flared. "I'm not asking if you fucked him, Keely. That would be one thing; I'm asking if he's taken a real interest in you. Don't think I don't see that you've suddenly started trying to improve yourself with those online courses. Not that that's a bad thing, it's just...guys like Lugh Hart can make a person want to..."

Keely watched him grope for just the right word for a few moments before she cut him off. "Lugh asked me out on a date, Cutter, which pretty well means he only wants to get in my pants, if my history with men means anything at all. So, whatever is knocking around in that space you call a brain—" Keely paused in her tirade to wave a dismissive hand before ending with a croak, "get over it." God, her throat hurt.

Cutter just stared down at her, like he might be trying to figure out what to do next. Then she watched as, without further explanation, he picked up the clunky desk phone and stabbed at the keypad. It was an old-fashioned black brick of a thing. The cord that connected the handset to the phone was always a tangled mess, and it was that tangled knot that Keely couldn't seem to tear her eyes from.

After a moment he said, "It's Cutter. Tell her I've got a situation. He's gone and gotten attached to someone here in Salem." There was a pause as the person on the other end said their piece, then Cutter grunted before adding, "Can't say that I know." Keely chewed her lower lip as her gaze traveled up the phone cord to watch Cutter. He was listening hard, his brows drawn together and his mouth a grim line. His gaze met hers. "Yeah, we'll be here."

As the receiver was quietly placed back in its cradle, a sinking feeling settled in Keely's gut. She couldn't quite shake the notion that somewhere over the last few hours, a line had been crossed, one that she hadn't known was even there until she'd found herself on the wrong side of it. Keely lowered the bag of ice from her throat, and in a voice closer to breaking than she would have liked, she asked, "What's going on?"

In the minutes of silence that followed, Keely watched Cutter's weathered complexion turn two shades paler. When he glanced over her head, it grew paler still. Reaching forward, he slowly spun the office chair so she, too, could see what he saw.

"I think the one to ask is her," Keely heard Cutter's voice respond.

Directly in front of her stood a very tall, very well-endowed redhead. Keely hadn't heard the skull bells jingle out by the bar, nor had footsteps registered as she'd entered the back area. It was as if the woman had just appeared out of thin air. To add to the eerie effect, the storage room's dim fluorescent lighting gave the stranger's hair kind of a red glow, like it was alive and on fire or something.

The devil woman smiled at Keely, though none of the warmth of her voice or smile seemed to reach the redhead's cool green eyes. "Hello. My name is Rhiannon. I hear we have a mutual friend."

Chapter 9

Ken Larkin stood shoulder to shoulder with the rest, the suffocating black robe hiding more than his middle-aged paunch. It also cloaked his deeply held revulsion toward himself, or at least the part of him that made him resemble the others in the room.

Talon had called the seven of them to the chamber this afternoon, the chamber with the pentacle carved into the wooden floor so they could bear silent witness as the leader of the United Shifter League performed some asinine, sky-clad ritual. Witchcraft was a delusion, in Larkin's opinion, empty play-acting to comfort the weak minded and the desperate. Talon was both.

From within the cowl of his robe, Larkin scanned the six other witnesses. Except for him, they were all proven shifters—little more than beasts barely contained in human form. The heavily perfumed candles scattered about the chamber and the floor-length robes did little to mask the musky scent of them. In the shadows of his cowl, Larkin's nostrils flared with distaste.

When it came to shifters, breeding and purity of line were everything. Only like forms could produce offspring who could be taught to morph at will—bear on bear, tiger on tiger, wolf with wolf, and so on. Copulation with anything outside a shifter's own kind produced nothing but junk DNA, a by-blow of little importance, a child incapable of protecting itself in the bloodthirsty shifter communities. That is, unless that child possessed the skills to see and understand how the game could be played, could see the big picture and then manipulate the pieces on the board. He would have to be patient enough to play the long game.

Larkin looked on as Talon, in the guise of the Horned God, began to fuck the nude high priestess from behind. It was a literal interpretation of the union of athame and chalice. Larkin understood that the public copulation was Talon's way of reinforcing his leadership status. The distinct tang of sex and sweat reached Larkin's nose just as the priestess moaned. If the young witch found the touch of a fifty-year-old shifter disgusting, she hid it well. Gritting his teeth, Larkin let the edges of the oversized cowl hide his eyes from the scene.

They were all aroused, the men and Shea, the only woman Talon had asked to stand witness. Larkin had to give Talon credit. When it came to the manipulation of his fellow animal, the bear knew what he was about. Even Larkin, who prided himself on his superior mind, found himself succumbing to the animalistic passions Talon's theatrics were inducing. The familiar rage swept through Larkin, a fire of the blood that was not human. If not checked by Talon, the ultimate alpha in the room, it would herald the start of a physical metamorphosis. All but the priestess and Larkin would turn—the priestess because she was human, Larkin because he couldn't. No, Larkin had to just suffer the flames of an impenitent fire, unable to shift, unable to embrace the beast inside him and gain sweet relief. And it was in such moments, when Larkin felt those chains tying him to Talon, that he hated the naked, fit, well-muscled man fucking in the center of the pentacle. *He should have let the dumb bear die when he'd had the chance.*

With a good bit of difficulty, Larkin calmed the impotent flame, the blood-fever, the urge that was nothing but a grotesque reminder of the animal crouched and locked forever inside of him. He heard Talon grunt and raised his gaze to see a low growl escape the handsome man's lips. Talon was in a full sweat and probably fighting his own urge to change as well as keeping everyone else in the room in check. It would be an unfortunate end for the priestess if the bear were to lose that fight.

Just as he was pondering this possibility, Larkin's eyes happened to catch a glimpse of Shea's expression. She was across the circle, her stance rigid and her cheeks flushed against the black of her robe. The air was full of denied need, and Larkin's lips drew back in a sneer.

With his help, Talon had taken control of the league. What better way to silence Shea's objections to the Great Unveiling than by forcing her to become Talon's mate? Bound, then, by shifter law, the young she-bear would no longer have the right to voice her opinion in public, except for what her mate might allow. Larkin let his gaze drift back to Talon's rocking backside as a plan began to form.

Time slowed, marked only by the methodical rhythm and sounds of slapping flesh. No doubt the blond bear was drawing this part of the ritual out for his own enjoyment, Larkin ruefully thought. Finally, the priestess's body shuddered under Talon's grip. Two thrusts later, Talon withdrew and shot his semen all over the priestess's mocha-skinned buttocks and backside, only marginally lowering his chances of siring a blow-by.

Reclaiming the calm, almost bored expression he'd worn at the ritual's start, Larkin knew Talon's elaborate ceremony would do little to reveal who had killed Seraphine, nor would it hold the power to assuage the big bear's grief, the depth of which Larkin had yet to wholly understand. It might, however, give Larkin the opportunity to dangle his plans for Shea in front of Talon. If he was going to keep moving the bear toward the unveiling of the shifters to the media, then Talon needed to solidify his standing as undisputed USL leader. Surely a strong but (more importantly) silent mate would help do just that. Ever since Seraphine's unfortunately timed death, Larkin had been searching for a way to refocus the big, dumb bear. Persuading Talon to take Shea to mate could do that. A win-win, Larkin thought. For the first time since entering the chamber, he smiled.

Beneath the robe, his cell phone abruptly vibrated. Catching Talon's eye, Larkin gestured with a nod toward the door before slipping out of the chamber. They both knew that the ritual was essentially over and that his continued presence was no longer needed.

Once in the hallway, Larkin fumbled beneath the folds of the robe to find his pocket. Finally withdrawing the phone, he shoved the cowl off his head and answered, "Tell me."

"You were right. There's a girl. I wasn't able to snatch her. Rhiannon has some watchdog keeping an eye on things here in Salem."

"Did you make an impression?" Larkin halted beside the single elevator and jabbed his finger at the only button.

"Yeah. Think I did. Cutter is the guy's name. Pretty sure he's an aged wolf."

Larkin smiled. "Good. Get back here before you're missed." With his free hand, he fumbled with the cloak's clasp. The damn thing didn't want to let go.

"I can still snatch the little rabbit if you want. It's not like she's all that bright. Without prompting, she told me Lugos was gone on business. I could locate his base camp and confirm on my way out of town."

Larkin was tempted to let the pup try, but he sensed that it might be overplaying his hand. The girl and this Cutter guy might identify Prideaux; best not to risk it. "No. Leave it," Larkin barked into the phone. The clasp finally released with a pop. Larkin ended the call, tugged off the stupid cloak, balled it up and stuffed it under his arm just as the elevator door opened. He could always send someone other than Prideaux, now that he knew a secret lay in Salem.

Chapter 10

Talon sought him out approximately twenty minutes later, dressed in a dark suit and tie. The bear caught Larkin deep in thought. He'd been staring out the window at the manicured lawn that separated Triton Security Corporation, the public mask of the USL, from the nearest brick office complex, which housed a dentist's practice and a small law firm.

Looking up, Larkin could clearly tell that the excitement of the ritual had dissipated for Talon, like the smoke and mirrors that magic was. The bear's eyes were bloodshot. Larkin could just make out the dark circles that had begun to form below them. Relaxing his shoulders, Larkin leaned back in his leather chair as Talon sank into a chair opposite the mahogany desk.

"Give me something, Larkin. You said you only needed a few days. I gave you that."

Larkin took a deep breath and let the silence gather before answering. "Her death has been hard on you, I know. It's been hard on all of us. Those of us who knew her." Larkin paused in his lie to let the silence say what he didn't feel. Seraphine had been a pain in his ass. He was glad she was gone. "I believe Rhiannon has called on Llew, or Lugos. I'm not sure what name he's going by these days. Perhaps he can find us a lead to follow."

"They *knew*, Larkin. They knew she was a shifter. They knew how to kill her to keep the police from asking questions. Which means that it could be one of us." Talon abruptly abandoned the chair and began to pace.

Larkin watched him lumber back and forth for a moment before commenting. "That's a bit of a leap in logic." He pointed at the operations room beyond the closed door. "Every Triton employee knows how to kill a shifter and make it look like a suicide, but only a handful knew Seraphine personally. And if it turns out that it could only be someone she knew, well, that's still a long list of suspects, considering…" Larkin paused to choose his words with care. "She had a lot of enemies, Talon. No shifter reaches middle age or rises to leadership without pissing off the ones they've clawed over."

Talon grunted his agreement. "It has to be one of us."

Larkin shook his head. "No. I don't see it. Your rise all but guaranteed her safety. You called her sister, despite…" Again Larkin paused, this time to take another tack instead of rushing into the quicksand of the unknown. No need to state the obvious; Talon and Seraphine were not brother and sister, at least not by blood. Larkin only suspected that there had once been something else to tie the two together, something that Seraphine had never let Talon forget. "My sources point outside the USL and the shifter community."

"But why bring Rhiannon into it?"

"We've talked about this. We need Llew to stir up the witches. Their dislike of him is legendary. If Seraphine's murderer happens to lie there…well, you can, of course, take your revenge. In the meantime, his investigation will keep Rhiannon busy putting out the fires he inadvertently causes with his questions."

Talon stopped his pacing. "Do you truly believe it was one of Seraphine's coven mates?"

Again, Larkin lied. "I'm not completely convinced, but there is a strong possibility, yes." It wasn't enough to tease an animal, you had to let it think that a kill was in sight. "In the meantime, we need to talk about your next maneuver."

"And what would that be?" Talon asked, his brown eyes narrowing.

"I've been watching Shea. She's going to be a problem if you don't take her in hand. And soon."

Talon waved off the warning. "She's a cub. She'll do as I say."

Larkin shook his head. "I don't think you're reading her right. She's not a soldier. She's an analyst, and as such, she has the irritating habit of forming her own, very vocal opinions. She's already grumbling about her doubts concerning your plans to reveal us. She's saying that it isn't in the community's best interest."

Talon set his large hands on the front of the desk and leaned forward. "We knew there would be naysayers. It was to be expected."

Larkin gave a calculated shrug of his shoulders. "There should not, however, be naysayers in your own organization, your own breed. And she's not a cub. She's twenty-two, and fertile." He paused to stare into Talon's bloodshot eyes. "And from a respected bear clan."

Talon held Larkin's gaze but said nothing.

"Just think about it, Talon," Larkin added. Then, switching topics, he said, "Right before you came in, I received a call from my spy in Rhiannon's camp. Llew was there. So was Alex. I'm sure she's taking him to the house you and Seraphine owned." He made a show of checking his watch. "If I guess correctly, you have a window of opportunity to help his investigation along."

Talon pushed off the desk with his knuckles and stood to consider the possibility. "You think it's necessary to send someone?"

"I think Seraphine's kitten might point him toward us if there isn't some counterbalance put in place."

"Fine. Do it. I'll be in my office. Call me later with the details."

Larkin nodded and then watched Talon exit. The hum of the

control room filtered through the partially open door. Security was about information gathering, but it was also about making sure the right people received the right information at the right time. Rising from his chair, Larkin crossed the carpeted office floor and pushed the door until it shut with a quiet click. He then pulled out his cell phone and dialed.

Chapter 11

It was nearly three o'clock when Alex directed him to a quiet, tree-lined street on the northeast side of Louisville. The houses were all brick ranch types that had been built during the 1940s and '50s, and the lawns were small but well kept. Lugos drove slowly past the house Alex pointed out, but he did not stop until he'd circled the block. After parking the dually on the opposite side of the street and two houses beyond Seraphine's, he cut the engine. His plan was to leave Alex in the truck, slip in, see what he came to see, and then start driving them toward Murray.

"I have a key," Alex said, exiting the truck before he could stop her.

Lugos bolted out of the driver's side and barked, "Get back in the truck, Alex! I'd rather do this by myself." Opening the rear door, Lugos dug inside his bag until he found the shoulder harness with the Glock still snug in its holster. Alex climbed back into the cab, a pout on her lips.

"It will be better this way," he told her.

She didn't argue with him. Once he'd settled his jacket over the firearm, she held out a set of keys.

"Expecting trouble?"

Lugos took the keys, though he had no plans to use them. "I

always expect trouble."

"There's a code for the alarm. 54-97-83."

Lugos nodded, slammed the driver's-side door, and headed across the deserted street at a jog. At not quite three o'clock, the neighborhood was probably as quiet as it was ever going to be. Moving quickly, Lugos headed into the backyard through a chain-link gate partially hidden along a line of shrubbery. Not bothering to use the key Alex had given him, he glanced through the nearest rear window to gain his bearings and then dematerialized, only to materialize once again in the center of a very small laundry room. Lugos was fairly certain that after Seraphine's death, Talon, the new USL leader, would have changed the alarm code Alex had given him along with the house keys.

Weaving his way through a cramped kitchen, he hastened to the front of the house. As he neared the front door, he spied the alarm panel. Once he reached it, he flipped open the top cover, which read, "Triton Security Corp.," popped off the control pad, snipped three separate wires with a small set of cutters from his pocket, and then rejoined two of the cut wires with a practiced twist. The third wire he grounded. When the arming light changed from red to green, Lugos replaced the control pad and snapped the cover closed. A small sigh of satisfaction escaped his lips. None of his kin would have known how to do what he had just done.

In the silence, Lugos allowed himself the luxury of taking a deep breath before letting his gaze wander about the living room and then the adjacent dining room. There was the subtle but telling aroma of cleaning products still in the air. Talon had probably brought in a cleaning service to deal with the aftermath.

Judging by what he saw, Seraphine had kept a tidy but comfortable home. What surprised him was not what he saw but what was missing. Nothing hinted at the fact that she had been a witch—no candles, no incense, no altar, no pentacles or nature trinkets. As he meandered through various rooms, Lugos started to question whether Alex had brought him to the right house. It was all so very Norman Rockwell. He then began to wonder if

Talon had done more than just remove the bloodstains. There were no dishes left in the sink or the dishwasher, no laundry left in the dryer, no lint in the lint trap, no dust on the furniture, no toothbrush beside the white vanity sink. Even the bed appeared to be staged for some future catalog shoot or a real estate agent's open house.

He paused inside what he suspected had been Seraphine's bedroom and picked up a framed photograph of Alex and Seraphine. It was the only personal touch he'd seen during this tour. Two things struck him as he stared at the faces of the women. The first was that Alex appeared truly happy. She was smiling—beaming, actually—at whomever had taken the picture. The other impression was that Seraphine's eyes held a haunted, almost sad expression despite the upturned curve of her lips. Removing the photograph from the frame, he looked for a time stamp but found none. Folding it in half, he slipped it into his jacket pocket, put the now empty frame back where he'd found it, and then went to check the bathroom one more time.

The tub where Seraphine's body had been found was, like the rest of the house, pristine. It took only seconds to confirm that the medicine cabinet had been emptied of all its contents. Lugos leaned against the white porcelain sink and wondered if he was wasting his time.

What did he know? Not much, really, just what Griffin had uncovered and what Lugos had gleaned from Alex. For some forty-odd years, Seraphine had decided to split her life between two worlds, the witches' and the shifters'. Talon and she had claimed a brother–sister relationship, though they were clearly not of the same clan. What had brought the two together? Lugos didn't know. What kept the two of them together despite the fact that they were obviously at odds at the time of Seraphine's death? Again, Lugos had no answer.

Seraphine also appeared to have been inclined toward her own sex, which should rule out any carnal relationship with Talon. Lugos pushed away from the sink. He was missing too much. He knew next to nothing about the woman whose life had ended in this house, and that bothered him. Someone as prominent in Pale relations as Seraphine should have been known to him. But somehow she hadn't been. There had been a flutter of something when he'd seen her face in the photograph, but nothing beyond the ghost of a memory. And as much as Rhiannon would like him to use Seraphine's death as a reason to probe into Talon's affairs, Lugos couldn't help the drive he felt to discover the truth.

Griffin had sent him a copy of the coroner's report and the PD's take on what happened the night Seraphine died. There had been nothing unusual in the officer's description of the scene. However, the coroner's report had mentioned finding a bullet lodged inside the body cavity very near the heart. The coroner had also noted the lack of an exit wound, and the presumed entry wound showed all the signs of having recently healed. The slash marks on Seraphine's wrists had been declared the official cause of death, but Lugos understood what the mortals did not: the unexplained bullet had been the culprit. Seraphine had been shot first, then had morphed in a desperate attempt to heal the damaged tissue so she could continue to fight.

Lugos moved back through the house looking for any sign that might tell him where the shifter had been shot. She would have been in her cougar form. Lugos didn't think she would have had time to morph more than once after being shot so close to the heart. If she had been shot mid-attack, mid-leap, where would the attacker have stood? He scanned the living room. With nothing out of place, no bullet hole or shell, he was left guessing.

While he was trying to picture a plausible scenario, a sudden sense of dread washed over him. For a moment, it was Keely he saw in his mind's eye, fighting for her life. His own heart stuttered and then righted itself, only to gallop inside his chest. His vision narrowed as his breathing became difficult. Then, just as quickly as the disturbing scene had risen, it was gone. Lugos put a hand to his chest, took several deep breaths, and then pushed the fear away. Keely was perfectly safe in Salem. No one knew about her. It was only because of the investigation into this woman's death, and his having taken a step toward claiming what was his, that the old fear of losing her had resurfaced so abruptly. She was his center. Because of that, Lugos knew he would always fear for her, no matter what form she took or in what lifetime she found him.

At least, that's what Lugos told himself as he tried to get back to the task in front of him. What would the killer have done after the gun was discharged?

So close to death, Seraphine—*not his Keely*—would have morphed back into her human form. The process would have knit new skin neatly over the entry wound, concealing the bullet inside. She would have been weak but not dead. *His Keely was perfectly fine,* he told himself again. The killer would have had to drag a still fighting, nude, and probably dying Seraphine to the bathroom tub, run the warm water, slice her wrists, and let blood loss finish the job the bullet had started. Lugos wondered if the murderer had stayed with her until the very end. Or if, thinking the task done, he had left her to die alone. *Perhaps he should tell Rhiannon that he'd found her again.*

In his mind's eye, he could see Seraphine's fall of dark hair spilling over the edge of the white tub, the pink water turning irrevocably darker as the minutes ticked by. At some point, the killer had shut off the flow of water. He would have then reached into the water to pull out the plug, red-tinted water spilling onto white tile as the rising water escaped over the edge of the tub's borders. The photos in the police file had shown a wet floor, despite the chain of the drain plug having been left looped over the faucet. They also showed Seraphine's head rocked back against the edge of the tub, eyes open but sightless. The killer stayed to the end. It had been personal. The killer had wanted to watch the life drain out of her.

The temptation to dial Keely's number was strong. He wanted to hear her voice. At that moment, Lugos needed to touch her spirit with his own. He now had the power to do such a thing even from this distance—to send his spirit winging out beyond the limits of his body to brush against her spirit—but Lugos resisted the temptation. If he did that, if he gave in to that temptation, he'd feel whole again; once whole, he'd never be able to give Keely the freedom she deserved. He'd never give her up willingly once…

"She's fine," he grumbled to himself. She was better off, safer, in her world. His was just too dangerous. If Seraphine, the witch-shifter, couldn't protect herself, then—

Raised voices out on the lawn brought Lugos out of his musings. He checked the clock on the bedside table on his way back to the living room. It read 3:46. He'd been so focused on uncovering the truth behind Seraphine's death that he'd lost track of time.

Lugos unlocked the deadbolt of the front door and swung it wide to find a tan and white sheriff's car parked curbside. Alex was doing her best to delay the officer marching toward the front door. Before the young shifter got herself—or perhaps both of them—arrested, Lugos barked, "Alex, why are you out there?" He pulled her away from the deputy and through the front door as soon as she was within reach. With all the authority of someone who belonged inside this house, Lugos then turned his full attention to defusing the situation.

"I'm sorry for my friend's rude behavior. May I help you?"

Officer Stanton's ruddy cheeks billowed like a bulldog's muzzle as he talked. "Yes. We received a call from the security company that monitors this house."

Lugos raised an eyebrow. "Did you? Odd. As you can see, Officer, everything is as it should be. I have a key and the alarm code, given to me by the owner." Lugos showed the key he'd taken from Alex. "Talon asked that I investigate the death of his sister, Elizabeth Dunbar."

Lugos then produced a card that read, "Lugh Hart, Investigator." The information had been embossed in gold lettering and on heavy card stock. There was a phone number as well. It would send the officer straight to Lugos's voice mail. The officer took the proffered business card. "This is Alex," Lugos continued.

"Elizabeth's close friend." He avoided the descriptor *lover* or *partner* or, worse, *familiar*. "As you can see, Elizabeth's death has been hard on her."

This particular ruse worked better on younger, less experienced civil servants. Officer Stanton was not exactly young; perhaps in his late thirties, Lugos judged. While silently waiting for Stanton to come to some decision about their presence there, Lugos's eye registered the black sedan rolling down the street toward the front of the house. When it turned into the house's empty driveway, it gained the deputy's attention as well.

With Stanton's gaze averted, Lugos hastily motioned Alex to head toward the living room. If things were going to get ugly, then he wanted her out of harm's way. Stepping forward so that his shoulders completely filled the doorway, Lugos leaned against the doorframe. He crossed his arms over his chest to block both the officer's and the new arrival's view of Alex so she could disappear into the house.

A slightly pear-shaped, middle-aged man, perhaps not yet in his fifties, exited the car. The new arrival carried a briefcase and the air of middle management. He wore his hair cropped almost militarily short. His brown suit was of an average cut, both fabric and color unflattering to the man's coloring and girth.

With impatience clearly discernible in the billowing of his bulldog cheeks, officer Stanton confronted the new arrival. "And who might you be?"

"Ken Larkin," came the terse reply. As quickly as a car salesman, Larkin produced his own card. "I represent Mr. Talon Dunbar and Triton Security Corporation."

Hearing this, the officer's lips thinned.

"I believe there has been a misunderstanding, Officer…Stanton," Larkin said, reading the deputy's name badge. "Mr. Hart is here at Mr. Dunbar's request. On behalf of Triton Security, let me apologize for the call from my company. It is not our policy to waste the time of local law enforcement."

The officer just nodded, annoyance drawing his lips

downward. "As long as you say everything is all right…"

"Everything is as it should be," Larkin assured the deputy. "Thank you."

The officer took one last, unconvinced glance at Lugos before departing. In silence, Larkin and Lugos watched the officer pull away. Just as the sheriff's car turned the corner, Lugos said, "So, Mr. Larkin, what does Mr. Dunbar want me to know?"

Chapter 12

"It's hot. Shall we go inside?"

Lugos stepped forward and then aside before waving an arm toward the entryway. "After you, Mr. Larkin."

Despite the bad suit, there was something about Larkin's manner that reminded Lugos of a manservant, a traditional valet or butler. It was an odd notion but one he filed away to ponder later.

Passing by the security panel, Larkin commented, "I see you have bypassed the alarm. But I guess that would be child's play for a god. I have heard much about you, Mr. Hart."

Upon reaching the living room, Larkin turned. "Or should I call you Llew? I really am not used to addressing one such as you. I hope you will forgive my ignorance."

Lugos's lips thinned. Whoever Larkin was, he was not the humble servant he was pretending to be. Lugos suspected a keen intellect behind the act. "I have the sense that you are far from ignorant, Mr. Larkin."

Where the hell had Alex disappeared to? While Larkin was busy setting his briefcase down on the coffee table, Lugos scanned the rooms within view. He could feel her in the house still, perhaps upstairs. The click of a lock brought his attention back to Larkin.

Withdrawing a file from his briefcase, Larkin said, "Mr. Dunbar was prepared at first to accept the local authority's verdict of suicide in his sister's death—that is, until he received a copy of the autopsy report. He asked me to give it to you."

Lugos took the file from Larkin, but he didn't open it. He'd already seen what it contained. "So he knows it was murder."

"Yes," Larkin confirmed. "And as one can only imagine, it has weighed heavily on him since. I assume you know that he is the new head of the USL?"

Lugos nodded.

Larkin hesitated, as if he'd expected more of a response from Lugos. When there was none, he continued. "Well, he has had quite a lot on his plate lately, so when Ms. Dunbar came to him with concerns about the emails, he didn't give them the attention that, in hindsight, they deserved."

Larkin now had Lugos's full attention. "What emails?"

"Oh, you didn't know? Well, it appears that Ms. Dunbar received two threatening emails from an unknown source. We tracked the IP address, but that gave us only a rough estimate showing that whoever sent them did so in an area just west of Murray, Kentucky. I believe the coven Elizabeth belonged to is located in Murray."

"And it's safe to assume that copies of the emails are in this file."

Larkin appeared startled. "Why, yes, of course. Mr. Dunbar very much wants his sister's murderer found."

Lugos cocked his head. "Where was Talon on May 1 and 2?"

Larkin hesitated and then cleared his throat. "I'm not completely sure. As I think you know, Mr. Dunbar shares his sister's affinity for the craft. He is quite a stickler in that regard, and so on May 1 I believe he was participating in rituals. However, from noon onward the following day, I can attest to his presence in the office. He stayed until quite late."

"How late?"

"I would need to check to confirm, but I believe it was nearly three in the morning before he headed home."

"Triton Security is that busy?"

"No, but cementing his authority as leader of the USL is, at least for now."

"Makes one wonder why anyone would want to take on such a challenge."

Lugos caught the small smile on Larkin's lips as the man bent to shut and lock his briefcase. "Yes, I suppose," Larkin replied as he straightened, his lips set once again in a straight line.

"Did Talon oversee the cleanup himself, or did you do that for him?" asked Lugos.

Larkin scanned the rooms before his eyes settled back on Lugos. "Yes, he was here at first. It was, I'm sure, quite painful for him."

Lugos nodded. "Please thank Talon for the information." He waved the folder between them. "And tell him that I will need to see her Book of Shadows. I noticed that it is missing, as are any journals she might have kept." If Lugos's request ruffled Larkin, the man did not show it.

"As you wish." Larkin moved toward the door. When he was once again on the front steps, he paused and turned. "I have been instructed by Mr. Dunbar to secure the premises after you and Ms. Blaylock have departed. I trust Alex is still somewhere in the house."

It was the first sign that Larkin had known Alex was with him. "We will only be a moment more," Lugos assured the man. He then swung the door closed and left Talon's too well-informed servant standing alone in the heat.

It was her clothes Lugos found first. They had been dropped in succession on the kitchen floor. Scooping them up, Lugos wove his way through the house until he came to what had been Elizabeth's bedroom. There, curled near the pillow, lay the quintessential witch's black cat.

Alex was a large cat, as cats go, but she was no cougar like Elizabeth. He tossed the clothes on the end of the bed. One white

Converse tennis shoe bounced off the edge and hit the carpet.

"Get dressed. I've got questions, and I'd rather not ask them here." Lugos turned and stalked back to the living room to read the contents of the folder.

"You didn't tell me about the emails. Did she pay after she got the first one?"

The emails had been short and telling. The first was aimed at blackmail, but the second, sent less than a week later, had threatened retribution. Either Seraphine had refused to pay up after the first email, or she had paid, but the blackmailer had decided that it wasn't enough and had then wanted Seraphine to pay with her life. Of course, there was the unlikely option that the emails had been sent by two different people. The odds were slim, but Lugos had seen stranger things while investigating a murder. Seraphine would have had plenty of enemies, despite what Alex thought. He looked across the cab of the dually at the shifter.

Alex nodded. "She did." Turning sad eyes on him, she added, "Seraphine paid because she wanted to know who had sent them. She'd taken it first to Talon, but he waved it off. She'd expected him to help her find the person. The fact that he was too preoccupied to care was what truly upset her."

Lugos's grip on the steering wheel tightened. "You lied to me, Alex. How am I to find out who did this if you don't tell me everything?" He took his eyes off the interstate to glance at her again.

"I'm sorry. But I never felt…" Alex paused. "I mean, Seraphine told me not to worry. She'd dealt with threats before. She said that these had everything to do with Talon's rise in the USL."

"Tell me about Larkin." Lugos's gaze flicked back to the road and the emerging traffic. It was nearly rush hour, and they seemed surrounded by the unaware, just average people leaving work and heading home. That home probably included a family, dinner, perhaps a pet that could be counted on to remain only a pet and nothing more. Lugos had a three-and-a-half-hour drive to get to Murray and Seraphine's coven.

"I don't like him. Never have. I never understood why Seraphine and Talon put up with him."

Just then Lugos's phone vibrated, and he held up his hand. As he fished it from his pocket, he said, "Hold that thought, Alex." Swiping the pad of his thumb across the cell phone's slick surface, he answered the call from Rhiannon.

"There's a complication," her voice announced as soon as he brought the phone to his ear.

"What is it?"

"Keely was attacked by a wolf. I don't think he was acting on his own. He was sent by someone."

As soon as he heard Rhiannon utter the words *Keely* and *attacked*, Lugos's insides turned to ice. He could feel the blood drain from his face. His heart filled his ears with its drumming. Gingerly he maneuvered the dually onto the shoulder of the interstate. Once there, he rolled to a stop and blindly forced the gearshift into park.

"Lugos, did you hear me?"

The truck's motor rumbled underneath him while cars continued to stream past. Despite the freezing temperature of the truck's air conditioning, a sickly sweat had broken out on Lugos's brow. "I heard you. Where is she?" Even to his own ears, his voice sounded far away. He was afraid to ask how she was. If she was still alive.

"I brought her to the farm to keep her safe. But if you could, I think it would be a good idea to pop back here. All and all, it's been something of a shock to her system."

"She knows nothing, Rhiannon."

"I realize that now, Lugos."

"Keep them away from her. As a matter of fact, keep all of them away from her."

"I will."

Lugos could hear the sympathy in Rhiannon's voice. "I'm trusting you." It was the closest he could come to telling the goddess just how precious Keely was to him. It had to have been the Mustang, the one slip on his part. He'd put her in harm's way again.

Determined to get to her as soon as possible, Lugos slammed the dually into drive and checked the side mirror for a space large enough to pull out into traffic. "I'll be there as soon as I can. Tell her I'm coming. Tell her that I'll explain everything when I get there and that I'll make it all right somehow."

He floored the accelerator and drove into the flow of traffic.

"I will."

After a long pause, Lugos finally asked the terrifying question. "Is she hurt, Rhiannon?" He never should have lent her the damn car.

"A few bruises, that's all."

He didn't ask Rhiannon how she'd known to intervene. She'd kept tabs on him in the past. He could be furious with her later—and probably would be—but for now he was just grateful she'd been watching when he hadn't.

"I'll be there as soon as I stash Alex." Lugos glanced at Alex. "I'm going leave her in a hotel for the night."

"Sounds good. I'll be waiting by the pool."

Lugos ended the call and then glanced at Alex and explained how the next few hours were going to play out. "We're going to pick a nice hotel at random. I'm then going to check you into a room, and you're not going to leave that room until I return. Do you understand?" He was in no mood for an argument, and his tone reflected it. He didn't bother to acknowledge her nod of acceptance before he added, "While I am gone, Alex, you are going to decide to tell me the rest of the story. Whatever it is your hiding might be the very piece of information I need to find Seraphine's killer." He glanced at her again. "That is, unless you sent the emails yourself."

"Of course I didn't!"

The shifter's outrage seemed genuine, but the attack on Keely had skewed his whole outlook; everyone was a suspect now. Lugos didn't believe in coincidence. Why now? Why had a shifter gone to Salem today? Who had sent him? Did the attack on Keely have to do with Talon's plans, or Seraphine's murder, or—

Abruptly Lugos slammed his hand against the steering wheel as a third option suddenly occurred to him. Surely Rhiannon would have warned him if one of his own kin had been behind the attack.

Chapter 13

Larkin was forced to call a technician to replace the control panel. Despite the fact that the god's system tampering had cost Larkin close to an hour, he felt that on the whole the interview with Llew had been a productive one. He'd been able to send the god's investigation in the direction they'd wanted. Should he need it, Larkin had information on at least three witches that would provide a motive for murder. Then there was Alex, the familiar. Early on, he'd recognized the signs of buried resentment in Seraphine's kitten, probably because it was an emotion that he'd gone to great pains to hide in himself.

While the technician worked, Larkin had received another bit of good news. As luck would have it, Rhiannon had sequestered the mystery girl at the Lexington farm. Yet another pot he could stir to keep Llew busy and out of their way.

At a quarter till five Larkin rapped three times on Talon's office door before entering. Sitting behind the massive oak desk, he found Talon reviewing the carefully scripted reveal speeches, which were slated to run in voice-over fashion while patriotic images of strength, honor, and country flashed across the screen. The USL was banking on the public's love of military service to smooth the bumpy path to the league's coming out.

Larkin hid his smile behind a polite cough. By the time Talon looked up, the smile had been safely suppressed. "Llew has the emails and is on his way to Murray to grill the coven members."

"Good. Who did you send?"

Larkin slipped his hands in his slacks pockets. "I went. I thought it too important to delegate. Llew isn't as stupid as Angus the Pretty. He can't be bribed or bought off. The best we can hope for is to distract him for a time."

"Angus finally talked this morning. Rhiannon is asking questions. And as you predicted, she brought Llew into it."

Larkin read the worry on the big man's face. Shrugging his shoulders, he replied, "We knew Angus would in time. It's unfortunate that your argument with Seraphine was overheard and that the witchlet talked in front of Angus. Eventually, Rhiannon will see through our reveal denials and send Llew in our direction, whether or not he's found Seraphine's killer. We need to speed up our timetable."

"How long do you think we have?"

"A week at most."

Talon nodded. "But he'll find the bastard."

"Yes," Larkin lied, feeding the longing he read in the bear's eyes.

"Good. In the meantime, I see no reason to back off. Before Seraphine took up with that kitten, she used to believe that this was the only way to save ourselves, to save our bloodlines."

Larkin was glad to see that the bear was focused again. Perhaps the earlier ritual had been just the right medicine, though Larkin didn't think there was anything partially magical about the cause and effect of sex. Talon had enjoyed demonstrating his power in front of his underlings. And when it came to power, one always wanted more. It was as addictive as any narcotic.

"I'm glad to see you back at work," Larkin said, silently congratulating himself when the bear's eyes were drawn back to the script in his hands. Talon's expensively tailored suit only enhanced the bear's good looks. But Larkin knew not to let the camouflage of civility fool him. Talon was a savage and temperamental beast, a predator.

"I think this should be the first one we release," Talon announced, holding up the script's title sheet for Larkin to view.

"I'll make sure it gets done." Larkin couldn't care less which piece aired first; the result would be the same. He turned to leave. Pausing at the door, he asked, "Have you given any more thought to Shea?"

Talon looked up again, his brown eyes narrowing. "You think it truly necessary?"

Larkin nodded. "Yes. Tomorrow night, and very publicly. Don't give her a way out."

Talon's square jaw flexed in thought, and then dispassionately he replied, "Let our people know that there's going to be a big announcement at tomorrow night's fight. We'll sandwich it in between the second and third fights."

Larkin doffed an imaginary hat and bowed to the bear's theatrical flair. "Excellent. I'll get the buzz started to ensure that everyone is in attendance."

Talon looked back down at the papers on his desk. "Just make sure Shea shows."

"Done." Larkin remembered the god's request, and his hand lingered for a moment on the doorknob. "Oh, he wants to see Seraphine's Book of Shadows. Should I make it available to him?" Larkin didn't need to explain who "he" was, for Talon both wanted and feared the god's involvement.

The big bear hesitated only a fraction of a second. "Do it. But make it perfectly clear to him that I want them back."

"Of course." With effort, Larkin suppressed his smile, but once the door clicked shut behind him, he allowed the grin to bloom. He was going to enjoy every humiliating minute of Shea's collaring. And then, when the general public realized the threat they were under, he was going to savor every beautiful second of Talon's fall from grace, and that of the entire shifter community.

Chapter 14

As soon as the dually was locked and he'd deposited Alex in the room at the Holiday Inn, Lugos dialed Rhiannon on his cell. She answered on the first ring.

"Lugos."

Concentrating all his thoughts on her exact location, Lugos said, "I'm on my——" And then, before he could finish the word *way*, he flung himself through space like a star streaking across the night sky to where Rhiannon waited for him.

A thousand and one times Lugos had rehearsed the conversation, his disclosure to Keely of who and what he was. Each had ended badly in his mind. And now, because he'd allowed himself to entertain the delusion that he could keep her close but at the same time somehow beyond the dangers of his world, they were going to have to traverse that dreaded conversation for real. But no matter how she reacted to what he had to tell her, Lugos intended to embrace her, to just hold her close. It was the only way he would be able to extinguish the terror inside him.

Cane in hand and at the ready, Lugos found Rhiannon poolside. A six-foot hedge separated the pool from the back of the house, where Bride and Angus were still in residence. Clouds immediately began to darken the sky. On his right stood a cheery yellow pool house. Keely was inside. He could feel her distress as easily as he could feel his own legs propelling him forward. Lightning forked between the newborn rain clouds.

Rhiannon had posted a guard near the door, a male shifter clad only in swim trunks. Whether he was there for Rhiannon's enjoyment or Keely's protection, Lugos didn't care. A single shifter would make no difference if Angus or Bride wanted to cause trouble. A sudden gust of wind startled the peacock atop the pool house's blue awning. All this Lugos had absorbed at a glance as he stalked toward the pool house door.

Rhiannon heaved herself out of her lounge chair while trying to tame her auburn locks, caught by the storm's lashing winds. The shifter moved to intercept Lugos. Another bolt of lightning abruptly crackled between the boiling clouds.

"Let him pass, Slade!" Rhiannon called.

The shifter quickly obeyed.

Lightning slammed into the ground just beyond the hedgerow, another just beyond the pool house. Lugos took no notice of Rhiannon's next words. His fear and helplessness had twisted itself into raging anger. A combination of Rhiannon's earlier gift and what godlike power he could still call forth was burning bright in him, ready to leap from his fingertips like claws from a tiger. Every muscle was taut. He wanted a reason, any reason, to bludgeon someone to death for daring to harm what was his.

With his hand firmly on the brass doorknob and a last murderous glare in Slade's direction, Lugos rammed his shoulder into the locked door. It splintered under the force.

"Take a breath, Lugos. You're going to scare the hell out of her."

Lugos caught only a portion of Rhiannon's last warning, most of it drowned by the wind and, now, the rain. Lugos froze when he finally saw her and she him. He was only vaguely aware of the lightning that still flashed in his eyes and outside on the lawn. Struggling for self-control and in a voice not quite human, he managed to ask, "Are you all right, Keely?"

What must she think of him? There was terror in her eyes. She stood across an open room, a small table knife clutched in her hand. Seeing her alive helped Lugos beat back the violence and fear. His tunnel vision began to recede, and he became aware of a small billiard table to his right, a big-screen TV mounted on a far wall, and a cluster of seating too new to have been used much. Behind him was a kitchenette; behind her, a window. After what seemed an eternity, Keely finally answered him.

"Was going to slip out the window, but—but the damn thing's painted shut." Tears made her eyes look like jewels. She took two hesitant steps toward him, knife still at the ready. "What's goin' on, Lugh? How'd I get here? Who's she?" Keely pointed the knife tip at him.

Lugos briefly acknowledged Rhiannon. The goddess had followed him in. The scraping of wood let him know that she'd managed to find a way to close the door behind her. Lugos could feel the shifter, Slade, still outside. It was just the three of them in the room—one too many for his liking. He was struggling with too many emotions. Seeing Keely alive and whole had enabled Lugos to rein in most of his power display. He knew that for her sake he needed to look normal. Still, the thunderclouds he'd created in his rage were going to have to rain themselves out.

Speaking to the goddess but unwilling to tear his eyes away from Keely, Lugos growled, "Go away."

"My house," Rhiannon calmly responded. The goddess then moved silently beyond him on bare feet to lean a chiffon-wrapped hip against the nearest rail of the blue-felted billiard table. She crossed her arms under her scantily covered breasts and made herself comfortable.

The sight of the dark purple marks so clearly on Keely's neck threatened to reignite his rage. The one who had made those marks would die for daring to harm her. Lugos glanced away so Keely wouldn't see the power sparking through him, the flashes of lightning crackling in the depths of his eyes. Rain pelted the pool house roof and lashed at the windows. Slade, no doubt, was drenched. Lugos took a deep breath and then glared at the goddess.

"Don't look at me in that tone. I plucked her out of the danger you put her in. You should be thanking me. And by the by, I know wolverines who behave better."

Lugos clutched the cane in his left hand a little tighter. "Where are they?" A loud crash of thunder shook the walls. He didn't have to say their names for Rhiannon to understand. She knew all too well where his concerns lay.

"Angus is—was—napping before he heads out tonight. And the Saint is busy decorating for a party that I have no intentions of throwing." The goddess inclined her head in his direction, queen to peasant. "Again, you're welcome."

"Is she your boss or something?" Keely asked.

"It's complicated." Their simultaneous response brought a smile to Rhiannon's lips.

Not to be put off quite so easily, Keely took another step toward him. "Well, I suggest you uncomplicate it, first by telling me why I'm here. And then why someone would want to take me to get to you. Are you some kind of drug dealer? 'Cause if you are, that would be mighty disappointin', Lugh."

If the stakes hadn't been so high for them all, Lugos might have laughed at her bravado, but having been the cause of Keely's abduction, he couldn't muster the same levity. "No, Keely, I'm not a drug dealer." He was so damned relieved that she was standing in front of him—relatively normal, relatively Keely—that he felt almost weak. The initial danger to her had passed, and it was tempting to ignore the fact that another danger sat squarely on the horizon. The attack on her life meant that he could not continue to give her the freedom she deserved.

"Well?"

Lugos eyed the knife. The rain was still falling in sheets such that Lugos had to talk over it. "Can you put down the knife?"

Keely looked down at her hand as if she'd somehow forgotten

it was there. "No. I think not," she answered. With her free hand, she flipped her hair behind her shoulder.

It was a nervous habit he'd seen her repeat a thousand times. The fact that it was so singularly Keely, and that she did it now, help ease the tight knot around his heart. At the same time, the storm outside eased a bit.

Lugos nodded. He now had a clearer view of the extent of the bruising on her neck. There was no doubt in his mind that he would hunt down and kill the one who'd put them there.

"All right, then," he began. He slowly leaned the cane against the nearest chair and then took off his jacket, revealing the concealed handgun safely tucked in its holster. He tossed the sport coat into the chair. With great care, he slid the Glock free, safety still on. Aware that Keely was watching his every move, Lugos held out the weapon to her, butt first. She'd grown up in the country. Though he'd never known her to hunt, he assumed she knew how to use a gun.

"If you feel unsafe, even with me, then this will do more damage than that." He nodded toward the knife. "But, Keely, you'll need to empty the entire magazine into me, all fifteen bullets; the same goes for Rhiannon, here. Even if you aim for the head and heart, that will only buy you a little time."

"Excuse me?" Keely and Rhiannon asked in unison. Keely made no move to take the weapon from his hand.

It was only then that Lugos started to breathe again. He'd been afraid to breathe. He'd been terrified that he'd lost her yet again. The thunderstorm outside began to dissipate as rapidly as it had materialized.

"What Lugh is trying to explain to you in his sweet and clumsy way is that he's immortal, as am I. You can't actually kill him, only slow him down."

Lugos watched helplessly as a series of emotions flickered across Keely's face: disbelief, alarm, fear, and then again disbelief. "I don't believe that nonsense. Ain't no one ever escaped death but Jesus Christ," she said firmly.

"Oh, I like her, Lugos," Rhiannon snickered. Then to Keely, she prompted, "Ask how old he is. Or, better yet, *what* he is."

"I'd rather ask you how the hell you drugged me and why you're keepin' me here," Keely snapped back.

Lugos groaned. "Rhiannon, please stay out of this!" He took a few more steps toward Keely and the conversation he'd never wanted to have with her. "You're here because of me, because someone wants to send me a message. I'm sorry you've been pulled into this, Keely. I shouldn't have loaned you the car, or even asked you out. I know better, but—"

Behind him, Rhiannon gasped. "You're *dating* her?"

"Leave it," he growled at the goddess. Then, because he needed to yell at someone, someone who wasn't likely to burst into tears, he pivoted to level the full force of his anger on the redhead. "Did you actually drug her?"

Despite the lingering lightning flashing across the pupils of his eyes and the balled fist at his side, the other of which still held the gun, Rhiannon remained unruffled. "Of course not. The girl just can't process how she could possibly be in one place in one instant and then another the next. I don't need drugs to teleport someone."

Thrusting the gun at Rhiannon, Lugos barked, "Hold this so I don't bludgeon you for interfering."

"Gladly," she replied, giving him an air kiss while taking the hard metal from his grasp.

When he turned back to Keely, he found her less than an arm's length away. She was staring up at him, her eyes both accusatory and watery. "Are you backin' out, Lugh?"

And in that instance, Lugos realized that he desperately wanted her. He longed to see trust and affection in those beautiful eyes. But even before that, her safety must come first, always. Before the needs of the Pale, or Rhiannon's demands on his time, or even Keely's own protests. He had brought her into direct contact with a world in which she couldn't possibly survive alone. It was a dilemma that he could have avoided, should have avoided.

Despite knowing all this, he said—because, try as he might, he could not bring himself to lie to her—"No. I'm not trying to get out of our date, though I know I should." That second confession he'd not meant to make at all, but Keely had that effect on him. She had always had that effect on him. He'd never been able to look her in the eye and lie. Not in past lifetimes and not in this one.

Lugos heard Rhiannon's little whistle of knowing. "I haven't seen that in a long time. Keely, while he's looking directly at you, ask him who he is," Rhiannon's voice instructed.

Lugos turned in the feeble hope of dissuading Rhiannon from her fun. "Don't do this, Rhiannon."

"Think of it as an experiment, Lugos. I know you like those. Go on, Keely, ask him."

Lugos's gaze returned to Keely with the hope that her stubborn streak would kick in, but she had followed this exchange back and forth, and so he saw the moment she chose to follow the goddess's suggestion. His heart sank. And just that fast, Lugos knew he'd placed himself once again in the untenable position of having to trust Rhiannon with his most precious secret.

To the clapped delight of Rhiannon, Keely set the knife aside and reached out to cup his cheeks with her hands. Lugos froze. He was trapped. Happily trapped. His soul reached for hers and, in doing so, found a home.

"Lugh, why does she keep callin' you Lugos?"

"It's my name." The answer slipped out before he could stop himself.

"You got other names I should know about?"

Again, try as he might, he could not stem the tide of truth that fell from his lips like pebbles from a jar. "Llew, Master of All Crafts; Lugh, Bringer of Light; Apollo, Sun God; Thor, the Mighty; Loki, the Trickster; Lugos, Lugh, and a slew of others that make no sense to me or anyone of my kin." It had all come out in a rush, the titles tumbling one after another in quick succession.

Keely's hands dropped from his cheeks, and her already pale

complexion turned whiter still. "What just happened?"

In the background, he heard Rhiannon's gales of amused laughter. Ignoring it, Lugos took a deep breath and answered willingly, though Keely had directed that particular question at Rhiannon. "It means I can't lie to you, Keely. My spirit is tied to yours, as yours is tied to mine. I cannot tell you an untruth." He ran his fingers through his hair, ruffling the blond mass. "It's absolutely infuriating."

"It's fucking marvelous," Rhiannon howled delightedly. "So, she's back!"

"When she said you're immortal, like vampire-immortal, is she telling the truth?" Keely looked him doggedly in the eye. "Well?"

"Yes. It's true." The rain outside had stopped, leaving behind a hushed silence that no bird had yet seemed willing to break.

Keely's legs gave way, and she dropped onto the nearest cushion.

"I'm not a vampire, Keely," Lugos hastily assured her.

"No, he's better!" Rhiannon interrupted. "He's a *god*," she announced, drawing out the last word with unabashed relish.

Keely's eyes were once again large and tear-filled. "There is only one God," she whispered, more to herself than to them. "All the pagan gods are naught but the fallen and cursed, part of Lucifer's minions."

Then, like an arrow to his heart, Lugos stood by as Keely linked his name to that of Lucifer. Lugos knew it was bound to happen. Lugh, Lucifer—the similarities were there, if you cared to look.

Rhiannon must have felt the ripple of his distress, because her laughter ended.

"At least she got the fallen part right," she offered him.

"It's said that Lucifer was the best of them. He was the Angel of Light, before the betrayal."

The weight of Rhiannon's hand touched his shoulder. "I'm sorry, Lugos. I didn't see this coming."

He hated the sympathy he heard in the goddess's voice. Shrugging off her hand, he went to kneel in front of Keely.

"Ask me if I'm Lucifer." He reached for her hand to rest it once again against his cheek, but she pulled it away from him. Swallowing his disappointment, he tried again. "There is more in this world than your church teaches, Keely. Scary things and wondrous things. Please remember that I didn't attack you." Not sure he was getting through to her, he added, "And you saw that I cannot lie to you. So, ask me." Once again he held his hand out to her.

None of this was going as he'd planned. Keely had so quickly jumped to the worst possible conclusion. While he waited for her to find the courage to ask, Lugos remained silent, hating himself for making her go through this. He was so very old, and she looked so inescapably young, her lower lip quivering. Not yet twenty-nine, and mortal, how could she possibly handle such world-altering truth without her mind breaking? Slowly the room grew a little brighter as the clouds that had been blocking the sun began to disappear.

She slipped her hand into his open palm, rewarding his patience. "Ask it," he prompted, his heart aching for her.

"Are you Lucifer, the Deceiver?"

It had been a hushed whisper but loud enough for him to hear. Relieved, he quickly answered, "No. I'm not."

"But you're not human," she said in a stronger voice.

"No. I'm not human."

"But you want to date me."

Lugos smiled. "Yes. Very much." The need to heal her bruised neck was riding him hard. But he couldn't afford to scare her again.

"Can you explain the not being a human part?"

"Yes, but do you believe me when I tell you I'm not the devil?" He watched her hesitate before nodding in the affirmative. Her hesitation worried him, but he could deal with it later. Lugos kept his voice soft and encouraging. They were now on firmer ground, or at least more familiar ground. "Think of all of humanity as one race, not Black or Caucasian or Asian or Hispanic, but the human race in all its variety. Now, there are others, races who look like humans and act like humans, at least most of the time. We—they—" he amended, "have lived alongside humans since the very beginning. Rhiannon and I are members of one of those races." It had been a simple answer, a true answer, and one he'd perfected over numerous lifetimes.

"Do you drink blood or anything disgusting?"

"No. We are not vampires. We do not drink blood. We eat what you eat. But we are different. Don't be fooled. Our bodies regenerate at an accelerated rate. The result, of course, is that over time even a wound that would have killed a normal man will eventually heal itself." He wondered if she was trying to fit his version of multiple races into some contexts of multiple Edens within her bible's Genesis. If so, Lugos hoped Keely wouldn't connect Rhiannon with Eve's willful and lusty red-headed predecessor.

"She said you're a god. I recognized some of those names you said from comic books and movies."

"I've lived for a very long time and accomplished things that gained me accolades. Some of my exploits—"

"Deeds," Rhiannon said, contributing once again to the conversation.

Lugos ignored the interruption. "Were embellished upon, so now it seems as if no ordinary man could possibly do the things I did. You have to understand that in ancient times, any great deed was attributed to the gods. But, Keely, the truth of what actually happened and the myth of what happened are very different."

"But gods have powers and are all-knowing, aren't they?" she asked, an accusatory note in her voice.

"None of us is all-knowing. And, yes, gods do have powers, but some of what you would call power is only a more complete understanding of natural law." This, too, was a simple explanation. Something he'd tell a child. The magick or science of the matter was rather complicated, and he didn't think Keely wanted an in-depth explanation of quantum physics, multidimensional space, or the warping ability of space/time/gravity right now.

"I don't understand. Do you have powers or not?"

"Yes," Rhiannon answered for him.

Lugos grimaced. "Yes. But unlike the rest of my kin, I hardly use them."

"Why?"

"Because I chose not to."

"But why?" Keely persisted.

"Because of a promise I made a long time ago—"

Rhiannon cut in, "Now, girl, he's answered your questions. Give it a rest. Just because you have the power to unearth every secret Lugos has ever had doesn't mean you should do so right here and now. Show a little restraint."

Lugos took Rhiannon's intervention as an opportunity to slide his hand out of Keely's grasp and take a breath. Quite frankly, he was a little dazed from that much truth telling.

"Sorry. I guess I just never had a man be that honest with me. It's kinda weird."

"Well, with power comes responsibility," the goddess lectured. "You can't just grill him incessantly." Rhiannon's gaze shifted to Lugos. "What do you want to do now?"

He ran his hand through his hair once again and avoided direct eye contact with Keely. "She can't stay here. It's too dangerous." He rose to his feet.

"Agreed. You want her stashed at a safe house until this is over?"

Keely rose from her place on the sofa. "I'm goin' with Lugh. Don't even assume that I'd stay here one minute longer than I have to."

She stood so close to him that her body brushed against his. Lugos nearly groaned at his own body's reaction. She was dressed for her work at the bar. And now that she was past her initial fear, Lugos found all that exposed skin far too tempting.

Averting his gaze, Lugos agreed, "She's with me. If you will give us a minute alone."

Rhiannon's eyebrow arched at his announcement, but otherwise she offered no comment on the soundness of his decision. She had stepped in to protect what was precious to him, though she had not known the extent of his interest in Keely. Rhiannon was sure to exact a price for her help at some point, of that Lugos was certain.

Rhiannon handed over the Glock. "We need to talk before you disappear." She then let herself out through the ruined door.

Alone at last with Keely, Lugos holstered the gun and turned to let himself really look at her. With a feather-light touch, he traced the bruise on her neck. "I can help make this go away. I should have never let my life get so close to yours. For that, I'm sorry, Keely."

She had not moved beneath his touch. He couldn't tell if she trembled because of fear or because she was starting to recognize the pull between them. To distract her from his subtle attempt at lessening the bruising on her neck, he asked, "Can you trust me, Keely? It's the only way that I can see us moving forward. I need you to have complete faith in me to protect and care for you."

Her hands unknowingly clutched at his shirt. He could almost see her heart beat inside her chest and feel her pulse flutter against his fingertip. All the while, Lugos directed a tiny amount of healing energy into the damaged skin as he traced the handprint left by her attacker.

"Damn, Lugh, that almost sounded like a proposal."

He ignored her attempt at levity. "What I meant to say is that you're no longer in a safe, human-only world. Life is going to get very weird very fast." He avoided telling her just how dangerous it was because he thought she'd already seen enough for one day. "It will help me...." He paused to amend the request. "I could better access my powers if I heard you say that you believed in me." It was kind of humiliating for him to ask her for something that he'd once taken for granted. It was also unavoidable. He would need the power to protect her. Her unwavering belief in him had always been a potent source. He slipped one arm around her waist and pulled her close.

She didn't fight him. "I'm just asking for a little faith, Keely. Faith that I'm going to look out for you." Every moment they remained here, she was in danger. It would be disastrous if Angus or the Saint discovered that his woman had found her way back to him. His mother and Blodeuwedd would love nothing more than to torture him by cursing the one person he truly cared about. Lugos took a moment to allow himself the luxury of holding her. He felt her body soften against him, her head lying just above his heart. When she began to ease back, he let her go, letting his hands fall to his sides. He was pleased to see that the bruise on her neck had faded considerably.

Keely managed a smile. "You seem capable, considering that entrance of yours. Looked to me as if ya could've taken on a whole Seal team all by your lonesome."

Her smile seemed a little tentative, but he'd take whatever he could get. "Thank you for thinking so." Lugos itched to touch her again, to reach out and enfold her in his arms, but he resisted. He needed to take this slowly. "All right, then, let me speak with Rhiannon, and then we'll go." He turned and moved toward the door but stopped short when he heard her boots scramble after him. Pivoting, he caught her just as she ran into his chest. "Where do you think you're going?"

"With you."

He shook his head. "No. If I'm to keep you safe, then you have to do exactly as I say."

"Oh, hell, no. We're partners in this," she waved her arm through the air. "Whatever *this* is. I'm going where you go."

He didn't have time to argue right now, so he stooped to attempting to scare her into obeying him. "Keely, there are two of my kin in that big house, and they wouldn't hesitate to turn you over to those who hate me." Whether it was his sharp tone or the message itself, the return of color to her cheeks evaporated.

Hating himself for frightening her yet again, he strove for patience. "I promise to tell you everything that Rhiannon tells me.

And just so you know, like my not being able to lie to you, once I've given my word, I cannot renege on that promise."

Chewing on her bottom lip, she studied him. "Can't lie, can't break a promise. Damn, Lugh, now you've gone and made me feel sorry for you. Go on, then, but hurry. This place gives me the heebie-jeebies."

Lugos was so relieved that he tugged her forward and planted a firm kiss on her inviting lips before he stepped through the door. He'd worry about the right or wrong of that kiss later—much later, when his Keely was out of danger and he had had time to think straight.

Chapter 15

Staring at the door Lugh had slipped past, Keely blinked and then blinked again. The fact that she could still feel the pressure of his kiss on her lips was strangely comforting. Lugh had actually kissed her! Keely put her fingers to her lips as if she could hold the moment in place. "Help me, Jesus," she whispered, and for once in her life she truly meant it. And it hadn't even been a long kiss. Just a peck, really, but she'd felt it right down to her toes.

Now that Lugh was here—well, she just felt better, safer, like somehow he'd see her through this mess. She hadn't yet wrapped her mind around Lugh's explanation, but his not being able to lie to her had come across loud and clear. Keely picked up his discarded jacket. Holding it to her nose, she inhaled deeply.

She'd be lying to herself if she didn't admit that Mama's earlier warning didn't still plague her. Lugh said he wasn't the devil, but then Lucifer was a tricky bastard, always using what you wanted against you. A wave of terror rolled through her, and her fingers dug into the jacket, crushing the fine fabric in her fists. "He can't lie to ya," she reminded herself, her voice cracking in the empty room. "Lucifer or not, wouldn't it be better to know a devil who can't lie than one who can?"

Keely made herself loosen her grip and then blinked away the tears that threatened to fall. This was no time to show weakness, not here, not now. But she couldn't quite corral her galloping heartbeat as easily as her thoughts, so to give herself something to do, she concentrated on smoothing out the wrinkles she'd caused in Lugh's jacket with one shaky hand.

He'd burst through the door like some wild thing, bright as sunlight, only to stop dead in his tracks as soon as he'd seen her. Frozen in place, she'd stood as much terrified as mesmerized by him. It had been like watching a howlin', cracklin' storm turn itself into a man. And at that moment, the moment when only Lugh stood before her, he'd looked so utterly vulnerable, almost scared, even. Keely swallowed the ache that formed in her throat.

"Gone an' done it again, girl," she said, her voice no more than a whisper. "Gone and gotten yourself all heartsore for someone you ought to've steered clear of."

Keely tried not to think about Cutter or the Witch's Whistle…or home…or her mama, for if she thought about those things she'd surely start feeling sorry for herself and begin to cry again. At least for now, if she was going to find a way back to normal, she'd have to take it one small step at a time.

Keely heard what was left of the door begin to open, and she scurried back until her calf bumped into a piece of furniture. She held Lugh's jacket to her chest like a shield. When she saw it was him and only him, she took an unsteady breath and forced a smile.

That's step one, she thought; but she said, "That didn't take long."

"No. It didn't."

He scooped up the cane he'd been carrying, strode across the room, and relieved her of the jacket she'd been holding. He then draped the still-wrinkled garment over her shoulders like a kind of cape. There were only a few inches between them. She could feel the heat of him as the pleasant scent of his aftershave surrounded her.

"Are you ready to leave?"

Step two, get the hell out of here. Keely hung on to her weak smile. She noticed again that the slightly worried expression had rooted itself between Lugh's brows. "Your friend didn't let me grab nothin', so I guess I'm as ready as I can be. Where we goin'?" she replied with more spirit than she felt. Keely was afraid to ask *how* they were going, afraid he'd blurt out one more thing she'd rather not know.

Lugh's hesitation spoke volumes. Perhaps he didn't exactly know what to do with her. On some level, even Keely understood that things were different between them now. Maybe her cool and controlled Lugh wasn't totally comfortable with whatever this new thing was between them. Then it occurred to her that maybe she should call him Llew, or one of those other names or titles he'd blurted out earlier.

"I don't know what to call you." The horrid confession popped out of her mouth before Keely could think to stop herself.

The worry resting between Lugh's brows caused his mouth to turn downward. "Anything you feel comfortable with, Keely. Lugh is fine. You're used to it." He reached out and pulled her into the warmth of his arms. Keely didn't fight him. If anything, she seemed to melt against him. "Close your eyes."

Keely was very aware of the hardness of him. His body felt like hot stone. Being this close to him was like sunbathing. She felt absolutely boneless; yet despite this, a new fear welled up from some deep dark place inside her. *Oh God, not again*, she thought as she squeezed her eyes tightly shut. It was unnatural to be in one place one minute and another the next. It was witchcraft or some other twisted demon magic. It was the same instinctual fear that had kicked in when Mr. Red T-shirt had attacked her. But instead of fleeing as her racing heart was prepared to do, Keely pressed herself closer to him. A mix of aftershave and warm skin filled her nose as she clutched at the starched fabric of his shirt. Her skin prickled in a cold sweat as she fought the urge to scream.

"Shhhhh."

Through the fog of terror, a gentle sound brushed the top of her head and then repeated itself. She felt Lugh rub one hand up and down the length of her back. She didn't dare loosen her grip. Fear held her firmly in place. In the corner of her mind, Keely knew she was wrinkling his shirt just as she had his jacket, but this time she couldn't make herself let go.

"We're here. Shhhhh. You can look. You're fine, Keely. I would never let anything harm you."

Again, she felt Lugh's hand move reassuringly up and down the length of her back. It felt solid. She managed to take a loud and shaky breath. The floor had not yet dropped away. They hadn't fallen into the blackness, the awful blackness. He gave her a little squeeze with his arms.

"Keely, you said you'd trust me."

"I do." It was a squeak of a reply and muffled by his shirt. He felt solid, and she was so afraid of falling. As long as she held on, she wouldn't fall, not like before.

His chin came to rest on the top of her head. "I can stand in this parking lot all night long, but people are starting to stare."

Keely took another shuddering breath. "Wh...wh...what parking lot?"

"The one we're standing in," he breathed into her ear.

She didn't ask if he was joking. She knew he wasn't. He'd answered her without any hint of humor in his voice. And then, as suddenly as the panic had washed over her, it began to drain away, leaving her limbs heavy and her mind sluggish. With a determined effort, she began to breathe more normally. She stood so close to him that she could feel the tightening of his body. Lugh made no apologies for his rising lust, nor did he seem embarrassed or make her feel dirty for the way she responded to his wanting her. She was no virgin, but neither could she be called easy. Despite her fear of falling, she'd felt her womb clench and the sudden wetness between her legs when he'd whispered across her ear.

Tentatively, Keely made herself ease back and open her eyes. Yes...she was staring at his chest, and it was a nice chest, a broad chest. Even with the thin layer of cotton, she could tell that she'd fit perfectly against it. Hadn't she decided to take this whole dating-the-god-Lugh-my-neighbor thing one step at a time? *Step three, let go of his shirt and take a step back. Step four, quit acting like a ninny.* The only other option was to let him have sex with her right here in the parking lot.

With what had to count as a superhuman effort on her part, Keely uncurled her fingers to release Lugh's pressed white shirt. "You're wrinkled now." She glanced up just in time to catch his easy grin.

"I'll live."

"Ya think?" Of course, he'd told her the truth. They were standing in a parking lot. Embarrassment for the way she'd clutched at him slowed her galloping heart to an uncomfortable trot. As his smile faded and an expression of concern took its place, the notion of life returning to normal seemed to mock her.

"That was a pretty impressive panic attack. You still with me?" he asked, his arms remaining loosely around her middle.

Keely's embarrassment rose to her cheeks. "Sorry, I don't like falling. It scares the shit out of me. Never could ride a roller coaster or even the Ferris wheel at the fair without it terrifying me."

Lugh took one arm from around her waist to fish out a set of keys from his pocket. He then deftly guided her to a white truck. "You're afraid of heights?"

"No. Just falling."

She stood leaning against the truck as he unlocked the driver's-side door, retrieved a black bag, and then relocked it.

"There's a difference?" He reclaimed his jacket from her shoulders and slipped it on. The gun strapped to his torso disappeared from view. The keys he dropped back into the pocket. The cane and the black bag he gripped together in one hand.

"Hell, yes, there's a difference! One's a nice view, the other is falling and then dying," she snapped. Keely accepted his free arm around her waist once more and allowed him to guide her across the parking lot toward the hotel.

He took his eyes off the Holiday Inn and grinned down at her.

"I'll remember that."

She was about to ask him if he'd hurt himself—you know, the cane thing and all—but she was sidetracked by the weird trick of the parking-lot lights, or maybe it was the hotel lights themselves combined with the coming dusk, but it suddenly looked to Keely as if Lugh had kind of a faint glow about him, almost like an angel's halo. As she stared up at him, his hand gave her waist a little squeeze of encouragement. Lugh then marched her into the hotel lobby, and the strange effect was washed away under the bright lights.

While he asked about a room and then paid for another, her mind tried but failed to make sense of it all; of gods and angels, of wolves and men, and of demons and goddesses. Unbidden, Lugh's words floated back to her: *There is more in this world than your church teaches, Keely. Scary things, wondrous things.* She pondered that, wondered which one lay ahead as she watched a disappearing sun set the evening sky on fire.

Chapter 16

During the brief elevator ride, Keely eyed the couple sharing their trip to the third floor. They seemed normal. The white-haired husband ignored Keely altogether. He acknowledged Lugh with a grandfatherly nod and a wink his wife didn't see. The wife smiled at Lugh, and at Keely, too, though not warmly. Lugh kept Keely tucked up beside him, so she wasn't sure he noticed when she pulled on the jagged hem of her shorts, suddenly wishing they were longer. When the elevator stopped, he waved the couple off first; as a common courtesy or a precaution, Keely couldn't tell. She watched the couple turn left and walk down the hallway. She and Lugh went right.

The carpet muffled their footfalls. More uncomfortable with the silence than with not knowing, she whispered, "Are they?"

"Are they what?"

"You know." She wasn't sure how to frame the question. Good God, she must sound utterly stupid to him.

Lugh glanced down at her, then back to the numbers posted on the passing doors. "They're human. 'Most everyone is."

"Oh." The uncomfortable silence returned.

A few feet farther on, Lugh paused to listen at the door of room 314. The noise of a television was all that seeped through the door. Keely wondered if he heard something she could not, but she decided not to ask. As he listened for a few more tense seconds, Keely stole glances down the empty hallway.

Lugh finally abandoned his eavesdropping, guided her to the door of room 316, and slipped the key card into the lock. Standing aside, he motioned her to pass through the open door. Not sure she had much choice, Keely complied.

The room itself was nicer and larger than she had envisioned. She'd been expecting only one large bed, now that they were, well, an item...together...dating...or whatever they were now. But instead there were two queen-sized beds, with a small nightstand sandwiched between them. A small table and chairs stood opposite and nearest the balcony, while directly across from the beds was a large wardrobe, most likely housing a television. The bathroom she'd only glimpsed as they entered, but it, too, was larger and grander than she'd anticipated. There was a fully glassed-in shower instead of a tub and curtain.

"Went all out, didn't ya?" she said, sinking down on the edge of the closest bed. "So, is this part of our date?" For the first time since entering the room, she caught and held his gaze. He had that worry line between his brows again.

"No, this is not part of any date, Keely."

She sat up straighter.

Before she could think of what to say next, he asked, "Are you hungry? I could order room service." He stowed the duffel and cane in a chair before moving to the phone. He then sat down on the edge of the unoccupied bed, reached for the receiver, and looked at her expectantly.

Keely just shrugged. Truth be told, she was too nervous to eat. Her stomach wasn't so much in knots as it was unsettled. She didn't even want to acknowledge how needy Lugh made her body feel.

Despite her lack of suggestions, Lugh dialed. Then, without waiting for her to suggest anything, he ordered them two perfectly normal cheeseburgers, fries, and a couple of cokes before giving the person on the other end their room number. After hanging up, he stared at her, his worried expression fixed in place.

The minutes ticked by without either of them saying a word, the silence growing between them like a malevolent beast. Finally, Keely decided that she couldn't take any more.

"What?"

"I need to prepare you for what's coming next, but—"

"What's coming next?" she blurted, swinging her gaze to the window as if some demon might crash through it. She looked to Lugh and immediately realized her mistake. She'd given him half a second to break eye contact with her, and break it he had.

In the silence, Lugh sighed, then reached for her hand, tugging on her arm so that she was forced to abandon her spot on the bed. When he positioned her directly opposite him on the edge of the adjacent bed, he seemed satisfied. Still cradling her one hand in his two larger ones, he stared down into the space between them. "Remember, I told you there were other races, races that weren't human?"

A chill skittered up her spine. Keely swallowed noisily before nodding. Try as she might, she couldn't forget such a thing.

Lugh hadn't seen her nod, but he continued as though he had. "Collectively, we call them the Pale. Rhiannon is their leader. Members of the Pale go to her when there's a problem. If the problem is big enough, she comes to me, and I fix it."

She was staring at his forehead, her eyes probably as big as saucers. He was talking to her as one might talk to a child, but at the moment his gentle manner made her feel safe. *He* made her feel safe.

"And you're fixin' something for her right now."

Lugh gently rubbed her hand between his larger ones. "Yes. I'm investigating a murder, for starters."

"Like a cop," Keely supplied, trying desperately to put what he was telling her in as normal a context as she could manage.

Lugh glanced up and gave her a crooked grin. "Yes, like a detective." He paused; the grin faded, and the worried expression returned. "What I find will determine what I do. But what I want you to understand is that whatever I do, your safety comes first for me. If I tell you that I want you to do something, I need you to trust that I am asking it for a very good reason."

To avoid the promise she could feel him moving her toward, Keely leaped ahead. "What are the other races?" It was an unforgiving question, one she'd asked while he held her hand and her gaze. She watched him struggle only briefly before the unguarded answers came rushing at her.

"My own kin, the ones called gods. Shifters, the dragonkin, the fae, the demon clans, demi-gods, and of course the witches—but they're usually human." He must have read the expression of horror on her face, because he hastily added, "I will protect you, Keely—from all of it." Lugh reached out and stroked her hair with one hand. It was a capable hand. It was a hand that could make her feel safe.

Before he could look away, she whispered, "And what's in room 314?"

"A shifter named Alex."

"What's a shifter?"

"Someone who's capable of changing into an animal form."

"A werewolf?"

"No, a house cat."

In the stunned silence that followed, Lugh abruptly withdrew his hands and rose to his feet, but not before Keely caught the flash of anger inside those impossibly blue eyes of his. She mumbled a feeble apology. "Sorry. It's all so...so weird to me."

Through the mirror's reflection, Lugh glared at her. "You can't do that to me, Keely!"

His anger felt like the lashing of a whip, and just that quickly the dam of tears she'd been keeping at bay threatened to break once more. Keely dropped her gaze to the floor to hide her confusion. She didn't want to know more. She wanted to go home, forget all of it, pretend it had never happened.

Lugh was back beside her again, one arm enfolding her, the other holding her clenched fist. Keely closed her eyes. A tear or two escaped but no more. She allowed herself the comfort of resting her head against his shoulder.

God, please let him be an angel and not a demon come to drag me to hell, she prayed.

"I'm sorry. I shouldn't have taken my frustration out on you. It's just—" One strong hand rubbed her arm from shoulder to elbow several times before he continued. "It's just that I'm trying to ease you into all this, Keely. There's this whole world you don't know about. I'm terrified that it's all going to be too much."

They sat for a moment, neither saying a word. Keely was fairly sure she didn't want to know any more. As far as she was concerned, the thing Lugh was calling a shifter was a monster at best, a demon at worst. How the hell would she ever be able to tell who was normal and who wasn't?

Lugh kissed the top of her head, and despite her fear and turmoil, that simple gesture was enough to cause her stomach to do a tiny, joyous flip. Even that made no sense. Why did she feel safer with Lugh? Shouldn't she be running from him as fast as she could?

"Trust me."

"I do. It makes no sense, Lugh. But I do." Despite what had happened to her, or the fact that Lugh or Lugos wasn't human, or the bone-deep worry that her mama had been right all along, Keely trusted the warmth and belonging she experienced whenever she was near him. He managed to make her feel cherished, like she was the most important person in his life.

His hand rubbed up and down her arm once more before stopping with a pat of finality. "Your trust means everything to me. Thank you for that gift, Keely."

She managed to smile up at him. Then a rap-tap-tap shattered the moment, and Keely flinched.

"It's just our dinner," Lugh told her. He didn't rise immediately. Instead he drew her closer, pulling her into his lap so that his body heat seeped into hers. Again, Keely had that sensation of melting into him. Lugh made no demand, just held her as if he had all the time in the world to feel comfortable.

Another rap-tap-tap. This time it was a little louder, a little impatient.

Though she didn't want the perfect moment to end, Keely also didn't want him to think her a burden, someone in constant need of comforting. "I'm fine now, Lugh. Get the door."

He raised one doubtful eyebrow.

"Go." Keely shoved at his chest to make her point. He didn't seem to notice. It was like trying to move a mountain. He hadn't budged an inch. "Really, I'm fine now." She tried to wiggle out of his lap but got nowhere. Just how strong was he?

Rap-tap.

Lugh sighed. "Stay here." Reluctantly, he set her back on the edge of the bed.

Keely looked on as he conducted the conversation through a mere crack with whomever was on the other side of the door. Lugh only opened the door fully when he was in possession of a tray of food and the hotel employee had been tipped and dispatched. Lugh then deposited the tray on the empty table and looked at her expectantly.

The familiar aroma of burgers and fries did nothing to entice her unsettled stomach or ease her nagging apprehension of the future. "I don't think I can do this."

When he just stared blankly at her, she waved an arm through the air to make her point plainer. "All this. It ain't normal, Lugh. There's some cat-woman in the next room, and God knows what else walking through that door," she said, pointing. "I was attacked today by a guy Cutter says was a wolf. Some demon-woman appears out of thin air, takes me two states away in a blink of an eye, and then tells me there's a tiger outside who'll eat me if I even try to escape." She was up and almost yelling at him now.

"And if that ain't enough for a soul to deal with—there's you!" The lump in her throat had suddenly made it hard for her to breathe, much less speak, but she couldn't keep a lid on her fears any longer.

"You say you're not a man at all but some old pagan god. And again, I'm taken from one impossible place to another impossible place and told that it's all okay." She backed up a step, then suddenly felt trapped between the two beds. "Well, it ain't okay, nothin's ever gonna be okay again." Her voice had been steadily rising. She was yelling—screeching, really. Even to her own ears she sounded hysterical. Keely knew she shouldn't scream at him, but she just couldn't help it. "A hamburger and fries and a romp in the sack ain't gonna make this okay, Lugh! My mama was right all along! I'm damned."

When he took a step toward her, Keely instinctively retreated and ran into the nightstand between the two beds. The panic was closing in on her, the scream rising. She hugged herself, a last desperate attempt to hold it all together. She wanted to be near him, needed him to hold her, but another part of her wanted to run. The room seemed to tunnel, sending the door an impossible distance away.

"Keely, look at me."

The command was a gentle one. Like a trusting child, she raised her eyes to stare at where he should be, but she couldn't see him. She could only see the horror of what he'd already told her. There were monsters and demons all around her. They looked just like everyone else until they suddenly didn't. And then you die, she thought. Or worse. The "or worse" scared her most of all.

"Keely, look at me!"

The demand in his voice made her jump. Lugh's worried brow and blue eyes came into focus. He had moved closer, much closer to her. She could feel his body crowding hers.

"Don't scream."

His arms slowly slipped around her waist. Then one hand moved to cradle the back of her skull, and he pressed her against him. Keely's head lay against his chest so that she could hear his heart beating into her ear. It was as steady and solid as he was. The pleasant scent of him surrounded her. His hands were impossibly hot, as was his skin beneath his shirt. Her body reacted by gluing itself to his harder frame.

"You're safe, Keely. I promise, you're safe."

A palpable warmth began to seep into her. It spread downward from the top of her head and through her like warm chocolate, softening the jagged edges of her panic and easing the tension from her muscles. Keely could not see his face, but a strange golden light seemed to surround them both. Eventually, she found the courage to look up.

Lugh didn't try to restrict her movement or hide the strange light from her. Keely realized that it was more than just a halo around his head, more than the glow she'd thought she'd seen in the parking lot. The warmth and light somehow radiated from inside him. It was how she'd imagined angels looking; that is, if angels wore two-hundred-dollar jeans and expensive but slightly wrinkled sport coats.

"Do you now understand why I wanted to take this slowly?"

Keely nodded, not trusting herself to speak. She would think of him as a guardian angel. An archangel like Michael or Gabriel, she thought. Hadn't Lugh been there every time she needed him? He'd shown up right after she'd kicked Carlos out, her lip still split, her eye puffy and black. Hadn't he been there to fix the heating, the plumbing, and her car whenever she'd asked? Given a friendly ear and advice when needed? For five years, hadn't he also tried to hold her at arm's length? She now understood why: to keep her safe from knowing about the shifters, witches, and all the other things she was afraid to ask about. That alone made him good. And he couldn't lie to her, the ultimate proof of his divinity. He had to be an angel.

"You're glowing." Keely watched the worried brow ease and a half-smile appear.

"It's a power thing. The more power I use, the more visible it is."

"You used it on me. Just then?"

He gave her a hesitant nod. "You were on the verge of another panic attack. I thought it best to head it off before you got up a full head of steam. Forgive me for not asking permission?"

Keely blinked. "Forgive you. Why?"

He smoothed a lock of her hair with his fingertips. "I try not to exert my influence. It's not fair." Then he added, "And it's a usually a waste of my limited power. You should know that I try to be the most human of all my kin."

"I don't understand. You have less power than the...others?" Keely almost said angels but caught herself. If Lugh wanted to let the others think he was one of those pagan gods, then that was his business. She knew the truth of it. She knew his true identity. "And what do you mean by *most human?*" Too late, Keely realized she was forcing him to answer questions that he might rather leave for later.

"It's a choice I made a long time ago when—"

"Sorry, sorry. I didn't mean to make you answer that," she blurted, hastily laying her hand over his mouth. His moving lips were warm on her palm.

Lugh smiled beneath her hand. He then removed her palm from his lips, only to absently play his thumb back and forth along the tops of her knuckles. "I don't mind this question. It is the one fact you need to know about me: I chose to fight for the advancement of humankind. Most of my kin would rather I gave up that fight. But for humanity to advance, I have to allow them to learn and evolve at their own pace. That means keeping my kin, and the whole of the Pale, out of their way. It also requires me to live as close to a human life as my kind is capable of doing. If I absorb too much power from those who would give it as a gift to me, then I'd glow in the dark like an activated nightstick. And as you can see, it makes it hard to stay unnoticed." He smiled down at her.

The glow around him had already dimmed considerably. "So, when you use your power, you glow, and if you absorb too much power, you glow."

"Yes. And you need to remember that bright light can hide a god's aura, but darkness will show what he truly is."

It was an odd conversation, one Keely kept trying to make fit into her angel theory. She sensed that he was not telling her everything, but she was fine with that.

"Trust me?" he asked again.

"Yes," she answered without hesitation.

He still held her against him with one arm, and she was happy to remain. With a wave of his hand, the lights in the room went out, though he had neither moved nor touched the light switch. In the dark, she could clearly see Lugh's soft golden glow. It wasn't just a halo, but all of him. And it was beautiful.

"Now." He paused to hold up a glowing hand. "Place your palm on mine."

Though a little nervous, Keely complied. She immediately felt the warmth that she was beginning to associate with him. But then it increased. It wasn't exactly uncomfortable, but as the heat built, it was hard not to move her hand away.

"No, not yet. Keep it there," he encouraged.

Keely took a deep breath and pressed her palm more fully onto his and tried to ignore the sensation. Slowly Lugh's golden glow moved over her hand and then crept down her arm. When he took his hand away from hers, the glow remained for a moment but then started to fade. It hadn't actually hurt at all, just kind of tingled pleasantly as her skin cooled in the air-conditioned room.

Lugh waved his hand again, and the lights came back on. The otherworldly glow was immediately gone.

"What was that?" she asked, still staring at her hand. The odd sensation was taking a little longer to fade.

He circled her waist once again with both arms. "Only a small sharing of my power. I can't do that with anyone but you, Keely."

"But why me?" she asked, glancing up into his impossibly blue eyes. "What makes me so special?"

"Your soul and mine are tied to one another."

"You're talking about soul mates. I don't believe in that." Weren't angels forbidden to mingle with humans, except to deliver a divine message? Her mama would know. If this thing between her and Lugh was forbidden, then how could they be soul mates?

Before she could ask him how that was possible, Lugh lowered his lips to hers. Keely promptly forgot her question, forgot to be afraid, forgot everything that had happened to her as Lugh swept her into a sea of pure feeling. He kissed gently at first, but then he began to kiss her as if his life depended on it. There was a longing, a branding, to his kiss. Keely's world narrowed to encompass only Lugh. He needed her, and something inside her rose to meet that need.

When he ended the kiss, she was left dazed and clinging to him. Keely laid her forehead against his chest until she thought her legs might once again support her without his help. She was aware that if he wanted to throw her down on the nearest bed, she wouldn't fight him. She wanted him so much that she ached. But sex was one thing. That kiss was another. No one had ever kissed her like that. No one had ever reduced her to a puddle of need. "You can't do that again," she said, her voice husky.

His chest rumbled with laughter.

"No, I mean it, Lugh," she insisted. She slapped at his chest to show him that she meant it. "If you kiss me like that again, you might just kill me."

He dropped a kiss on the top of her head. "I plan on kissing you a lot while we date."

"No. No, I'm quite certain that's a really bad idea." She looked up and shook her head. Clearly, he didn't understand what he'd done to her. "Does everyone like you kiss like that?"

His expression abruptly darkened. "You will never find out. You and I belong to one another. I have no intention of allowing you ever to meet another of my kin."

Keely just blinked up at him. It stood to reason that he would want to keep this thing between them a secret from his kin, or from any person or demon or abomination who'd want to cause mischief, or worse. Obviously their "dating" each other was going to be the very definition of complicated. But he said he had powers of some sort, she thought, angel powers he was willing to use. "So what powers do you have?" she wondered aloud.

Lugh took a moment to clear his throat before answering her. "Most of my abilities reside in my skills. I am...was...honored as a god because I was a master of all crafts: war and weapons, song and storytelling, metal, alchemy. But it's my intellect that is my most prized power and the gift I give mankind."

A wave of disappointment washed through her. "Oh." She'd been expecting more. So much more.

He gave her a look that was part sympathy and part amusement. "Disappointed?"

"No lightning bolts, no balls of flame? Or wings?" An angel should have a secret set of glorious wings with which to righteously swoop down and smite his enemies.

"Only when all else has been attempted and nothing else will suffice." He grinned down at her.

She frowned. "You're making fun of me now." When Keely moved to sink down onto the edge of the bed, Lugh released his hold on her.

"No, not really," he said, stepping back.

He had replied so quickly and so matter-of-factly that Keely was sure he meant it. She dropped her gaze, suddenly aware of the sharp contrast between his soft leather loafers and her scuffed and worn cowboy boots. "Do you at least know what I'm thinking before I think it?"

"Sadly, no. I'm not all-knowing, though at times it might seem that way."

He sank down beside her, his jeans-clad thigh touching her bare one. The warmth of him was reassuring.

"Being immortal has its perks. I've had a millenia to understand how mortals think, to know what motivates them, to understand what drives them, what they dream of, and how they go about bringing those dreams into reality. So, no. I don't know what you are thinking right this minute. But I hope that by now you've concluded that I can and will do all that is in my power to keep you safe and whole. You are the most important person in my world, Keely."

Keely gave him a small smile. "Yeah, I believe you mean that." She couldn't quite believe he'd actually said it, though. Even that wasn't normal. No man said things like that and really meant it. How was she ever going to find her way back to normal if he kept saying things like that, or kissing her like that?

"Now that I'm not going to scare you to death, I need to finish healing the bruises on your neck."

Keely's hand touched her throat. It had stopped hurting some time ago. She'd been so wrapped up in Lugh's coming to get her that she hadn't noticed that he'd already eased the soreness. "When you were tracing my neck with your finger?"

"Yes. I couldn't stand it. I could not allow it to continue, a reminder of the attack on your life."

Her eyes welled with tears again.

"Keely, don't cry. I don't think my heart can take it if you keep crying."

She made a desperate effort to blink back her tears, but the sweetness of his actions went right through her. "I'm sorry," she whimpered. But the dam had broken, and Keely could no more stop the tears than keep the sun from setting.

Lugh sighed, pulled her into his lap, and just let her cry it out.

Chapter 17

After what seemed an eternity to him, Keely's crying subsided, and her spirit rallied. Lugh wasn't sure if Keely thought him insane for calling himself a god, or if she'd found a place for him somewhere within her faith's parameters, a supernatural category of sorts. At this juncture, Lugh didn't actually care what designation she'd decided on. What mattered to him was that she'd found a way to accept him yet again. She had humbled him with her ability to trust, with her capacity to take on faith what he had told her. Instead of running from him, she was running to him. Unfortunately, she had yet to understand what it meant to be in his world and under his protection.

As always, Lugos felt the need to claim her: her body for the comfort it gave him and her soul for the peace it granted him. He would demand nothing less than everything from her, a complete surrender. Her soul belonged to him. It was a part of him. She had not been there to witness the suffering it had caused him each time her spirit had been ripped from his. The pain of it had come close to destroying him. He had not lied to her when he confessed that she was everything to him. She was in every breath he took. Her light had guided every choice he made. Even more than wanting to irrevocably claim his woman in this lifetime, Lugos wanted to protect her from all hurt and harm. Holding her in his lap while she cried out her fears had been torture for him.

His first instinct was, as always, to lock her away somewhere safe where his enemies would never find her, where she'd never have to endure the terrors in his world.

Lugos had entertained the idea of taking her to Griffin until this thing with Talon and the USL was over, but his Atlanta building was known to too many within the Pale. What he needed was a deserted island or a remote tower, but he wasn't sure his independent-minded woman would go for such a plan. At her core, she was a warrior, a fighter whose courage bordered on the ridiculous. He'd tried to cage her before, many lifetimes ago. It hadn't worked out well, and he wasn't going to make that mistake again. There would be no hideaway, no island, no castle, no vault in which he could stash her that would keep her safe and still happy. The only place for his Keely was right beside him, where he could defend her when the time came. Because if he lost that battle again, lost her again, Lugos knew without a doubt that he wouldn't survive it.

Lugos didn't knock on Alex's door to announce himself. Instead, he simply used the key card and strolled in.

"Alex."

She was not in the room. Lugos brushed past Keely to check the bathroom.

Keely turned off the blaring television. "Where is she?"

"I don't know." The room was identical to their own except for its single king-sized bed. Keely had accepted the first step of meeting Alex, but Lugh knew that her faith in him as a protector was still quite fragile. She had no idea what he could actually do, or to what lengths he would go to keep his promise to her.

"She's gone," he grumbled after a moment, annoyed with himself for misplacing his only tangible connection to Seraphine's murder. "Her clothes are on the bathroom floor, so she left in her cat form."

"How big of a cat? Wouldn't that be noticed?"

Lugos stalked over to the room's phone and snatched up the receiver. He glanced at his watch. It was twenty till eight, almost three hours since he'd last laid eyes on her. "Probably, if she ventured out on her own. But if she were stuffed into a bag—" He left the sentence unfinished and dialed the reception desk. As soon as the clerk answered, he identified the room and asked, "Has a woman of medium build with black, shoulder-length hair checked out or left her room key at the desk?"

"One moment, sir."

Lugh waited as the clerk brought up the reservation.

"No, sir. Have you lost one of your cards—" There was a pause as the clerk obviously searched for the name on the reservation. "Mr. Hart," he finished. "I can have one ready and waiting at the desk."

"No, thank you." Lugos set the handset back on its

cradle. It was not what Lugos had been hoping to hear. He explained the problem to Keely. "Either she figured out, as a cat, how to pass unnoticed down the elevator, through the lobby, and out the door, or someone came and took her."

"A big cat or a house cat?"

"An average-size house cat. Black, no white markings."

"Oh." Keely cocked her head. "What about her bags? Her phone? Surely she just changed and then left to eat or somethin'. She'll be back. Won't she?"

Lugos glanced around the room again. Keely didn't understand. And why would she? "No, she won't. I gave her strict instructions to stay put. And not many in the Pale are willing to disobey a god's orders. She didn't have another set of clothes," he explained, his initial frustration with the situation rising. There were so many questions he should have asked Alex. Now the shifter was gone, and probably not because she wanted to be. Lugos went to the bathroom and dug through each pocket of her discarded clothing. He then methodically searched the rest of the hotel room for any sign that Alex had put up some sort of struggle, perhaps torn something off the clothing of her abductors. Had she been caught her in her dual form, or had her kidnappers forced her to turn in order to make it easier to remove her from the hotel without drawing attention? Or had she arranged for someone she knew come to get her? The last thought he discarded. If she knew the person, why leave in her dual form? Why not just walk out of the lobby as Alex?

Guilt stabbed at him. It was his fault she was missing. Another glance at Keely's bemused expression had him explaining aspects of his world that an outsider simply wouldn't know about. "Shifters aren't modest. They don't really care what skin they're wearing, human or animal. But I doubt Alex would prance down to the lobby naked. It would draw too much attention. As would a house cat waiting for the elevator. Anyway, I found her key card in the back pocket of her jeans. And her phone is missing." He showed the key card to Keely before letting it disappear back into his own jacket pocket.

"Why didn't you ask the desk if they'd seen a cat?"

"I will find a discreet way of doing just that when we check out," he replied.

Keely raised both eyebrows. "So we're leaving now?"

Lugos gave a curt nod. "I think it's best. The most likely scenario is that someone knew that I'd brought Alex here and that I'd be returning for her." He thought about the silver sedan that had tailed him and kicked himself for failing to spot another attempt to follow them. The attack on Keely had been his only concern. And then after, her emotional state was all he'd thought about. "I don't believe she left because she wanted to. It's safer if we move on as well."

The cell phone in Lugos's pocket suddenly rang, and Keely flinched. He'd turned it off in order to navigate the delicate conversation he'd been forced to have with Keely at Rhiannon's place, and had only turned it back on upon leaving their room.

The sight of the familiar Atlanta number was reassuring, though it did little to lessen Lugos's building frustration.

"What?"

"I'm having trouble chasing down the names of the women in that Sacred Grove Coven," Griffin began. "Only a few have made what they call their magickal name their legal one as well. But that's not why I'm calling. Your perimeter alarms have gone off. I've checked the video feed, but I don't see anything. It's too dark, and for some reason the infrared's not working. You installed it, didn't you?"

"I did, but I forgot to turn it on," Lugos lied.

"Oh. Okay. Probably nothing anyway. A deer or some possum, 'most likely. I told you the calibrations on those sensors were too sensitive. Do you want me to send someone out there anyway?"

"No, don't bother. And, Griffin—"

"Yeah?"

"They're just sensitive enough," Lugos replied with practiced god-like patience. Sensitive enough to catch a member of the Pale, he thought to himself. "Keep an eye on the feed and let me know if the house alarms are triggered." He didn't want any local law enforcement wandering around his home and sanctuary.

Sounding vaguely distracted, Griffin muttered, "Uh-huh...okay, boss."

"Are you playing one of those games while you're talking to me?" Lugos was fine with that as long as he got the answers he needed.

"Well, kind of. I just got killed."

"In an hour, send me what you have on the coven."

There was a brief hesitation on the other end, then Griffin said, "Sure...sure. Will do."

Lugos ended the call, scooped up Alex's clothes, and escorted Keely out of the room. He then dialed Rhiannon. When she answered, Lugos didn't wait for her greeting.

"Alex is missing."

"Because she wanted to be, or because someone thinks she knows something?" Rhiannon asked.

"The latter, I think." Lugos unlocked the room he shared with Keely and then stepped back so she could pass through the doorway first. "If by chance she resurfaces at your place, let me know. I have more questions for her."

"I'll let it be known that I'm looking for her."

"No, don't. I'd rather we searched without drawing attention to the fact that she's missing. I could just as easily stumble across her in Murray when I go down to speak with the coven." Lugos didn't think so, but it was a possibility. "Let whoever took her think they have time, and if I'm completely wrong and she went to ground on her own, I'll eventually find her."

"Yes. But will you find her still alive?"

Lugos wasn't ready to entertain that possibility yet.

"You didn't scare her, did you?" Rhiannon pressed. "You were pretty upset."

"No." Although, in hindsight, the goddess might have a valid point. "At least, I don't think I did," he amended. "I was firm, but I'm hardly scary."

Rhiannon's rich laugh filled his ear.

Interrupting her laughter, Lugos informed her, "We're heading out to question the covenmates."

"Do you think it's necessary? You're closer to Talon at the moment. Why not show up on his doorstep and see if Angus was right?"

"Because you put me in charge of this investigation of yours," Lugos snapped.

"She's still with you," Rhiannon replied.

"Yes."

"It really is her again, isn't it?"

Lugos paused too long, which only confirmed the truth for Rhiannon. "I'll keep in touch."

"Of course. I'll wait to hear from you."

"And Lugos, keep her safe. I don't want to lose you." And then the line went dead.

She's making a habit of that, he thought sourly. Lugos let his cell phone slip into his pocket, the same pocket that held the two key cards. Keely had already collected his black bag and the disguised spear. Thank goodness she had no idea what she was holding.

"What now? And why are you carrying this thing?" she asked, raising the cane. "You aren't limping."

"Be careful with that; it's dangerous," he cautioned, taking the spear from her. Not understanding, she then thrust the bag toward him.

She was starting to act like his old Keely, and that brought a grin to his lips. "Beyond leaving here, I don't know. And this cane isn't a cane. It's for protection." He accepted the bag and then held the door open for her to pass through once more. She walked beside him in silence toward the elevator. He paused just long enough to stuff Alex's discarded clothing into a trash bin along the way.

Once they were inside the elevator, she pressed, "You said it's protection. I don't understand."

"Don't ask. It's more than you want to know right now."

Lugos could only hope that her return to silence was for his benefit, allowing him time to think, and not because she was upset with him.

When they reached the little lobby, Lugos went through the process of paying for both rooms. Alex hadn't ordered room service, used the minibar, or charged a movie to the room's bill. In his inspection of the room, he'd noticed that the shower and the sink had remained dry, and housekeeping's triangular fold still remained on the toilet paper roll. In fact, the only signs he'd found of Alex were the slightly wrinkled bedspread, the too-loud television, and her small pile of clothes. Lugos was beginning to suspect that she'd disappeared only moments after he'd abandoned the hotel. Which meant he'd been followed—and that he'd missed it.

So now what? Keely's question weighed heavily on him. Someone or something had gone to the trouble of snooping around his home. He needed to know who and why. He should also get himself to Murray. Solving Seraphine's murder wasn't Rhiannon's primary objective, but a woman of dual communities deserved some sort of justice. And now another shifter was missing. Lugos had not forgotten about the one who'd attacked Keely. That had been done to get his attention. Well, they had it now. And Lugos had no doubt that he'd make them regret it before this mess was all over.

Lugos was tempted to forgo the investigation in Murray, as Rhiannon had suggested. He was beginning to suspect he'd find more satisfying answers if he tracked down Talon. What exactly was Talon's USL up to that might have gotten his sister killed? Perhaps it was just instinct again, but Lugos's gut told him that Seraphine's murder and Talon's takeover were deeply connected. But then, there was the question of what to do with Keely while he hunted.

Lost in his own musing, Lugos laid his hand on the small of Keely's back and escorted her from the hotel into the parking lot. He needed to commit to an avenue of inquiry: Murray and Seraphine's coven, or Talon and the USL. No matter which he chose, having Keely with him was going to be a definite distraction.

"It's not real noticeable, but you're kinda glowing, Lugh."

"Am I?" he asked absently. He felt her slip out from under the weight of his hand only long enough to lace her fingers with his. They were nearly across the parking lot.

"Where are you walking us to?"

His chin jutted out to indicate a row of parked automobiles and the white truck. "We have to park this thing somewhere so Rhiannon can have it picked up."

"Okay, then what?" she asked, following his gaze.

Lugos unlocked the driver's-side door while Keely waited patiently. Only after he'd stowed his bag and cane and Keely was settled safely in the passenger seat did Lugos make up his mind. "If you're not tired, we're going back to Georgia so I can check something out, then stopping off at your place so you can pick up clothing that makes you look a little less tempting." He paused to grin wickedly at her. "And then we're going to pay a visit to a woman in Murray, Kentucky."

If the meeting with the witches started to get dicey, he'd take Keely to Griffin with some plausible story that the kid might swallow. Then again, Griffin had no real means of protecting her if some member of the Pale truly wanted to get their hands on her. No, until he knew more about what was going on, Keely was safer with him. He'd have to be both Plan A and Plan B. His Plan C would be Zee and Murmur. At least Murmur understood just how high the stakes were. He'd protected her before. But Lugos was hesitant to reintroduce Keely to the demon. She wasn't ready for that yet.

"How long will all that take?" Keely asked, unaware of the battle raging inside Lugh's head and gut.

He turned the key, and the motor roared to life. Lugos shrugged his shoulders. "A little over an hour, I think. Unless you're a slow packer."

Keely grinned back at him. It was an honest gesture, devoid of the earlier reservations he'd glimpsed in the depths of her brown eyes. In response, the tight cord around Lugos's heart suddenly eased. He put the gearshift in reverse and carefully coaxed the oversized vehicle into motion.

Chapter 18

Lugos guided the Audi down the gravel drive until a red farm gate finally blocked the road. After a moment, he switched off the headlights and put the car in park. From where they sat, moonlight allowed an unobstructed view of the coven's farmhouse three hundred yards beyond the gate. One white SUV was parked nearby. No porch light, but a few lights still shown through the windows—just enough light to suggest that someone was still awake.

It was nearly eleven o'clock. He had arrived later than intended because Keely, suddenly insecure about her clothing, had taken longer than necessary to pack. Striving not to give into the frustration he felt, Lugos had finally realized that she was worried her usual attire might not be acceptable to him. In truth, her second-hand garments had never bothered him. He'd always seen beyond the financial circumstances of the woman he loved. Wanting to make her happy, he'd asked what she would wear if money weren't an issue. She had immediately showed him a catalog of soft, very feminine clothing, a little Bohemian in style and, in her view, terribly expensive. He'd quickly thumbed through the catalog, noticed the pages that were dog-eared, and given into temptation. To her delight and awe, he had simply manifested the clothing she most desired out of thin air. She'd kissed him, then, and he'd allowed that to go on far longer than he should have.

"Keely, stay here. Don't get out of the car. I want to see what we're dealing with." His mother's followers were not always happy to see him, even at the best of times. He didn't want Keely to suffer their anger if he had to rouse them from their beds.

When she started to argue, he held up his hand. "Remember, I explained that they might be hard-core followers of my mother, which means you need to stay put."

"Yeah, I get that. We all have mother issues, Lugh."

"Yes, but your mother doesn't throw lightning bolts. Or curse people, or mess with their fate just for entertainment."

Keely laughed. "You can't say that. You haven't actually met Mama yet."

Although he was shaking his head no, Lugos found himself smiling at her. "Remember, you promised to do as I said," he persisted. He would take no chances with her safety.

She gave him a solemn nod of understanding. "Yeah, yeah, I remember. It's like UGA and Florida's rivalry. Go Dawgs!"

For the umpteenth time, he wondered if he should have left her back at his cabin instead of dragging her with him. Murmur could have watched over her without her knowledge. Sure, she might have snooped a bit in his absence, but how much could that really matter now? He had every intention of moving her into his home as soon as this USL business was concluded.

"I'll be fine. Just go have your chat," she said, smoothing out the fabric of her new pastel rose skirt. It was ankle length, and she wore matching sandals with straps that wound around her calves. The white halter top was just short enough to show off a small portion of her waist.

Following the slow motion of her hand, Lugos groaned. "I'm not sure these clothes are any less tempting than those shorts of yours, Keely."

She cocked her head and just smiled at him.

Reading the invitation in those warm, chocolate eyes, Lugos groaned again. He then cleared his throat and exited the quietly running car. The soft thud of the door was unusually loud in the darkness. He had been extravagant with his powers: first the clothes, then transporting himself, Keely, and his Audi to Kentucky. He could have just rented a car, but Lugos couldn't pass up the opportunity to give her a little sample of what he was capable of doing. He wanted to spoil her. He craved that look of adoration and awe he saw shining in her eyes. Lugos had already decided that they'd travel when all this was over. He'd show her the world.

The red gate was unlocked, merely shut for the night, and the air was still heavy and moist with the day's heat. The packed gravel hard and dry under his loafers, Lugos moved quickly past the gate and up to the farmhouse, the persistent drone of cricket song masking the steady crunch of his steps. He was aware of his own golden glow. With Keely to protect, he would just have to forgo any attempt to hide his identity.

Just as he reached the front porch, the door opened and a woman stepped out.

"You!" She didn't bother to soften the accusation in her greeting.

Lugos replied in kind, glad that Keely had remained behind in the car. "Were you expecting someone else?" He stepped onto the wooden porch and decided that the graying brunette could only be Cassie, the coven's priestess. She had the bearing of a leader, despite her blue terry-cloth robe and fluffy gray slippers.

After an extended period of strained silence, the priestess remembered her manners and prudently decided to extend him a basic level of cordiality. "I welcome you, Lugh, Bringer of Light. You honor us. Please enter."

It would have been believable had it not been for her chilly delivery and the expression of disdain, which managed to suck all warmth from her welcome. She tightened the belt around her middle with a sharp tug of annoyance before stepping aside to allow him entry.

Lugos accepted her grudging hospitality and stepped through the doorway, only to find another witch waiting inside. She was young enough to still have the narrow hips of an adolescent, but this was no innocent babe. Pale, blonde, comely, and wearing far too much eye makeup, she bobbed an awkward curtsy in her Tinker Bell pajamas. Definitely Angus's speed, Lugos thought.

Cassie rushed forward to insert herself between Lugos and her student. "Jewel, this is the god Lugh, the Mother Goddess's *exiled* son. Run and wake Harmony and Fawn." Jewel was slow to respond, so the priestess sharply clapped her hands together, startling the young witchlet into action. "Now, Jewel. And be quick about it."

Catching the scent of her teacher's anger, Jewel darted for the stairs like a frightened doe. Lugos's gaze followed her retreat before returning to the high priestess. "Rhiannon has questions about Seraphine," he announced, hoping that dropping Rhiannon's name would soften the priestess's initial resistance. "I don't wish to be here any longer than necessary. Assemble your coven so I can get on with this."

Cassie shuffled over to a wooden chair and sat straight backed. "What questions?" she asked, her gray eyes accusing.

Lugos glided forward to stand over her, little caring how uncomfortable he might make her. "How often did the two of you argue?"

"We hardly ever did," she replied, craning her neck upward.

"But you did disagree over accepting your latest two pupils, Jewel and Josey."

She blinked up at him. "Yes, but I don't see that's any concern of yours."

Lugos shrugged. "I don't care who my mother takes into her service. I do want to know what Seraphine's objection was."

Cassie's mouth drew down in a thin line. Her eyes darted toward the stairs before returning to him. "Lack of pedigree, nothing more. They didn't have anyone to vouch for them."

"Did you contact their last mentor?"

The sudden flush of anger that stained her cheek told him that she had not.

"I don't see how any of this is your business."

She started to rise, but Lugos took a step closer, forcing her to sit back down on the chair. She might not like him, but he was a god and she a mere mortal.

Lugos shrugged again. "What's my business and what's not isn't for you to decide." He then stepped away from her so that he could study the newest arrivals and still keep an eye on the priestess. "How many witches are in the coven?"

"Seven."

In a flurry of pounding feet, Jewel arrived with her coven sisters in tow, Harmony and Fawn. Lugos took a moment to absorb the details as Cassie launched into introductions. Fawn and Jewel were of like coloring and build. Fawn's complexion remained completely free of makeup, giving the false impression that she was far younger than either of her covenmates. Her locks had been pulled into a ponytail, while Jewel's was loose and fell well past her shoulders. The fuller-figured witch, Harmony, was darker in coloring. She wore large silver hoops in each ear as well as silver studs in both lip and nose. A series of tats rose up her thick neck and arms.

Lugos directed next his question to Jewel. "Who's missing, other than your sister Josey?"

"Do you know Josey?" Jewel's mascara-laden eyes widened.

"Cygnet went for a walk," Harmony chirped, talking over her covenmate. "She does that every night."

Lugos did a quick mental count: Cassie the priestess, Tinker Bell Jewel, the missing twin Josey, young-looking Fawn, tatted Harmony, night-strolling Cygnet, and the deceased Seraphine. Again it occurred to Lugos that he might be wasting his time trying to determine who among them might be the source of those emails.

"Enough!" Cassie snapped, attempting to take charge of the conversation once more. "With all due respect, I don't see why you have any right to ask questions about our coven. We are under the Great Mother's protection and owe you nothing."

Lugos interrupted the priestess before she could regurgitate all the imaginary crimes and shortcomings his mother had laid at his feet. "I am trying to learn what kind of coven Seraphine would choose to align herself with, when it is crystal clear to me that she would have been better served if she'd remained within the shifter community. After all, Talon, her acknowledged brother, is now their leader. But instead of remaining within the community she was born to, Seraphine decided to live a life divided between two very different worlds. Why?"

His question seemed to shock the younger witches. They appeared genuinely baffled, if not a little horrified. In contrast, the high color staining the priestess's cheeks was proof that his inquiry had touched a nerve. Did the witchlets not know that one of their own covenmates was a shifter?

"And why expel Alex?" he added before Cassie could answer. "Was it because she was a shifter as well?"

The priestess jammed her hands into her terry-cloth robe. "I asked her to leave because she was not inclined to learn the craft. As Seraphine's familiar, she had a place, but without..." Cassie raised her chin defiantly. "There was no reason for her to stay. I told her that. Anyway, she's better with her own kind."

"Unless it was her own kind who murdered Seraphine," Lugos shot back. Race prejudice was everywhere, even in the Pale. Lugos found himself hoping that Seraphine had shielded Alex from Cassie's racist views while alive, for it was clear to him that there was little warmth to be had from this group since the elder's death. "It's safe to assume you haven't seen Alex of late."

"No," the priestess declared. "We haven't."

"Did you know your elder was a shifter?" Lugos turned his gaze on Harmony.

All three witchlets stole a glance at their priestess. Cassie hastily answered for them. "No. Seraphine was private about that part of her life. She divulged her flaws to very few."

"But you obviously knew." Lugos wondered what other "flaws," other than being a shifter, Cassie thought Seraphine had possessed.

Cassie nodded. "Yes, of course."

"And all of you knew Alex was a shifter."

He didn't need Cassie's confirmation, though she gave it anyway.

"How could they not?"

He swung his gaze back to Cassie. "If Seraphine could keep them in the dark, don't you think she could have done the same for Alex's sake?"

"Alex did as she pleased," Fawn blurted. All three witchlets were huddled together, still at the bottom of the stairs. "Not even the Lady Seraphine could make her follow the rules."

"It's true," Jewel agreed. "I heard Lady Seraphine scold Alex for showing Harmony how the transformation was done."

"That's enough, Jewel," Cassie butted in. "You are divulging coven business. From here on out, I will answer all his questions. Go locate Cygnet and your sister."

"I'd rather they remained here," Lugos said. He didn't want any more of the coven wandering about outside with Keely alone in the car.

The priestess drew her shoulders back. "I don't see that you can keep me from sending—"

Abruptly Lugos tapped into his god-powers and allowed the raw energy to flow through him. The air crackled as his power surged upward from his core and then around him, amplifying his golden glow tenfold. His vision altered, and something akin to euphoria flooded his senses. Seeing the awe and shock on their faces, Lugos fought the urge to laugh at them. He had dispatched gods. Did these four women really think they were a match for him?

Lugos carefully repeated his request. "I would rather they remain here."

Having made his point, Lugos reluctantly wrestled down the surge of power until it was a mere trickle humming in his veins. Slowly his golden aura receded, and the world as it truly appeared came back into focus. Lugos took a deep breath as a disturbing mixture of regret and relief filled him.

The priestess and her charges now all wore identical expressions. Ignoring the stunned and worried eyes aimed in his direction, Lugos plowed on with the interview. "I'm sure they will be along soon enough. Tell me more about Seraphine and her role in your coven."

A scream shattered the night. And then another.

Keely! was his only thought. Lugos drew deeply on his power stores and teleported himself outside. What he saw upon materializing drove the breath from his lungs. Keely, followed by another woman, burst from the tree line and into the open yard at a dead run. Even at this distance, he could read the terror on Keely's moonlit face. She was running full out and straight toward him, her skirt hiked up around her knees. Her pursuer was gaining ground.

Lugos's whole world seemed to shrink, and his focus narrowed to a razor-sharp edge. In a flash of brilliant white light, he teleported again and inserted himself between Keely and her pursuer. He hurled himself into the other woman. There was a satisfying whoosh as the breath left the witch's lungs. They fell to the ground together in a heap, her full skirt and arms folding around him like a wet, heavy blanket.

Another scream ripped through the air behind him. And then another.

"Josey!"

All Lugos's attention was on locating Keely, not the enemy who lay beneath him. He disentangled his legs and sat up. Even through his altered vision, he could see that he'd knocked her out cold. Then one of the witchlets tugged at his arm, and he balled his free hand into a fist, more than ready to continue the fight.

"Lugh! Stop it!" Keely's voice pleaded.

Lugos froze in mid-swing. A young witch lay at his feet, pale and unmoving; another tugged at his arm, terror in her eyes. Lugos was already moving to get to Keely.

"She isn't dead," he announced. With a good deal of effort, he reined in his power. The fact that his power had sprung forth so readily worried him a little. He'd successfully tamped it down again, but the addictive hum of euphoria that had flooded his system lingered still.

Without asking her permission, Lugos collected Keely in his arms and moved her away from the gathering witches. From Cassie, there was a flurry of cooing concern for the downed witch. The others huddled around their fallen covenmate. To Lugos's annoyance, even Keely seemed sympathetic to the young woman's injuries.

"Why did you leave the car?" he barked.

"What are ya doin', Lugh? She—" Keely turned to him and then fell mute.

"What happened?" he demanded. He didn't know what she had read in his expression, but he was thankful that it was just concern he read in her eyes and not fear of him. She was winded and still shaking, but he didn't appear to be the cause. He gentled his hold on her arms, afraid he might have accidentally bruised her.

"We...we were attacked," Keely replied, still working to catch her breath. "One of the girls stayed to fight it off." She looked past him toward the tree line the two had fled, then added, "I think."

In the moonlight, her eyes were large and brimming with apprehension. She had yet to let go of his shirt, and he had no intention of making her do so.

"It?" he asked, latching on to the vagueness of her description. He expected that she'd stay put. The young witch he'd mistaken for her attacker was now slowly coming around, her covenmates still too preoccupied with their fallen comrade to notice much else. He doubted that he'd have more than a moment or two before the accusations started. He stroked his hand down the fall of Keely's brunette hair until it came to rest on her lower back. With his heart still hammering and still flush with the terror he'd felt, Lugos tried to sound as if he were in complete control of himself and the situation. "Describe what you saw, Keely."

Keely dropped her gaze. "It was dark, we were walkin' and talkin', then this thing, big as a bear, came out of the trees and knocked me down. Cygnet, that was the other girl, yelled at it." She glanced up from his chest to lock eyes with him. "I guess she got its attention 'cause Josey hauled my butt off the ground and we got to runnin'."

Lugos spared a quick glance at the group huddled around Josey. She was sitting up now. When he turned back, he saw that Keely had followed his gaze. "I'll apologize later," he assured her, though he wasn't sure that an actual apology was in order. It had been an honest mistake. "Can you tell me where this Cygnet is? She may need my help."

Keely hesitated.

"We should hurry," he prompted. Cassie was going to turn her attention from Josey to him in a minute, and he wanted Keely clear if possible.

Keely nodded.

He let Keely set the pace. It was a slow trot across the open yard. As it turned out, Lugos didn't need much guidance to retrace the route Keely and Josey had taken. Just beyond the tree line was a well-worn path. Here, he took her hand and slowed them.

Every time she'd been out of his sight, someone had attacked her—first at Cutter's place, then this. Once again, it occurred to him that placing her with Zee and Murmur might not be such a bad idea. Lugos scanned the area, expanding his senses to find the danger waiting for them. He could feel a disturbance, but not the *it* that had attacked Keely.

Lugos was the first to detect the sounds of pursuit behind them. The crashing sound of rapid footfalls didn't slow; whoever was following them didn't intend to take them by surprise. Within moments, Harmony's larger frame came into view.

Breathing hard, she called, "I can see you, ya know."

Lugos resisted the urge to yell back, "and I could hear you a mile away." He'd gotten so adept at operating at his former low level of god-power that glowing in the dark had been almost a nonissue for him—until now. The more faith Keely put in him, the more power he seemed to draw from her. Lugos kept Keely glued to his side.

Harmony slowed her rolling pace. By the time she'd drawn abreast, the witchlet was holding her rib cage with her right hand. "It's not much farther," she explained between pants, pointing. "Cygnet likes to walk by the pond. The path ends there."

"You should go back," Lugos told her. He had a good idea what they would find, but Harmony was already hurrying down the path.

True to the witch's prediction, the tree line ended to reveal a secluded pond perhaps two acres in circumference. On the other side of the pond stood a barbed-wire fence, the coven's property line. Beyond that lay only empty pasture. The shifter, Keely's *it*—for Lugos was already convinced of that particular fact—would have made his or her escape across the open pasture instead of risking traveling through the coven's land.

All was still. Deathly quiet, Lugos thought. Harmony called out to her missing covenmate, but there was no answering call. While Harmony repeated Cygnet's name, Lugos began to look for signs of a struggle. To help, Keely pointed to where she'd been knocked down. Whatever had attacked them was long gone. Only animal tracks remained along the path. Though the moon was full, very little light penetrated the trees and underbrush.

Lugos was the first to spot Cygnet's body through the soft glow of his own aura. It had only taken a few moments because he'd known what to look for. The missing witch had been thrown well off the path and into some brush. He could see that the body was torn, the neck wrenched awkwardly up and back, exposing the fatal bite mark on her neck.

Hearing Harmony's approach, Lugos moved to block her view and caught the witchlet by the arm. "Go fetch Cassie." When she was slow to respond, he shook her. "Go!" he barked, giving her a shove in the direction he wanted her to go. She stumbled at first but then regained her balance and sprinted noisily back up the path. Unfortunately, when he turned back to send Keely far enough away to keep her from seeing the entirety of the carnage, he found that his opportunity to shield her had evaporated.

Lugos hovered as Keely vomited at the base of a tree. When her stomach was empty, he guided her to a spot by the pond where he could still see her but where she might sit to recover in peace.

"Sit here." Gentle pressure to her forearm and shoulder had her folding downward onto the grass. "I need to make some notes before the police are called." He stroked the dark wave of hair as it spilled across her back. Keely didn't notice the gesture. He then kissed the top of her head and stood. *She's in shock*, he thought.

"Keely," he said, trying again to reach her. She didn't answer him, only stared vacantly across the pond. "I'll take you away from here as soon as I can. Just hang in there." Though the night was not chilly, he manifested a light shawl and draped it around her shoulders for a measure of comfort. He'd handle this quickly for Rhiannon, he thought, and then take Keely to Zee. There was no need to explain Murmur to her yet. Quietly he stepped back toward the trees and the path, worry creasing his brow while his gut twisted like an eel inside his belly.

Reaching the body, Lugos drew a tree limb aside and squatted on his heels. It was a fast kill, he mused, studying the gashes through the dim light of his own glow. The spray of black splotches dotting the skin and surrounding vegetation completed the gruesome narrative. The fact that the attacker had then taken time to maul the body told Lugos that the shifter liked the taste of killing—or perhaps this witch wasn't the intended victim, and this shifter had deep anger issues. The more Lugos examined the depth and angle of the ripped flesh and clothing, the more convinced he became of the latter explanation. What Lugos read through all the darkening bloodstains and ripped flesh was fury, fury and frustration. If this witch hadn't been the shifter's target, then who had been? Had it been a second attempt on his Keely? Or was Josey the intended target?

It wasn't until an audible gasp of horror arose behind him that Lugos realized Cassie had arrived. Lugos took a moment to scan for Keely beyond the terry-clothed priestess. She was still sitting alone where he'd left her. Good, he thought. He swung his attention to the priestess.

Faced with such horror, Cassie seemed to have physically shrunk. Fragile and pale and all too human, she knelt down beside him, heedless of the dirt, the leaves, and the blood she rested in. When her hand moved to close the victim's eyelids, he intervened. "Leave her. This has to be reported to the local authorities."

Snapping her head around, she began to protest, "But—" Then her mouth shut tight like a turtle snapping a twig.

Lugos rose to his feet, the glow that had illuminated the body rising with him. "You know I'm right," he said a little too harshly. "You will say it was an animal attack. She was by herself, walking as she always does. When she didn't return at the usual time, you became concerned. You then heard a scream. Harmony and Josey went out to search for her. This is what they found. When they returned to the farmhouse with the news, you called immediately and then came out here because you just couldn't believe it." The story he gave her was a simple one, one everyone would need to stick to in order to protect the secret that was the Pale. "I'll inform Rhiannon."

Cassie remained silent, then nodded. With a grunt, she gained her feet. "I'll go now."

He added another detail. "Harmony vomited over there." He pointed to where Keely's stomach had rebelled. He wanted this wrapped up quickly so he could get her out of harm's way as soon as godly possible.

Cassie acknowledged the added bit of information before heading back the way she'd come. He didn't care how much she resented him. He was more concerned with doing his job and keeping Keely out of as much of this as he could. Cassie hadn't asked him who Keely was or why she was with him, and for that he was thankful.

Lugos waited until the Priestess was out of sight before returning to the small clearing at the pond. He eyed the path along the way. It was so worn that he didn't think the number of footprints would matter. If the local authorities started counting impressions, then at least substituting Harmony's for Keely's prints would work to keep the story plausible. The question of what type of animal could do this much damage was something the locals would just have to guess at. It's the kind of thing local legends were made of. Lugos was quite certain they'd never hit on the truth of the matter.

Keely was still as he'd left her. Lugos lowered himself down beside her. It was a pleasant and secluded place. He could understand why the witch now lying in the brush had spent time here. He felt the pressure of Keely's shoulder as she abruptly leaned against him.

"You could have been fast asleep at my cabin or bored out of your mind watching late night television. I'm sorry, I shouldn't have brought you here with me." She didn't respond, so he cocked his head to study what he could of her profile. Her dark hair fell in waves, obscuring a large portion of her face.

"That's not the first dead person I've seen."

"Is that so?"

Her shoulder moved off his. "Yeah. My uncle shot himself a few years back. I was seventeen at the time. Blew one side of his head clean off."

Her admission surprised him, as did the matter-of-fact way she'd said it. "And you found him."

Keely nodded before turning her gaze toward him. "It was real gross." She gave an audible sigh. "And sad," she added, looking away again to stare out across the water. "And fascinating at the same time. There was something about the missing bits of him, ya know, that made it easier to look at it all. Like it wasn't him no more…like it wasn't a real person sitting there with half a face."

Lugos understood that the witch in the bushes was a bit different. Despite all the damage to neck and body, the almost doll-like face had remained intact. Cygnet was also someone Keely had just met. And although the dead witch appeared to be close to Keely's age, Lugos knew that with witches it wasn't always easy to guess their biological age just by looking at them. Many tended to gain a kind of agelessness after years of practicing the craft.

"That could have been me," Keely said, interrupting his wayward thought.

Lugos felt a chill spread through him despite the warmth of the night.

"When you said you had to go talk to some witches, I was scared at first, but they're just girls, Lugh. The one you tackled to the ground, she was the one who tapped on the car window, all smiles and friendly. She was so excited about meeting you. We were going to fetch her friend when…" Keely paused and then inhaled deeply before turning her gaze back to him. "I don't want you to tuck me away somewhere. And I know you probably are thinkin' you should, but somethin' unnatural killed that girl, and I want you to find out who or what it was."

Lugos tried to ignore his rising sense of dread. "I am perfectly capable of doing that without dragging you along with me. It would be safer if——"

"I'm stayin'."

And just like that, the woman he loved had reasserted herself. The headstrong, reckless, bad-boyfriend, too-brave-for-her-own-good Keely had resurfaced. He stared at her. She had no idea the power she held over him. It also occurred to Lugos that somewhere between this morning and now, he'd become her next and last bad boyfriend. "I'm not going to deliberately put you in harm's way. Don't ask that of me."

"As long as we're together, I'm safe." Her eyes narrowed to slits. "You said as much." To drive her point home, she'd stabbed his thigh with her index finger.

Lugos abruptly rose to his feet, both to gain some perspective and to keep her from seeing the rising anger that had slow-burned through his earlier chill and nausea. "I also said to stay in the damn car, Keely. What happened there? Did you forget, or did——" He stopped himself from finishing the accusation that sat crouched behind tight lips. He wasn't acting rationally anymore, at least not where she was concerned. He'd already tapped into his god-powers more today than he'd done in years. Now he was about to admit a deeply guarded insecurity that she'd somehow managed to stir in him. Striving for patience, he tried again. "I'm taking you back to the cabin. I will keep you updated. But for now——"

The distant sound of sirens kept him from finishing the declaration of intent.

"You can't now. The police are about to be here." Keely rose to her feet and dusted off her new skirt. "And you're glowin' a little too much right now. We need to get you into a lit room before they get here, Lugh," she declared, her back stiffening in stubborn resolve.

How often had he seen that? Lugos grumbled a curse word or two under his breath.

Keely slipped her hand into his and tugged.

Lugos knew that letting her have her way in this was a bad idea. And yet, he folded. "I am a bad boyfriend," he admitted with a groan.

They were halfway up the path before Keely saw fit to reply. "It's too soon to tell, Mr. Hart. I've only seen one dead body. If you recall, this mornin' you promised to show me all of them."

Lugos would have had to be both deaf and blind to miss her forced flippancy, or the tiny catch in her voice. Keely was headstrong and resilient, but he couldn't help but wonder just how much of his world she could take in one day.

When they reached the end of the path and gained the moonlit yard, he reminded her, "I also recall telling you that kind of information was second date material. We've yet to have a first date."

Not to be outdone, Keely replied, "And whose fault is that? You had five long years to ask me out, as I recall."

Lugos didn't know whether he wanted to strangle her or kiss her at that moment. Unfortunately, circumstances required that he do neither.

Chapter 19

Keely would have thought the farmhouse downright charming had it not been for the girl lying dead in the woods. Without asking anyone's permission, she'd immediately gone about turning on every single light she could find to hide Lugh's glowing skin. Harmony, the big-boned girl who'd led them to the pond, seemed to catch onto Keely's intent and jumped in to lend a hand. Harmony then went one step further and tugged the drapes shut. The effect was like pulling a heavy blanket over your head, protective yet kind of suffocating.

Keely found an out-of-the-way place to sit and glanced over at Lugh. She could now see only the subtlest glow around him, and only if he moved too quickly, lifting an arm to point at something or someone, turning his head to see who might be running down or up the stairs behind him. She managed a weak smile when he looked in her direction. She was far more tired than she wanted anyone to know.

"I think you need to stand closer to this lamp," she told him.

Her gentle teasing eased the worry in his expression, but she could still read it in his eyes. She might have missed it but for the way his gaze lingered whenever he looked at her. Keely didn't think anyone else had noticed the long glances; at least, she hoped none of these strange birds had.

Not that Lugh had given anyone time to notice much of anything. As soon as he'd bustled her into the farmhouse, Lugh had gotten busy being…well, Lugh. His commands to people had begun as soon as her pretty pink sandals touched the scuffed pine floor. And it was clear to everyone with any kind of sense that the one called Cassie didn't particularly like his high-handed interference. She was the oldest of the group of women living in the house, though Keely would be hard pressed say how much past thirty-something the woman might be. Some women just aged well. Cassie was obviously one of them.

By the time Cassie stepped out onto the porch to greet the first set of sirens, Lugh had thoroughly drilled everyone on the story they were to tell. While waiting for the coroner and the sheriff's department to descend, some of the girls had taken Lugh's advice and changed out of their pajamas. But the one named Jewel had just waved off his suggestion. Still in her Tinker Bell print PJs, Jewel was keeping herself busy fussing over her injured sister. At the moment, she was wrapping Josey's rib cage in gauze. Lugh had cracked a rib or two when he'd tackled the girl like a UGA linebacker. Keely was fairly sure Lugh regretted hurting her, probably even more so now that Josey had been so quick to forgive him, graciously saying it was a misunderstanding, a mistake anyone might make. Keely had almost laughed out loud at that, mainly because it had been such a bad lie. In Keely's opinion, the girl was wavering between fear of Lugh and complete and utter awe of him. Keely wasn't exactly ready to say which would win out, though the way the blonde peered at him through her lashes, it was probably the latter.

With a whump, Harmony fell back into the sofa's cushions. Her mascara was smudged from crying, which had left dark half-moons under her red and puffy eyes. Keely tried not to stare at the tattoos lining Harmony's fleshy arms, but they were many and kept one's mind off other, more troubling things. Lord Jesus, she was tired.

"So, you're one of Rhiannon's acolytes," Harmony prompted.

Keely nodded a halfhearted yes. That's how Lugh had instructed her to respond. Keely wasn't sure what an acolyte was, but she was supposed to confirm that she was one if asked. In an urgent whisper, he had also instructed her not to offer any information about herself, including where she lived, who she knew, and above all, that he was her boyfriend. Keely glanced down at her lap and smiled at the memory. If there hadn't been a dead girl in the woods, it would have been a perfect memory. She noticed the dirt under her nails and started to pick at them. When did that happen?

"Must be a real honor," Harmony continued wistfully, "to have a goddess claim you as her own."

Keely raised an eyebrow but not her head. Is that what acolyte meant? she wondered. She took another few seconds to set aside the surprise she felt before raising her gaze.

Harmony attempted to wink one puffy red eye in Keely's direction but succeeded only in squinting. "I know, this is the wrong time to talk about such things, but—"

The shadow of Lugh fell across Keely's lap. His mere presence was enough to discourage Harmony from further talk. Keely looked up and duplicated the smile she'd given him a moment before. He needn't worry; she had no intention of telling any of these odd ducks anything she didn't absolutely have to.

He briefly rested a hand on her shoulder, and Keely had to stop herself from covering it with her own. Without any warning, she began to feel that hot, tingling sensation from before. It was slow at first, seeping into her like warm honey. She glanced up to find him looking at her.

"You're tired, and we have a few more hours to go."

He was pushing a little of himself into her, as he had before at the hotel. But this time it was such a small amount that there was none of his god-glow, just enough energy to help her not feel so tired.

"Thanks. But a cup of coffee might work just as well," she breathed, once again pretending more interest in her nails than in the rest of the room. She'd whispered her appreciation, suspecting that Lugh could hear her. He seemed completely aware of every move she made. The girls, the ones Lugh kept insisting were witches, were all packed into this one room with them. Though they hardly looked scary to Keely in the brightly lit room—Harmony with her streaked mascara, Tinker-Bell-clad Jewel, cracked-rib Josey, and Fawn, who'd tucked herself away in a corner chair. Harmony seemed to be the only one who'd taken any notice of the way Lugh hovered. Harmony seemed to see a lot.

Keely turned to Harmony. "Rhiannon would be mighty upset if anything happened to me." She then flicked her head toward Lugh. "He knows it."

Harmony mouthed an "O" of understanding.

Above her, Lugh grunted. Keely could feel his amusement slide into her along with the heat flowing from his hand. A heartbeat or two later, the strange tingling in her shoulder began to fade, but his hand remained. "They're coming."

When the terry-robed Cassie entered, Lugh dropped his hand from Keely's shoulder, but he didn't move from her side or out of the lamplight behind him.

A stocky young man in uniform followed. The uniform was blue, not sheriff brown; for some reason, Keely had expected the latter. The newcomer was well muscled but not much taller than Keely herself. He had a sort of military handsomeness and a graceful way of moving across the floor, almost like a dancer.

Jewel was the first to break the silence. "Carson!" she said, smiling for the first time since her sister's injury.

The bright greeting was wholly out of place given the grim reason for his being here. Not unexpectedly, Cassie's mouth dipped downward even further. The woman must suck lemons, Keely thought uncharitably.

Carson replied to Jewel's greeting with a warm smile of his own before taking the time to eye the rest of those assembled. Fortunately his gaze only skimmed over Keely's as he took in Lugh above her. Once there, the deputy's gaze seemed stuck.

"I assume you've got a permit for that sidearm?"

Lugh had taken off his jacket back at the car but not the shoulder holster and gun. It was Kentucky, after all, so Keely hadn't even questioned his having it.

"Of course I do."

"Too bad you didn't use it on whatever it was that got Cygnet."

"Yes, it is. Is this your jurisdiction? I expected the local sheriff, not a Murray police officer."

Before Carson could reply, Jewel and Harmony spoke over one another.

"He lives just down the road," said one.

"Carson's family's from here," said the other.

Not to be ignored, Cassie's sour voice rose over the girl's explanations. "He's a nosy neighbor and was a close friend of Seraphine." She'd drawn this last out as if it contained some significance. Keely glanced up to study Lugh's expression. He'd heard it too.

Lugh's blue eyes narrowed. "Might have been you, then. You arrived on the scene quick enough. Should I assume this is a message from Larkin?"

And just that quickly, the whole conversation went off the rails for Keely.

Carson's professional mask seemed to drop away. "You misunderstand the situation, sir. I wouldn't have done nothin' to hurt these girls. 'Specially Jewels over there." Carson paused, then asked, "Who's Larkin?"

Keely had no idea what the two of them were talking about. Larkin? Then she realized that Lugh was accusing Carson of being the very thing that had attacked them in the woods.

"You're a shifter. I can smell you from here. This is your territory, is it not? Who attacked those girls?" Lugh hadn't raised his voice, but the accusation caused more than one person to squirm uncomfortably in her chair.

Carson chuckled uneasily. "I thought I was the one gonna be askin' the questions. But then, I didn't know someone of your significance was gonna be on the scene."

"He's looking into Seraphine's death for Rhiannon," Cassie explained. "Why, exactly, I don't know."

Keely didn't think the woman liked Carson any better than Lugh did. Carson, on the other hand, showed no sign of caring what Cassie thought of him. And he seemed to know right off that Lugh was important and not one to be disrespected.

"Are you thinkin' there was foul play? Official word is that she...that she did herself in. You know, cut her wrists and bled out." He then had the grace to grimace apologetically for spelling out the details for the entire room to hear.

"That's the official word," Lugh replied.

"But Rhiannon doesn't think it's that straightforward? That's why you're here." Carson supplied.

Lugh didn't confirm the deputy's assumptions, so Carson rushed forward to fill the ensuing silence that no one else seemed willing to fill. "Well, someone from the sheriff's department and Jack Tanner, the county coroner, are gonna arrive soon, and you'll need a good reason for being here—one they won't think to question. Guess that story's as good as any. I warn ya, they're gonna want to talk to you," he finished, eyeing Lugh once more with an intensity Keely didn't quite understand.

Lugh gave an almost imperceptible shrug of his shoulders. Although Lugh seemed okay with the idea, the thought of the local sheriff questioning him made her a little nervous. What if they spotted the glow around him? What if they questioned her? What was she supposed to do? Lying wasn't as natural to her as to some people.

"What about Cygnet?" Fawn asked, speaking up for the first time. "We can't just leave her out there."

"She's with Mother and past need, Fawn," Josey said, her voice breathy.

Fawn immediately teared up, and the rest of the rooms occupants ducked their heads. Keely stole yet another glance at Lugh. The mention of a mother confused her. Were Fawn and Cygnet sisters as well? She was about to ask when Lugh gave a discreet but definite shake of his head. Unfortunately, Carson caught the fleeting communication. The deputy jabbed his forefinger in her direction.

"And who's she?" Carson asked Cassie, his brown eyes taking every detail from the top of Keely's head to the tips of her bright red-painted toenails. "A tender new member of your coven?"

"She's Rhiannon's acolyte," said Harmony, Cassie, and Jewel in unison. Harmony said it as if she were envious, but neither Cassie's tone nor Jewel's held any such emotion.

Carson's eyebrows rose toward his hairline. It was clearly not the response he had expected.

Keely wanted nothing more than to dissolve into a puddle and slip down between the floorboards. She didn't like the way the deputy studied her. There was something feral in his gaze that sent a shiver up her spine. Fortunately, Lugh was there to save her.

"She has no connection to what happened tonight, so let's get back to you, Officer Carson Pratt," Lugh said, reading the officer's badge from the other side of the room. "You expect me to believe you're here because of neighborly concern?"

"Something like that."

In the conversational lull, Keely could clearly hear the wail of approaching sirens.

Carson was the first to speak. "Right. Okay, Cassie, I'll go out there with you to meet them. What's the story?"

Without prompting from Lugh, Cassie launched into the constructed tale. When she was finished, Carson nodded. "Guess that'll do," he replied, giving Lugh a nod that could be construed as approval. "Okay, stay here, I'll do my best to keep this short and sweet." He had been looking at the girls, but Keely had the feeling that he was really talking strictly to Lugh. Turning, Carson opened the door and he and Cassie stepped out to meet the growing noise and the swirling blue tornado of lights.

Chapter 20

In the void left by Carson and Cassie's departure, Fawn uncurled herself and announced to Lugh, "Carson and Cygnet had a thing."

"That's hardly important," snapped Jewel.

"You were screwing him, too," Harmony declared, jumping to Fawn's defense. Her eyes were squarely on Jewel, her rounded jaw hard. "And he's married!" she added.

Josey put a hand on her sister's arm, her voice still breathy. "He's mated, not married; there's a difference. Harmony, you should know that."

Fawn's delicately narrow nostrils flared. "It's basically the same thing. You're utterly stupid to think Blye would let his cheatin' go unchallenged."

Jewel's complexion paled. "You think Blye did this?"

"Isn't it obvious? She's a cougar like Carson. You think she'd willingly share her mate with you or Cygnet? Or even Lady Seraphine?" Fawn sniped.

Keely flicked her eyes up at Lugh. He was watching the girls but had yet to intervene. All their bickering and bed-hopping reminded her of high school back in Salem. How old were these girls?

Harmony wasted no time stirring the pot Fawn had started. "What about Blake?"

"What about him?" Jewel snapped, her head whipping around to glare at Harmony.

Harmony shrugged a tattooed shoulder. "Well, he's not exactly the passive type. What if he had a real problem with his mated brother screwin' half the county? What if he decided to put a stop to it for Blye?"

Jewel's cheeks turned crimson. "That's a lie! He wasn't— isn't screwing half the county!" she shouted.

"Maybe he is," Fawn replied under her breath.

"So, what if he is?" Tinker Bell shook off her sister's hold and stomped across the room to loom over Harmony. "What're either of them goin' to do, go on a killin' spree?" Harmony matched Tinker Bell's glare.

"And it's none of your business who I sleep with," Jewel went on. "Carson was pretty damn tight with Lady Seraphine before she banned him. You sayin' he screwed her, too?"

Finally, Lugh cleared his throat. The casual gesture was just enough to remind the girls that he was still in the room. Jewel's head snapped up, as did everyone else's. With all eyes on him, he quietly asked, "When did she ban him?" Keely watched Lugh's cool blue eyes single out Jewel for the answer.

Jewel's mascara-laden eyes widened.

Twisting around on the couch, Harmony quickly responded, "Beltane eve. At least, that's when we were told about it." Harmony glared at Jewel, daring her to deny it.

They were like two cats howling at each other, a lot of noise but never willing to actually scrap. But if they did, Keely's money was on Harmony. Tinker Bell just looked too fragile to defend against Harmony's bulk.

"The day Talon came to see his sister," Lugh supplied. "The day they argued."

Jewel's crimson cheeks lost their color, and she looked to her twin for help. In the fleeting silence, Keely saw what could only be described as twin-speak, the silent dialogue flowing from one twin and back, fluid as waves along a beach.

Josey answered, briefly saving her sister from Lugh's scrutiny. "Yes. Carson had just left," she explained as she held her battered ribs. "Jewel and I passed him at the gate. He wasn't happy."

"He was pissed," Jewel added, then fell silent again, drawn back to her sister's side.

After a shallow breath, Josey continued. "When we got to the farmhouse, we heard yellin'. I went to find Alex."

"How did you know she was nearby?" Lugh pressed. His eyes flickered in Keely's direction, but they didn't stay long before moving on. Something told Keely that he already knew the answer.

Fawn and Josey talked over one another.

"Alex was Lady Seraphine's familiar."

"If Lady Seraphine had arrived, so had Alex."

"And did you find her?" Lugh asked, drawing out the story.

While Lugh's attention remained on Josey, Keely watched Fawn. She was still curled up on her chair, but a smugness had replaced the timid creature she'd first shown herself to be. When Fawn caught Keely staring at her, she froze for the span of a heartbeat and then dropped her eyes to the ragged hem of her cutoffs.

"Yeah, she was on the back porch, listening at the open window," Keely heard Josey reply in her breathy way.

Keely glanced up again at Lugh. Those kissable lips of his had thinned. "Go on. What happened next? What were they arguing about?"

Jewel laid a hand on Josey's shoulder "They were arguing about Carson. Talon kept saying that he was her true brother and that she needed to trust him. He said it had always been the two of them, that nothing Carson claimed could or would change that."

Keely watched as one of Lugh's blond eyebrows arched upward. She was suddenly lost again. Had Jewel just suggested that Carson was Seraphine's brother? And they had...eeuw! Surely she'd heard wrong.

"Any mention of the USL?" Lugh went on, ignoring the suggestion of incest between Carson and Seraphine.

The twins studied each other, and then Josey shook her head. "Not that I recall. It seemed to be some sort of family quarrel. Alex left me and went around front."

"That's when she caught my arm and dragged me inside," Jewel finished.

Keely couldn't remain quiet. "Why would she do that?" She was hard pressed to ignore the deep downward turn of Lugh's mouth. Amid all the secret-telling, she'd temporarily forgotten that he had wanted her to remain silent.

Jewel immediately attacked, her strong feelings for Carson far too evident. "Because Carson and I had slept together. Alex thought Carson wanted Lady Seraphine, and Alex didn't want to share her. She was jealous and wanted to make a scene. She wanted Lady Seraphine all to herself. So she made damn sure that Seraphine knew that Carson and I were seeing each other. Alex was even jealous of Talon because he cut into her time with Seraphine. The bitch was crazy possessive when it came to Seraphine."

"But Carson is already mated. And Lady Seraphine is...was old," Fawn interrupted, a blush touching her cheeks.

Keely didn't know how Fawn had managed the blush. She couldn't put her finger on it, but there was something false about the girl.

"Yes, but if one cougar had come sniffing around, there would be others," Lugh surmised, gaining Keely's attention once again. "Do you know how large Carson's community is?"

Like conspirators, three of the girls locked eyes, a discernible degree of guilt in each expression. The fourth, Fawn, wore an expression of surprise. Keely instinctively distrusted Fawn.

In the end, the ever-helpful Harmony was the one to answer Lugh. "We don't really know anyone besides Blye, Carson, Blake, and Old Man Grady."

"And does either Old Man Grady or Blake have a mate?" Lugh asked the room at large.

"No," Josey replied, "but Old Man Grady is Carson's father." Her nose crinkled with disgust.

Lugh ignored Josey. And rightly so, Keely thought to herself. There were plenty of horny old geezers in the world; why not Old Man Grady?

Keely hardly expected Lugh's next question. It put a whole new perspective on things.

"To your knowledge, had Lady Seraphine ever taken a male lover, even for ritual purposes?"

The door opened. "Yes, on occasion," answered Cassie, walking in without Carson in tow. As the door swung closed behind her seemingly on its own, she eyed her pupils disparagingly. "Been gossiping, have we?"

"They've been very helpful," Lugh informed Ms. Sourface. "More forthcoming than you, I daresay. What I want to know now is why Seraphine banned Carson, and why have you allowed him back on the coven's land?"

A knock at the door preempted the answer. It was Carson again, this time followed by a brown-uniformed deputy and a flood of blue, swirling lights. Keely's heart began to pound.

***

Lugos wasn't comfortable relying solely on luck to keep the Pale's secrets, nor was he comfortable having Keely squarely in the middle of an ongoing investigation. Carson the cougar-shifting deputy was far too interested in who Keely might be, and that had Lugos on edge. Despite Jewel's not-so-subtle efforts to keep Carson's attention, the cougar's sharp eyes kept coming back to Keely. Carson would have dared more if it hadn't been for

Lugos's earlier lie. As far as everyone knew, Keely was under Rhiannon's exclusive protection, which made her off limits. In the end, it had been the threat of an unhappy Rhiannon and simple luck that had kept Carson from learning who Keely was and why she was traveling with a god.

The local county authorities, on the other hand, had no inkling of what had transpired either inside or outside the farmhouse. They had readily accepted Lugos's fabricated truth about his and Keely's presence at the scene. Cygnet's unrelated death was an open-and-shut case for them—a freakish animal attack, probably a pack of feral dogs, too early to tell for sure tonight, could just as easily have been coyotes, though that was less likely. The authorities agreed that the tracks had been oddly formed and difficult to see in the dark. Perhaps they'd be able to tell more once it was light, when they could track the animal or animals involved.

After an hour or so of thrashing about in the dark with flashlights, the authorities instructed the farmhouse inhabitants to be careful. Various members of the sheriff department shook their heads and mumbled their condolences while the torn body was bagged and carted away by the coroner. The sheriff then promised Cassie he'd be back at first light, along with a team and dogs, to investigate further. But for now, he assured her, they could do no more.

In a display of sympathetic grief that Lugos wasn't entirely sure Carson felt, the cougar-shifter told Cassie he'd make sure the coroner took good care of Cygnet, and then followed the sheriff out the door.

Cassie quietly closed the door behind the officers, once more sealing the blue lights and commotion outside. Fawn, curled into herself, quietly cried in one corner of the room. The twins had turned to each other, holding hands for support. Harmony had created something of an angry shield, within which she was now encased. Lugos couldn't see Keely's full face, though her cheek seemed pale. He put what he hoped was a reassuring hand on her shoulder again.

Lugos still wasn't convinced that Larkin hadn't had a hand in tonight's affairs. Unfortunately, the notion was more gut driven than based on sound deduction. In the absence of their priestess, the young witches had given him a treasure trove of information. They clearly didn't possess the same shifter prejudices as their mentor. He'd learned that a small cougar family lived just next door; he'd found out about love triangles, and he'd discovered just how much Alex had lied to him. According to the little band of witches, Alex the shifter-familiar possessed a compelling motive—that is, if Seraphine truly had flirted with the idea of taking a cougar lover or a mate.

Yet even with all the complicated relationships he'd discovered tonight, Lugos knew that he was still missing pieces of the greater puzzle. He just didn't know what they were. The circumstances of Cygnet and Seraphine's deaths were completely different, like night and day. His gut kept telling him Larkin was involved, but how and why would Larkin want to kill this witch? And why would Larkin risk another attack on Keely while she was so obviously under Lugos's protection? He needed to talk to Talon, to verify the coven's story. And of course, delving into Talon and the USL was his primary objective. He'd let Seraphine's murder and Keely's safety sidetrack him.

Glancing down, his gut clenched into a knot. What gnawed at Lugos most was that this investigation might be the thing that would get his Keely killed. He gave her shoulder a squeeze. He'd get her out of here in the next few minutes.

"Why, exactly, did Seraphine ban Carson?" he asked the room at large.

The priestess padded across the floor and dropped down onto the cushions beside Harmony. She appeared exhausted by the night's events, by the death of her pupil, by the authorities' questions, by his persistent demand for answers. But the priestess's emotional state failed to stir any sympathy in Lugos.

Witches were charged with the task of strengthening connections between all living things, but Cassie's hatred of shifters had made her blind and a bad mentor to the younger witches. This coven was deeply flawed. Again he wondered why Seraphine had chosen to join this particular group.

"She said his carrying on a relationship with both Jewel and Cygnet would cause problems inside the coven," Cassie admitted into her lap.

"Did he make overtures toward Seraphine as well?"

The priestess's head popped up. "'Course he did! But that wasn't the reason he was banned."

Lugo let one eyebrow rise but otherwise did not comment. Though he hadn't followed up at the time, Lugos had caught the suggestion that Carson might have been Seraphine's brother by blood. An interesting wrinkle to this case, he thought.

The priestess's cheeks splotched red. Cassie tried to hold his gaze, but after a moment her surge of defiance ebbed, and she resentfully answered him. "One night, about a month ago, when she had just come into heat. Mind you, this didn't happen often to her, but when it did she usually would disappear for days on end in order to keep her...well, that side of her from showing." Cassie paused and stole a glance at Jewel before continuing. "For whatever reason, this last time she didn't go off with Alex; instead she remained here at the farmhouse. She sent all of us off to Louisville to a gathering of the Greater Southern Council. Of course, what Seraphine claimed she didn't want to occur happened in our absence, just like I'd warned her it would. The Pratts are too close."

"You mean proximity, not blood?"

"Yes. They're just next door. They could tell she was in heat. When Blake and Carson realized there was a window of opportunity to mate with her, they got into a terrible fight. Carson broke Blake's arm. Alex jumped into the fray and was hurt pretty bad herself. Of course, Carson came by afterward to apologize for it all, but by that time the worst of the fever had left her, and Seraphine was having none of it. She banned him and all the Pratts from coven property and used spells to enforce the ban. When we returned a week later, she was herself again."

Cassie's distaste for the whole episode was apparent, as was her delight in having the Pratts finally gone.

"When was this?"

"Mid-April. About two weeks before May Day."

"But the spells are no longer in effect now that she's dead." He'd suddenly realized that Seraphine, not Cassie, had been the coven's true leader. For this coven, the title of priestess was a hollow one. It also explained why the witchlets had been so friendly with Carson and his kind. Lugos watched as Cassie shook her head from side to side, verifying his conclusion. "Did they know Seraphine was a shifter?" he asked again.

Cassie looked up sharply. "No! She never shared that side of herself with them. I never fully understood why." The priestess glanced back down at her lap instead of at her pupils, who had been listening intently to the exchange between her and Lugos.

For the young witchlets' sake, he was going to make Cassie admit her failings. "You don't have the power to keep Carson and his kind off coven land."

"No, I don't. Seraphine did, but I don't." Cassie looked utterly defeated. "I knew that she held all the real power. Without her, the coven will most likely disband, given enough time. I've seen it happen before."

Lugos found the priestess's self-pity as distasteful as her shifter prejudice. "Do you know who was blackmailing Seraphine?"

Once again Cassie's head popped up, just as Jewel and Josey's faces paled. Lugos could feel Keely's eyes boring into him. He kept himself from stealing a glance at her. She must have a million questions, he thought.

"Blackmail?" Cassie's eyes were wide, her thin lips frozen as if around an invisible lemon.

Lugos's attention moved again to the twins. "Why did you send the emails?" he asked the two.

Jewel's lips drew taut in a line of defiance, while Josey's mouth opened and closed like a fish out of water.

"What is he talking about, Jewel?" Josey whispered, looking to her sister for answers.

"Not a damn thing. He's just guessing," Jewel responded. Stubbornness had transformed her face; the wistful, pale beauty was now icy and cold.

Cassie rose to her feet, planted her hands on her rounded hips, and pinned the young witch with an equally frigid glare. The air in the small farmhouse crackled with tension as the temperature dropped sharply. Fawn curled further into her cushions, and Harmony squirmed uneasily in her chair. Lugos took the precaution of stepping a little closer to Keely's side.

"Don't you dare pull that attitude, missy! I may not have been a match for Lady Seraphine, but I will not tolerate any insolence from the likes of you. You've yet to earn your first degree, and the last time I looked you were still bound by the laws of this coven. Answer him! Answer him now!"

Lugos was astonished at the sudden support, but he knew that Cassie's unexpected aid stemmed from a rigid sense of order and hierarchy and not from any love of him. He stole that long-needed glance at Keely's face, and a rush of warmth filled him. Her cheeks were a little pale, but otherwise she showed no outward sign that the turn of events was causing her any alarm. Returning his attention to the stand-off between the two witches, he silently hoped that the two would avoid actual spell casting. But in case they did start hurling spells at one another, Lugos was prepared to teleport himself and Keely out of the line of fire.

Under the glare of her priestess, Jewel's lip twitched and then softened.

Lugos took another intuitive leap. "I know the emails came from you, Jewel. I also know from Seraphine's medical records that she gave up twin girls for adoption." In the back of his mind,

Lugos also knew that Larkin had read the same threatening emails. The man probably knew about Seraphine's past. If Griffin could find the birth records, it's possible that Larkin, who worked at a security agency, could as well.

"Adoption records are sealed. How can you know that?" Josey demanded, her voice a pained exhalation. Cassie's face went slack, and the air in the room warmed again to a more comfortable temperature.

Lugos shrugged a shoulder. "It's not important. What I want to know is what you thought you might gain by extorting money from Seraphine." He'd read the threats, but after having met the twins, he didn't think they had it in them to kill their target. At least, Josey didn't.

"Is he telling the truth? Was Lady Seraphine our birth mother?" Josey asked her sister, tears pooling quickly on her lashes.

Under the weight of Cassie's influence, her sister's question, and the truth, Jewel's defiance finally melted away. She slowly turned to her injured sister. "I thought so. I only wanted her to pay something for abandoning us. Enough for college, or a car, or a new start somewhere. I thought we at least deserved that much from her."

"Why didn't you tell me?" Josey asked, her voice breaking. "Did you find our father as well?" She blinked several times to keep the tears from falling.

The longing Lugos heard in Josey's question bothered him. Why hadn't Jewel told her twin? Lugos heard the faint scuffing of boots on wood as tires began to roll across gravel in the heavy silence.

"No," Jewel replied.

Griffin had a lead on the identity of the father but not much else. Given that only one twin had blackmailed their mother, Lugos wasn't certain that sharing the answer with the twins was a good idea—that is, if Griffin could discover the answer.

It was at this fragile moment that Carson re-entered the farmhouse. The shifter scanned the room, no doubt picking up on the tension. "We're heading out, now. Just thought you'd like to know." His gaze moved from Lugh to the twins and then back again. "You staying?" he asked Lugh.

Lugh had heard the faint challenge in the simple question and wondered how much the shifter had heard while on the porch. "Not tonight. But you can be sure I'll be around," Lugh assured the shifter-deputy. Now that he knew that there was a community of cougars nearby, he wanted to know just how much conflict it had caused between Seraphine and Alex.

Thursday

Chapter 21

It was two thirty in the morning by the time he and Keely pulled away from the Sacred Grove Coven and the site of the night's attack. An audible sigh escaped Lugos's lips as he guided the Audi down the gravel road toward the highway. He knew that his next move involved paying a visit to Talon at the USL's base of operation. He'd need to do that before returning to follow up on any loose ends he might have left behind in Murray.

He was convinced that Josey wasn't capable of murder, but was Jewel? Just how problematic had the cougar community been for Seraphine? Why had she chosen to change her routine of leaving? Had the temptation of a viable cougar male been too overwhelming for her? Was Carson a true blood relation of Seraphine, and who else might have that information? Was her murder motivated by jealousy, rejection, or something completely different? Where in the hell was Alex? Why had she lied to him if she wasn't the murderer? And how did Ken Larkin and the USL tie in to all of this?

From the safety of the passenger seat, Keely's voice broke into his musings. "You feel like talkin' a little?"

He glanced in her direction. Her tired smile was illuminated by the car's dash lights and his own golden glow. "Sure, if you're up for it. I guess you've got a lot of questions. I didn't exactly stop and explain everything that went on in there." He turned onto the two-lane highway, choosing Murray over the long drive to Louisville.

"No. I think I understood most of it," she assured him. "There's not much to do in Salem 'cept watch how people hide their particular brand of crazy. So where do you want to start?"

"My lady's choice," he said.

Keely smiled at his words and then worked to collect her thoughts. "One," she began, ticking off revelations on her fingers, "that Murray cop was an animal-shifter, like your missing Alex woman."

"She's not my—" he began to protest, then stopped, having caught the sudden eyebrow lift and downward turn of her lips. "Sorry, go on." He'd forgotten just how much his woman didn't like being interrupted. He tried to hide his amusement by checking for cars in the driver's-side mirror.

"Two. He was banging Cygnet, Jewel, and possibly your vic, Seraphine, which makes his wife a strong suspect. Three, the twins were blackmailing their birth mother." Keely paused. "Well, at least Tinker Bell was. I'm not sure if her sister even knew about it.

"Vic," he repeated, interrupting once again.

Keely shrugged a shoulder. "That's what the victim's called in all the detective books and TV shows."

Lugos suppressed his smile, fearing Keely might think he was laughing at her. "You watch many of those?"

She brought up one knee and turned in the passenger seat in order to study his profile. "Well, yeah. Don't you?"

Lugos shook his head slowly from side to side. "Not really. I have enough real-life mysteries to deal with."

"Oh. I guess that makes sense. Can I finish?"

"Absolutely."

"Four, Fawn knew about all of it but said nothing to no one."

Lugos pounced on her last statement. "Are you suggesting that Fawn had a motive for murder?"

"It's always the quiet ones you have to watch out for, ain't it? Leastways, that's how it is in all the—"

"Television shows," he finished for her. She nodded. "You may have a point," he conceded. "I shouldn't completely discount Fawn, though I don't have anything to tie her to Seraphine's murder." He eased the Audi around a slow-moving van.

"Not yet. That's a messed-up bunch of girls," Keely replied, not willing to let go of her idea. "Five," she went on with her list, bending her thumb back, "Sourface didn't do it. Neither did Harmony."

Lugos had to agree with her, but he also had to ask her to explain, just for the sheer pleasure of hearing her talk. "And how do you arrive at that conclusion?"

"Well isn't it obvious? Sourpuss needed Seraphine to back her as leader, and Harmony has wanted to help us since we arrived."

"She did lead us to Cygnet," Lugos helpfully admitted.

"She also didn't like that Tinker Bell was carrying on with a married man, shifter or no shifter. I think, out of the whole messed-up group, I trust her observations the most."

Lugos nodded in agreement. Keely hadn't yet mentioned the wife, Blye, or the brother-in-law as a suspect. "I didn't like that she was trying to draw you out," he said, meaning Harmony.

"Please. She was just trying to be friendly with all that acolyte talk. I think she's misguided, but then so is that whole lot. Witches, my ass. They ain't nothin' but a bunch of lonely girls on a power trip."

"Perhaps," Lugos muttered, overtaking another slower-moving car. Keely had completely discounted the possibility that those "lonely girls" might actually be real, live witches, students of nature and keepers of the universe's secrets. He briefly wondered how his Keely would have reacted if she'd witnessed an accomplished witch in the midst of casting. Would she have dismissed it so easily? Then his stomach churned, and he decided to be grateful that she hadn't, in fact, seen anything so extraordinary. Except for the death of one witchlet and the injuring of another, his dealings with the Sacred Grove Coven had gone better than expected, though Keely's exposure to them had gone on far longer than he had intended. It would be more dangerous still in Louisville, he knew; shifters could be impulsive and volatile.

They rode in silence while he guided the Audi through a small town and onto another highway. "Tell me honestly, Keely, are you okay? Witch or not, a girl was killed tonight." He still had a gut feeling that Keely, not Cygnet, had been the intended target, but he wasn't willing to say so aloud.

Keely remained silent for so long that Lugos took his eyes off the road to make certain she hadn't drifted off to sleep. He'd used up most of the power Rhiannon had given him and had been forced to draw from his Keely. When he had realized that he could draw from Harmony and Josey, he'd carefully replaced some of what he'd taken from Keely. He was going to have to be even more careful. He'd felt her body absorb his energy almost greedily tonight. There had been no force applied on his part, just an opening up to her. That had been different, a new sensation.

"I'm not sure if I'm okay. I'm not even sure all this is happening." She waved her hand through the air. "But I ain't been dragged to hell yet, and that's sayin' something."

He reached across the center console to take her hand in his. Their fingers comfortably laced together as if by memory. "There's no hell coming for you, Keely. I won't let that happen." He gently squeezed her smaller hand. He hoped that she believed him.

"I'm countin' on it, Lugh. Believe me, I'm countin' on it."

* * *

Larkin pushed from his desk and stretched to relieve the stiffness in his legs and lower back. He then removed the

Bluetooth earpiece from his left ear and turned the skin-warmed device over in his hand. The elegantly designed plastic rolled effortlessly through his fingertips like a polished pebble. Everything was set for tomorrow. Talon's script approval had been the last hurdle. All that was left to do was babysit the production process. Once the completed promo was safely in his hands, he'd have the power to begin. The unfamiliar sensation of a smile spread across his face. Almost giddy, he dropped the earpiece onto the desk and reached for his cell phone.

It was nearly three in the morning but Larkin was no stranger to keeping late hours, and neither were his employees. Once, one of them had asked if he slept at all. He'd responded by simply smirking, then walking away. The truth of the matter was that he slept, but never for very long and not often deeply.

Before he had a chance to do much more than thumb in his personal password, his cell phone vibrated. Intrigued but not wholly surprised by the caller identification, Larkin put the device to his ear. "Yes."

"He's in Murray and probably won't be tied up for much longer."

"A pity." Larkin started to terminate the connection but paused when he heard the voice on the other end ramble on. He brought the phone back up to his ear. "I'm sorry, I didn't catch that."

"I said, it got kinda out of hand."

Larkin frowned. "How so?" Then he hastily changed his mind. He'd rather not know the details. "Never mind. I don't need to know. Not my affair, as it were." Although the pun amused him, the humor never touched his face. "I'm sure whatever you did was…" He paused to find the appropriate word. "Necessary." Larkin terminated the call, and then deftly erased the caller history on his phone.

Necessity, in his experience, had often explained what some referred to as misfortune. It was a fact of life: collateral damage happened. In the end, the goal was what mattered. Keeping

Rhiannon's hound busy and off balance was necessary. He set his phone down and rested his elbows on the desk. It was 2:22 in the morning, and Prideaux had yet to resurface. Larkin pushed back, rose to his feet, and went to his closed office door. Opening it and himself to the hum of people and the active array of computer systems, he barked at the nearest body. "Where's Prideaux?"

Several heads in the control room turned in his direction, but it was the intended target who answered. "Sir? Prideaux just checked in. I believe he went to the mess hall to grab a bite before reporting for duty." The clean-shaven face reddened slightly under Larkin's silence.

There was something about a militarily structured life that simply stuck with a person. Even this twenty-something kid, who'd only done one tour and had been out of the army for a respectable amount of time, couldn't think to call the place where you stuff your face anything but a mess hall. "Tell him I want to see him. Pronto." Larkin delayed just long enough to hear the automatic response of "Sir, yes, sir" before retreating into the quiet sanctum of his office.

Approximately ten minutes after he'd relayed his wishes, a series of firm knocks struck his door. Bent over the notes he'd been compiling, Larkin barked for the knocker to enter. He was aware of the lock turning, boots entering, and the door closing; still, he let the silence return and lengthen before he set his pen down and raised his head to study Prideaux.

"Yes, sir." Prideaux's greeting wasn't as crisp as the young analyst's had been and was laced with a touch of humor. Larkin had picked this shifter because he was capable and ambitious.

"He's in Murray for now. I have someone I'd like you to babysit for a little while. She doesn't like dogs, so you should be perfect."

Prideaux grinned. "Yes, sir."

If the man had a tail, at that moment it would have been wagging, Larkin thought. "Don't torment her too much. I'm going to need her later for the Bear."

Prideaux raised an eyebrow. "Permission to speak candidly, sir."

Larkin gave a faint nod of approval.

"The girl in Salem. Why her? I'd have thought you'd target his pet geek instead."

Larkin leaned back in his chair. Prideaux was an effective but blunt instrument who didn't usually ask questions or offer opinions. The ability to follow instructions without question was a large part of why Larkin used him. Perhaps it was becoming time to find someone else.

When Larkin didn't answer, Prideaux began to backpedal. "None of my business, I know. Just curious, is all."

Larkin's lip twitched with amusement. He took a slow breath, then answered. "Lugh's weakness is that he genuinely cares about humans. More precisely, he cares about her specifically."

"The loan of the car, then."

"Yes," Larkin confirmed with a weary sigh. "If he thinks she's in danger, he'll keep her close, which divides his attention. And believe me, a distracted Lugh is better than a focused one."

"Yes, sir. But why the girl over the Atlanta geek?"

"Griffin is an employee. Employees can be replaced; loved ones cannot," Larkin replied, laying down the implied threat between them. Prideaux was smart enough to hear his message.

"Remember, I want her kept whole. The Bear wants someone to pay for his sister's death, and a jealous lover will work nicely. I'll text the address to you."

Prideaux responded with a curt nod.

Larkin lowered his eyes to the papers stacked on his desk and shuffled through the nearest one. "Dismissed."

Though he heard Prideaux take his leave, his mind was already elsewhere. The shoot was set for sunrise. If all went according to plan—and there was no reason that it wouldn't—the producer would hand Larkin a preliminary cut within forty-eight hours and the finished promo in seventy-two. In the meantime, he'd have to keep Lugh running around in circles, Talon entertained, and Rhiannon guessing. It was going to be a busy and exhilarating three days.

The Bear was easy. There was the fight tomorrow night, Shea's collaring, and a murderess he could serve up for Talon's entertainment and no small amount of gratitude. The key to keeping Rhiannon guessing was Lugh. The trick to keeping Lugh distracted was that Salem girl. But he'd need to be careful what strings he plucked. Larkin had no intention of leading Lugh back to him personally. He understood that eventually Lugh would arrive at Triton's doorstep to ask questions, and he was prepared for that.

He reached down and unlocked the bottom right drawer of his desk to remove Seraphine's personal journal and Book of Shadows. He'd already thumbed through them, removed some pages in order to destroy what needed to be destroyed. Others he kept, seeing that they might come in handy at some point in the future. He patted the two leather-bound journals, then reached for his cell phone once more and thumbed the address to Prideaux. The long game truly was the only one worth playing.

Chapter 22

Larkin probably wasn't someone to be caught off guard. Because of this, Lugos stopped after less than twenty minutes of driving and checked himself and Keely into a randomly chosen hotel in Murray. Keely was exhausted and needed food and a few hours of sleep. And he...well, he needed a shower and a moment to contact Rhiannon and Griffin.

Unwilling to place Keely in a room separate from his own, Lugos had gone to some lengths to ensure that the room he booked contained two beds. Even if she hadn't actually called him an idiot in front of the desk clerk, the look she'd given him had said it all. As soon as they were alone, he'd made a point of explaining to her that he was old fashioned and then asked her to just go with it for now, at least until he could properly date her. She'd promptly laughed at his archaic sense of propriety. It had been good to hear her laugh, especially after all she'd been through that day. Now, it warmed his heart to see her sleeping soundly in the adjacent bed.

Glancing back down at his phone, Lugos keyed in a reply to Griffin's latest text: *Thanks. Keep looking into it.* He hit the send button and smiled. Griffin tended to do his best hacking right before dawn. Thus far, it appeared as if the Pratts didn't own the land they lived on. Instead, they leased it, like a farmer might rent fields for a season. According to Google Earth, the Pratt property had six buildings on it: two houses and the rest barns or sheds of some sort. They'd been there for over twenty years; the lease was for thirty. The Pratts were settled, but Griffin hadn't found any additional monetary ties to keep them rooted there for the full thirty years. If they thought it necessary to pull up stakes and move, they would, probably in the middle of the night.

The situation Griffin had uncovered wasn't unusual. Most shifter communities moved around fairly often. First one family would move, then another and another, like a loosely tethered gypsy clan. As in everything else that concerned the affairs of the Pale, it was knowing what signs to look for that made the difference between finding answers and finding nothing.

A text from Rhiannon vibrated his phone. *Going to check in, or do I have to beg?*

He could almost feel her scowling at him through the device. He should have filled her in before now, but dread had caused him to put it off. Lugos paused to consider what he thought she needed to know before responding. *Young witch is dead. Shifter attack while I was at SG Coven. Cover story in place. Priestess will contact you with details. Have you found Alex?* He hoped that she had. Seraphine's familiar had lied to him about quite a lot, and he didn't enjoy feeling like a fool.

His phone vibrated again. *No. I'm also hearing nothing but denials about Talon's plans to go public. Makes me suspicious. Too forceful. Are you going there soon?*

Lugos thumbed a quick *yes* and hit send. He wasn't sure what she meant by forceful: vehement, shocked, or angry. He decided to wait and see for himself. He typed, *Did you know there is a community of cougar shifters near the SG Coven?* He hit send and waited. Keely turned in her sleep, and her soft snoring stopped. He smiled in the darkened room; dark, that is, except for his faintly glowing skin and the phone screen.

The phone vibrated again. *Yes.*

He swore in Gaelic and then hastily typed, *You could have told me!* But before he hit send, he deleted his response and instead typed, *Ever have any dealings with the Pratt cougar clan?* He then hit send and waited. Carson Pratt had gotten under his skin but only because of the shifter's blatant interest in Keely.

His phone vibrated again. *Can't recall. Why?*

"Can't recall, my ass," Lugos muttered. Resentfully he thumbed a reply. *Lots of suspects in Murray for your witch murder. Pratts near the top of the list. Another possible attempt on Keely. How much do you know about Ken Larkin?* It wasn't unlike Rhiannon to withhold information from him. It was irritating, but often it worked to the benefit of the investigation if she allowed him to come to his own conclusions about events and relationships instead of offering her own impressions beforehand. He wanted just the facts from her, no speculations. Lugos eased the tension in his neck and waited to see what she chose to tell him. Call it a gut feeling, but he had no doubt that Larkin had at some point caused a blip on Rhiannon's radar.

I met him once at a meeting of the Pale. He was an aide or something to the then USL leader, Rankor. I spotted him talking in an animated fashion to Seraphine in the hotel hallway during that weekend in Prague. Talon was also in Rankor's contingent that year. Seraphine was heading up the witch collective.

Lugos digested Rhiannon's text. The Prague conference had been held in '98, which suggested that Larkin had been an integral part of the USL for quite some time. Instead of asking anything else, he simply replied *thanks*, then set the phone face down on the bedspread.

A moment later, it vibrated. Instead of picking it up again, he simply flipped it over. *How's your feisty truth seeker holding up?*

Lugos read it and groaned. He glanced over at her sleeping form. Fortunately, his Keely had stopped asking him direct questions, questions to which he could not avoid confessing the answers. Either she was physically too exhausted, or she'd decided that there could be such a thing as too much truth. Lugos wasn't sure which, but he was grateful that she'd stopped mining him for answers. After centuries of guarding secrets, both his own and those of others, it was dizzying to reveal so much to satisfy his woman's curiosity.

His phone vibrated angrily in his hand. *Hello?* Her text was followed by an emoticon of a dragon blowing smoke.

"She's fine," he muttered aloud while keying in the response, *How's Bride?* It was Lugos's less than subtle way of warning the goddess away from the subject of Keely. Then an idea occurred to him. *I told the Murray Coven that she was your acolyte to minimize questions.* He hit send before Rhiannon could reply to the Bride dig.

Rhiannon's response came quickly. *I'm going to kill her.*

Lugos hoped she meant Bride and not Keely; otherwise, they were going to have a problem. The phone vibrated again.

Never have known you to name drop. She had added a kissing emoticon and a heart at the end of her text. A moment later, she sent, *I'm honored. Will have your back if asked. Got to go kill Bride now. Check in again after USL.*

Lugos didn't respond. Honored, my ass, he thought. She was probably laughing at him. Keely stirred again but didn't wake. He watched her for a time: the even rise and fall of her breathing, the curve of her jaw, the dark wave of hair lying against the smooth skin of her shoulder. He knew she would not turn him away if he slid into her bed. The thought of indulging himself in the softness of her, of finally claiming her, had his body hardening to the point of pain. Flashes of memory came to him, of her in various lifetimes lying under him. The eyes were the same, so full of love and trust. Her bone structure and skin tone only a little different, but it was the union of their bodies and souls that Lugos remembered the most. She was the only one he'd ever love, the only woman he'd ever desire. And somehow, despite the fact that he was a god and she a mortal, she was the only one he couldn't manage to keep safe.

Lugos tried to readjust himself within the confines of his jeans. It would be so easy to just take what was his this night. With a groan of frustration, he slipped off the edge of his assigned bed. For all that he would have to demand of her later, his woman deserved a period of courtship, a span of time for her current incarnation to come to love him for who and what he was before he took over her entire life. He wanted to give her that.

But because he couldn't seem to help himself, Lugos wound a strain of her silken hair through his fingers and watched, mesmerized, as the slow progression of his golden glow flowed like a living thing from his hand and fingers down the long tendrils of the brown silk until her entire body was illuminated with his god-glow. How many times had he watched this strange phenomenon, this physical demonstration of their unique bond? In each successive lifetime, it had become more pronounced, easier, and had lasted just a little longer. He'd often wondered where it might lead, if there was some significance to her ability to absorb and hold his god-power within her mortal form. With a sigh, Lugos released the contact, afraid that if he held it any longer, he would disturb her dreaming.

Sensing his withdrawal, Keely stirred and reached out in her sleep. Lugos had to step back to keep her hand from brushing his leg. Her mortal body required rest, and her mind needed time to adjust to all that had happened. He'd tried to give her a lifetime without him, without the dangers that loving him would bring. But that path was now closed to them. The bond between them was growing stronger the longer she stayed in his company.

With one last sigh, Lugos made his way to the bathroom to take a very long, very cold shower.

Chapter 23

Keely was slow to open her eyes as her mind tried to separate fact from fiction, dreams from nightmares. Her head rested on his chest. Lugh—the solidity of him and the rise and fall of it reassuring in its predictability. The weight of his hand moved along her shoulder and across a portion of her back in long, languid strokes. There was a tingling beneath her skin where his hand touched, an ebb and flow of something connecting them. She concentrated on that strange surge and withdrawal of something she could not name, something that was as consistent as the ocean upon the shore.

"What time is it?" Though she'd yet to open her eyes, Keely could tell that he was fully dressed and that the length of him lay on top of the covers. Still, she was pressed close, her body curling toward his, one arm draped across his chest.

"It's still early, eight-somthing. We have plenty of time, if you're inclined to doze a little longer."

She smiled, her cheek against his chest. She hoped she hadn't drooled on his shirt while she was asleep, or—heaven forbid—snored. "Don't you have somewhere you have to be?"

"Eventually," he replied, his hand still moving back and forth in that same slow motion that made her want to purr.

Keely stretched and shifted so she could glance upward, squinting against the morning light streaming into the window. Lugh was watching her, amusement perched at the corners of a far-too-kissable mouth.

"Hi. I'm sure I look a fright this morning."

He gave her that lopsided grin of his, the one that had the power to make her stomach somersault. "You're beautiful."

Keely groaned. It was just too much. He was too much. "You can't say that this early. I'm sure I need to brush my teeth, and I bet I have mascara smudges under my eyes."

He hugged her closer. And then, as if it were the most natural thing to do, he bent forward and dropped a kiss on her forehead. No one had ever done that. It was a curious gesture, one that somehow made her feel special and cherished.

"Don't try to argue with me, Keely. You're beautiful inside and out. Morning breath and all." His smile widened into a particularly irritating bit of male amusement.

She groaned again and had to look away to hide the blush that stole up her cheeks. She laid her head back down on his chest. "I was wrong. You're not gay. You're crazy, Lugh. Stark raving mad."

To her delight, his chest rumbled under her ear as he laughed at her teasing. She didn't know why, but she wanted him to be stark raving mad about her, wanted him to want her so badly that—

"I was going to take you back to my place in Atlanta this morning, but Rhiannon sent word ahead that you would be with me today," he said over the top of her head.

"You don't sound pleased about that."

"I want you safe, Keely."

She took a moment to digest that. He had told her that her safety came first with him. "And I won't be safe where you're going today?" Then, before he could answer, she asked, "Will you be in danger?" That thought bothered her more than she wanted to admit.

"I'm a god. The shifters I'm going to see will know that."

Still speaking across the surface of his shirt, Keely asked, "So I guess that's a no. Why take me, then?"

"I have to, now, but that's not the point. They'll know you're human. What I didn't want them to know was that you belong to me."

"You mean with you. I belong to myself, Lugh." When he didn't answer immediately, Keely glanced up to find that his blue eyes had darkened, though he still stroked her arm, her back, and her hair.

His touch continued to be gentle and slow despite the hard set of his mouth. "I didn't misspeak, Keely. In this, I cannot lie to you. Nor would I want to. You belong to me. You are a part of me. I still intend to court you because you deserve the experience of discovering what it is like to be with someone who puts you first in all things. But you have always belonged to me. I had hoped to give you the chance at a life without the dangers of my world. But that path is closed to us now."

Keely's pulse quickened. The stroke of his hand along her body no longer felt as soothing as it had only moments ago. It felt possessive, as though he had every right to touch her. "What do you mean, I have always belonged to you?" As soon as the question was out of her mouth, Keely regretted it.

His gaze was locked with hers. He had no choice but to tell her exactly what she was afraid of hearing. "This is not the first lifetime in which we have found one another. There have been others. Your soul, your spirit, that part of you that is immortal seeks to reunite with mine. We are bound to one another. It is a tie that neither time nor death can break."

Keely tried to duck her head. She didn't believe in reincarnation, and that was what he was talking about. But Lugh captured her chin, and once again she was caught in the turbulent sea of his gaze.

"Know that I have always loved you. There is no other for me, Keely. When I tell you that you are beautiful, I mean it. Everything about your spirit calls to me. I've had the unique privilege of loving you and caring for you over many lifetimes. Trust that I will do so in this one as well."

Keely pushed away from him then, and he let her retreat. "You may believe that, Lugh, but I don't. We get only one lifetime, and then we go either to heaven or to hell." She slipped out of the bed dressed in only a tank top and lace panties. She was shaking, not from cold but from fear. He'd just wiped out any and all chances of her ever finding a way back to a normal life, one without him. A normal life that did not include Rhiannon, or demons, or shifters, or God knows what else he'd yet to tell her about.

Lugh sighed and then rose from the bed in one fluid motion. "We have time. Your entire world was upended yesterday. I have not given you time to adjust. We will not speak of this again until you are ready." He then turned away from her to stare out the window.

She showered alone, then dressed inside the bathroom. She'd taken her time, turning over in her mind what he'd confessed to her. She was sure that Lugh believed what he'd told her. But if what he said was indeed true, then where was her free will? Didn't she get a say in all this weirdness?

Keely could feel him in the other room. Deep inside her body, deep inside her mind, she could still feel that strange tidal flow that seemed to connect her to him. Even after taking the hottest shower she could stand, her right side continued to tingle where he'd touched her. Keely studied her reflection, looked hard for any sign that Lugh's glow had somehow gotten on her, like before when he'd told her that she was different. Had he somehow changed her?

A rap-tap-tap at the bathroom door nearly gave her a heart attack.

"We should go soon."

His voice was not impatient, though she knew he had reason to be. She'd been hiding inside the little bathroom for nearly an hour. "Be right out," she promised. Gathering her hair into a ponytail, Keely abandoned her retreat.

She had assumed he'd rush her out the door, but Lugh had insisted on brushing and braiding her hair, piling her locks artfully into a sophisticated weave that she'd never be able to duplicate on her own. The flowing outfits he had conjured for her out of thin air were identical to the expensive clothes in her favorite catalog and neatly packed in a new suitcase he'd also conjured. She picked out another skirt to wear today, definitely not something her mother would approve of, too gypsy looking, too many colors, riding too low on her hips, its hem just skimming the tops of her sandals. But the moment Lugh saw it, his eyes went all warm. Despite her earlier fears, his reaction pleased her to no end.

"That neckline needs something shiny," he said, handing her a tiered silver necklace. The longest loop dropped down to disappear suggestively into the valley between her breasts. Lugh had thought of everything, right down to the bobby pins that kept her hair fashionably secured.

Keely worried the inside of her cheek. "I'm not sure I recognize myself anymore."

Lugh lightly caressed her jaw with his thumb and forefinger. "Never fear; I do."

Chapter 24

Triton Security was located smack in the middle of suburbia. It had a dentist's office for a neighbor on one side and a law firm just across the groomed lawn on the other. Keely squared her shoulders and took a deep breath as Lugh cut the Audi's engine.

"Remember, they're expecting both of us. You are Rhiannon's acolyte and therefore as important as I am—and in theory just as untouchable. But, Keely, any time I feel you might be in danger, I will not hesitate to pull you out of there. Do you understand me?

"Here." He pushed a small tablet into her lap. With his index finger, he tapped the screen once, and a note-taking app lit the black screen. "You can operate it by touch, just like your phone. I don't care what you write on it. Stay close to me and pretend to take notes for Rhiannon." She could feel the heat of him as he leaned in close to demonstrate a few of the app's basic commands. He then gave her a pen. She twiddled it in her finger a time or two to give her an excuse not to meet his eyes.

"It's a stylus, to use on the tablet. You can slide it in here," he began to explain.

"I know what the hell it is. I'm not an idiot," she said, finally finding her voice. She glared at him. Did he think she was stupid? Everybody knew what a stylus was.

"I didn't say you were."

Keely was starting to feel trapped in the close confines of the car. Lugh had once again used his magick to move the two of them and the car from Murray to Louisville. It was crazy how he could just do that, move them like that. What she'd marveled at last night scared her today. The clothes, the jewelry only added to her sense that she was no longer in control of her own life. She rubbed at her arm, the one that still remembered his touch. In the ensuing silence, she could almost hear him gather his patience.

He began again. "Rhiannon thinks she's being helpful by publicly claiming you as her own. That was all well and good when we were questioning the witches, but shifters are another matter entirely. They can erupt into violence if Talon suspects I'm doing anything other than looking into his sister's death."

"But you are," Keely interrupted.

"Yes. I need to find out if Talon has plans to take the shifters public. I can't let him do that."

"So, he can't know that's what we're looking to find out."

"We're not investigating anything. I am. Just stay close to me at all times, and try not to look surprised when you see something supernatural. Remember, as Rhiannon's acolyte you would be aware of such things."

Her mounting fear must have revealed itself, because he added, "I won't let anything harm you, Keely."

"I can do this," she replied, putting her hand on his. Keely hoped she sounded convincing. What the hell was she thinking? There were demons inside that plain brick building, body-shifting demons living and working in the heart of American suburbia. And she was going to walk right in there with Lugh. His skin was warm to the touch, in stark contrast to the iciness of her own.

"Of course. I promise to keep my mouth shut and blend into the woodwork, just like you want. Now, can we go?" She asked this as if she didn't care one tiny bit about what might lie ahead. For good measure, she raised an impatient eyebrow and waited for the eventual nod that she just knew would be his reply. After all, it hadn't been his idea to bring her along. He had wanted to stash her inside his cabin this morning, or in his Atlanta loft. Under normal circumstances, she would have been pleased as punch to go home to Salem and forget yesterday had ever happened. But nothing since yesterday had been normal. In truth, she didn't think Lugh wanted to turn her loose inside his cabin, though he kept dangling the offer in front of her like a lure before a trout.

And if Keely were truly honest, she knew that left on her own, she'd drive herself crazy with worry and conjecture. The whole secret-races-living-among-us thing was still a hard pill to swallow. She hadn't yet been able to wrap her mind around it, but some sleep had helped her to place a layer or two of duct tape over the whole hellish idea. Keely held on tight to the notion that as long as Lugh was with her, she would be fine. Even after he informed her that she belonged to him, and not just in this lifetime but before, in lives she couldn't recall ever having.

So here she was with her angel and protector, about to enter a den of demons who called themselves shifters. Or was he her neighbor, who may or may not be a pagan god of old? Regardless, he was the very definition of someone she should not be seriously dating. He was definitely not in any way human, and he answered to far too many names. Despite those serious flaws in his character and the fact that he thought he had a right to her body and soul, Keely wanted to be with him. She trusted him like no other. It made no sense.

"God help me," she muttered, one hand clutching the tablet like a Bible as she pushed open the Audi's door with the other.

"Miss Lee."

At the sound of her name, Keely's head popped up to see Lugh already at the building's tinted glass door. He was holding it open for her, an odd mixture of impatience and worry on his handsome face.

"How the hell?"

The impatience and worry were wiped away with his answering grin. Realizing that her mouth was open and catching flies, Keely snapped it closed along with the car door, then half-ran up the concrete walkway.

He was getting into his role as a bigwig awfully damn easy, she thought irritably. They had discussed this. She knew his tone and lordly manner were all an act for the benefit of the demons inside, but she bristled anyway. She glared at him in passing, only to feel his hand snake out to catch her elbow, bringing her to an abrupt halt before she ran smack into the bulky, nearly bald security guard, whom she had not seen waiting just inside the darkened doorway.

Completely flustered, Keely hastily uttered the lines Lugh had scripted for her. "Mr. Dunbar was informed by Rhiannon that we would be arriving this morning." In the silence, she was acutely aware of Lugh releasing her elbow and of the sucking sound of the heavy glass door as it swung closed behind them. Abruptly, a chill skittered down her spine.

Baldy glanced over at a second, much younger guard stationed behind the security desk. The younger guard said nothing, only gave a subtle nod of his head. Still expressionless, Baldy declared over her head to Lugh, "We are honored, Lord Llew. For the sake of any human clients that may be inside, Talon has asked that you wear name tags. Of course, your real identities will not be mentioned while you are here. Are there names you wish to go by?"

"Miss Lee," Lugh said, giving his full attention to Keely. "Will you sign me in as Lugh Hart, please?"

Even off balance and totally out of her depth, Keely had to suppress a smile. Lugh just had that damn effect on her. "Yes, of course," she simpered. Lugh then discreetly nudged her toward the security desk.

As Keely made her way to the second guard, she breathed a little easier, having escaped the cloying effect of Lugh's and Baldy's clashing colognes. Guard Number Two laid a clipboard in front of her. He was more pleasant to look at than Baldy: sandy haired, hazel eyed, and slightly less mountainous, though that impression, Keely realized, was due to the fact that he was seated and not towering over her. She took the clipboard while he reached into a drawer and pulled out two laminated tags. Hoping she was doing what everyone expected, Keely signed for both her and Lugh. In the space designated "Purpose of Visit," she'd written nothing, doubting it would have been good manners to scribble "To interrogate boss as a possible murder suspect"—or worse, why they were really here. Keely gave the clipboard back.

With what might have passed for amusement poised at the corner of his mouth, the guard handed her the tags. "Please wear these at all times, Miss Lee. Donald, here, will escort you to a waitin' room. I'm sure someone will be with you shortly."

His silent amusement spread into a toothy grin, but Keely didn't find anything particularly reassuring in the smile.

"Miss Lee."

Lugh's voice called to her once more. Baldy had already moved forward, but Lugh moved closer to her instead of following the guard. When she was once more striding beside Lugh, Keely thrust one of the visitor tags into his waiting hand before hastily slipping hers around her neck.

Their wait, as it turned out, was nearly thirty minutes. She watched Lugh out of the corner of her eye, but the waiting didn't appear to bother him; if anything, he seemed amused by it. Keely, on the other hand, couldn't stop fidgeting. She thumbed through a couple of tech magazines, played with the tablet, and then, just when she was about to start pacing again, a woman appeared with an apology and the offer of a tour, after explaining to them that Mr. Dunbar was currently out of the office on matters that could not be avoided. But both he and Mr. Larkin were expected back shortly. If Lugh felt any frustration at hearing this, he didn't show it. He smiled charmingly and accepted her offer.

Their beautiful tour guide breathed a sigh of relief. "Call me Shea," the woman replied, a measured smile firmly in place, one manicured hand held out first to Lugh and then to Keely. "We are honored by your visit."

When Lugh returned Shea's smile, Keely took an instant dislike to the woman. Shea was generously endowed in hips and chest, though she'd gone to a good deal of trouble to hide these attributes under dark, conservatively cut clothing. She was no taller than Keely, but the way the brunette carried herself spoke volumes: Shea was confident of her abilities, whatever they might be. Her look was direct, as was her manner. In the aftermath of Lugh's thousand-watt smile, a blush had briefly colored Shea's caramel complexion. And that grated on Keely's nerves. To Shea's credit, the woman hadn't exactly puddled at Lugh's feet like Keely always wanted to. That irritated her, too.

After the third room they visited, Keely began to understand why Shea was less fazed by Lugh's attention. Triton Securities was mostly populated by men. They ranged in height and color from stocky to unbelievably tall, from pale and freckled to rich, dark chocolate. Yet despite these surface differences and their smart business attire, they all appeared to be various versions of Keely's Mr. Red T-shirt, right down to the bad-to-the-bone swagger. Though no one thus far had held her gaze for long or moved threateningly, some deep and primal fear inside her mind had been triggered. By the fourth control room, all the hairs on the back of Keely's neck were standing on end.

At this point, she closed the distance between herself and Lugh. Twice he accidentally bumped into her when pivoting to follow Shea from a room. Once he stepped on her toe. Except for the brief apology she saw reflected in his eyes, he showed her no extra attention, no hand to her back, no whispered word of reassurance, no irritating display of male ownership. He wasn't rude to her; he just wasn't the Lugh who had only a few hours ago declared that she was the only woman for him. Surprisingly, the withdrawal of his focused attention, however necessary, hurt Keely far more than her pinched toe.

Why did it bother her? Being with Lugh was like lying in the noonday sun; it was wonderful and sometimes uncomfortable. But now clouds had obscured all that obsessive sun. Shea was getting all the benefit of his rays. Keely had to ask herself, could she be so far gone that she was jealous of Shea?

"And this is the central control room," Shea was explaining to Lugh, but by now Keely was only half listening. She was feeling a little sick, as her morning coffee continued to mix inside her stomach with her rising fear of the place and the people inside it, and Lugh's lack of Lugh-ness.

"And Mr. Larkin's office?" Lugh was asking.

Keely didn't hear Shea's response. They were standing very close together and talking in hushed tones. To protect her toes from further damage, Keely had hung back by the door and pretended to play with the tablet. During most of the tour, the building's fluorescent overhead lighting had managed to mask the slight glow of Lugh' skin, but not so much inside this darker room.

Catching movement to her left, Keely jumped, and her stomach pitched. It was just another Triton employee reaching for an object she couldn't identify in the darkened room, but then he grinned at her like a fox catching sight of a hare. She managed to return his grin with, she thought, a relatively good impression of annoyance.

When her gaze found Lugh again, he and Shea were still conversing with their heads together. The soft light of Lugh's skin only enhanced Shea's classic features, making her appear even prettier than before. If they were back in Salem, Keely would have known how to regain his attention, but not here, not in this place. She knew she was being the worst kind of silly. This was all for show, his leaning in close and playing up to Ms. Corporate

Bombshell. Even knowing the truth and how stupid she was being didn't stop the surge of ugly jealousy.

Taking a chance, Keely slipped through the door behind her and retraced her steps. She'd seen a bathroom along here somewhere. She'd take just a minute to collect herself, get her mind right. She'd hide in a stall for just a minute, perhaps say a little prayer, drink a little water. With this in mind, she moved with purpose down the empty white hallway and the closed, look-alike doors, her sandals clicking rhythmically as she searched.

She turned a corner, then another. Where the hell had it gone to? She glanced behind her as she kept going. She didn't want to be gone long—or, God forbid, run into one of these demons without Lugh nearby. Surely, it would be just one more turn. Quickening her pace, she all but jogged around the final corner, when her left foot slipped. Keely reached her arms out in an attempt to keep from falling. The tablet jumped out of her grasp and clacked against the hard floor just as a strong hand clamped around her flailing arm hard enough to make her yelp. A bark of laughter erupted above her head.

Chapter 25

"Look what I caught, Larkin."

Keely looked up to find herself attached to a big bear of a man. He was probably pushing fifty, but fit. The other one, the one he'd called Larkin, was of similar age but shorter, and doughy compared to the mountain that continued to hold fast to her arm so that she kind of dangled there, one foot hardly touching the floor.

"I think you've frightened this little bird, Talon."

"Oh, excuse me, miss," said the blond mountain as he grinned down at her.

The pressure on Keely's arm abruptly eased, and he released her.

Meanwhile, Larkin reached down and retrieved her tablet. "You must be Rhiannon's girl, with Lugos," he said, handing her the device. It was now ruined, a spiderweb of cracks originating in one corner covering most of the screen.

"Yes. Mr. Hart and I were offered a tour," Keely replied, rubbing her bruised arm. That didn't explain why she was on her own, but then, she hoped, Lugh would already be wondering where she'd taken herself off to. Keely tried to return Larkin's direct gaze but found the intensity of it a little unsettling. She turned to the one called Talon.

"Mr. Hart should be along—" she began.

"I'm sure he will be." Talon smiled indulgently down at her. "Larkin, why don't you make Miss Lee, here, comfortable in your office? I'll go search out Mr. Hart." Talon had said Lugh's name like it was some kind of inside joke among the three of them. Larkin only half smiled at Talon's jest.

"Of course." He took a step forward. "Miss Lee, if you will come with me, please."

"Ah..." Keely hesitated, not at all sure she'd be comfortable anywhere but standing directly behind Lugh. It wasn't that Larkin looked all that threatening. As a matter of fact, he appeared downright ordinary. But that didn't mean she wanted to go gallivanting off with him.

"This way, Miss Lee." Larkin took another step toward her so that he could loop his arm around her shoulders. He then more or less towed her in the direction he wanted her to go. "My office is this way."

Though she reluctantly moved with him, she said, "I really think I should go back. Mr. Hart will want to know where I am." Talon had already taken off in the opposite direction in search of Lugh and Shea.

"Mr. Dunbar will let him know that you are in good hands. Can't have you getting lost, or— gods forbid—hurting yourself. Rhiannon would never forgive us. Got to be careful on these slick floors. We keep everything polished to a high gloss around here. Our clients expect to see a state-of-the-art operation when they visit, and dirt or clutter detracts from that image. Hence the overzealous efforts of our janitorial staff, which have nearly landed you with a concussion. Can't have you cracking your pretty head on the waxed floors, now, can we?"

Keely knew when she was being talked down to by a man, even when it was served up with a fatherly smile and a wink. "I really think it would be best if we follow Mr. Dunbar," Keely said more firmly. Despite the persistent pressure of Larkin's arm around her shoulders, she managed to stop them both in the hallway. When she tried to sidestep his hold, his fingers bit into her arm.

"That wouldn't be wise, Miss Lee." He continued to pull her forward.

"I don't know what you're talkin' about," she replied, panic welling up. She began to struggle in earnest when she realized that the long, empty hallway was probably going to remain empty.

Keely also belatedly realized that Larkin possessed a great deal of muscle under his marshmallow appearance. Because he was so much stronger, he was largely able to ignore her efforts to politely free herself. His office was near the end of the hall and directly opposite the tour's first control room. Though only a wall of glass separated them from the room's occupants, no one looked away from their monitor to offer Keely assistance.

Larkin hissed next to her ear, "Let's drop the fiction, shall we?" Even with her struggles, he'd managed to tow her down the hallway. His free hand reached out to turn the brass knob just as Keely took the opportunity to kick at him. He grunted when the sole of her sandal scraped down the length of his trousered shin. Still, his grip remained firm.

"Lugos came to talk to Talon about his sister's murder." When the door was open, he gave her a little shake. "He suspects one of our own did it. It would be much safer for you, Miss Lee," he said, pushing her through the door toward a large ornate wooden desk, her hip hitting its edge hard enough to leave a bruise, "to wait in my office, away from prying eyes, while those two have what I'm sure will be a very candid conversation." Larkin shut the door with a thud.

Keely heard the lock turn.

"You are inside a shared den of predators, my dear. And not all in the residence are as friendly as our Shea."

Keely skirted the corner of the desk in order to retreat to the other side of the room. It didn't seem nearly far enough.

Larkin held up his hands. "I'm not going to hurt you, Miss Lee. Or can I call you by your first name?" He didn't wait for her answer. "Keely, Llew seems fond of you, or so I've been told, and I have no intention of getting on the wrong side of any god, much less Llew the God-Killer." He gestured to one of the two guest chairs in the room. "Please, have a seat." He glanced at his watch and then moved to claim his desk chair, a hint of a limp in his stride. "I'm sure he will come to collect you as soon as he's done asking his questions. Why the hell would Rhiannon send you along with him? Care to enlighten me?"

"Rhiannon's reasons are her own," Keely replied, her voice more confident than she felt. Keeping as much distance as she could within the confines of the room, she circled around toward the door again. The lock required a key. She couldn't quite figure out if she was afraid of Larkin, furious with the way he was treating her, or both. Crossing her arms over her chest, she scowled at him. "Who the hell are you?"

Larkin looked up from where he sat, a mixture of irritation and weariness in his expression. "I'm the one keeping you safe, Miss Lee."

Keely raised an eyebrow. "Why don't I believe you?"

Larkin replied with a forced chuckle. "Because, Miss Lee, you are an idiot."

Chapter 26

Where the hell did she go? He'd told her to stay beside him. Lugos barreled down the hallway, his senses flaring out. Shea was doing her best to keep up with his progress. He was silently fuming and imagining far too many scenarios, each less likely than the one before. If their tour guide thought it odd that he was worrying unduly over the whereabouts of Rhiannon's acolyte, she wasn't saying anything.

"The restrooms are to the left," Shea offered a little breathlessly.

"Shea!"

Lugos started to turn in that direction but stopped when he caught sight of Talon strolling toward them from the right. The picture Griffin had sent was apparently a recent one, but the image on Lugos's phone had not been a full body shot, nor had it offered any sense of scale. The leader of the USL was a full head taller than Lugos, a real bear of a man with or without the fur.

"So glad you're here." Talon held out a hand, the back of which was liberally covered in soft blonde hairs.

Lugos took it, shook, and then said, "Have you seen a woman, about this tall, brunette, multicolored skirt? I seem to have lost Rhiannon's acolyte. I'd rather avoid an argument about whether I got a scratch on her property or, worse, misplaced the girl."

Talon threw back his head and laughed. "Larkin had the same worry when we ran into her wandering the halls. He's babysitting her in his office so you and I can talk." Talon glanced over at Shea quietly hovering nearby. "Go tell Larkin that Mr. Hart and I are in my office. We'll collect Miss Lee shortly."

"Of course, sir." Shea turned to Lugos. "It's been a pleasure meeting you. If you'll excuse me." She gave him a faint nod, then turned down the hall to the right and, presumably, Larkin's office.

"My office is just down here," Talon said, leading the way in the opposite direction. "You're lucky. I kept Miss Lee from colliding with the floor just a minute ago. Guess you owe me for keeping you out of trouble with Rhiannon," he said, chuckling.

Lugos paused for only a second. Keely would be fine for a short time; he didn't think Larkin would risk upsetting Rhiannon or him. "So, how about I find out who killed your sister? Then we can call it even."

"I like it," Talon said lightly. He paused to open the last door on the right. Upon entering his domain, Talon growled rather menacingly, "I'd like that a lot."

It was a corner office. Nice view of a patch of green, a few trees, and the lawyers' building next door.

Talon watched Lugos for a moment. "Larkin's looks just like this one, on the other side of the building. Between the two of us, we keep Triton Securities humming." He moved behind his desk and sat down. "How about giving that door a push?"

Lugos closed the door and then leaned on it. "Let me ask the obvious question. Did you kill her?"

Talon sprung forward, meaty hands splayed on the top of his heavy wooden desk. "No!"

"But you argued right before she died."

"Yes, we argued. We are both strong-minded people." He lowered himself back down into his chair. "A shifter killed her. I want you to find the son of a bitch and bring him to me."

"Why are you so sure it's a man?"

The question brought Talon up short. "You think it's a woman? One of those witches? Any of them behind the emails?"

Lugos shrugged. "Don't know yet," he lied easily. "As for the other questions, why don't you answer a few more of mine first?"

"Fine. Fire away."

"What do you know about the cougar community that borders the coven's land?"

Talon leaned back in his chair. "You're talking about the Pratt clan. Not much to them. It's a tight-knit pride. Carson and Blake have been USL members in good standing for quite a while now. Carson collared Blye a few years back. Don't think they have any offspring yet. Kinda thing people make a fuss about when it happens, y'know. Carson's sire goes by the name of Grady, but he's a bit odd and getting up there in years. Never could get him to join us. Don't know why. If they've somehow located and wooed additional females out to their property, I don't know about it. Why?"

"I'm told Seraphine spent time with Carson during her last heat cycle."

"Her prerogative, I guess. Why would I care?"

"Rhiannon and Alex told me she was a cougar, but she wasn't, was she?"

Talon took a moment to answer. "She was cougar born, but she had enough control to change her coloring to black, so some assumed she was a panther. I don't know why she did that. I asked her once."

"What did she say?"

"She just said it felt better to her. I assumed it was an identity thing. You know, a trans thing."

"Were you two ever more than just adopted brother and sister? Oh, let's say twenty years back, when you were young and a little more foolish?"

"I have a feelin' you already know the answer to that question. It's ancient history now, and for her memory's sake, I'd like to keep it that way."

Lugos shook his head. "Not as easy as you might think. She got pregnant back then, had twins, and gave them up." Talon started to shake his head but stopped when Lugos said, "I saw the birth certificate." Just another nugget Griffin had dug up for Agent Lugh Hart. The kid was a wonder.

"They're the source of the emails?"

"Yes, the emails." Lugos hadn't been sure, had only suspected; but when he saw the picture of Talon he'd known the truth. It would take a DNA test to turn conjecture to fact, but Lugos was certain that Jewel and Josey were Talon's offspring. The cross-species affair wouldn't have produced a shifter who possessed the ability to transform, but it still could produce viable children. It also explained the girls' predisposition to the craft.

"I think it's safe to say you have two very angry and confused daughters looking for you." Lugos hoped he wasn't putting the two girls in danger by telling Talon that he was their father. "You should know that they didn't kill Seraphine."

"Why are you so sure?"

It was a gut feeling, but he wasn't going to tell Talon that. Lugos took a moment to put into words what his gut had already figured out. "Seraphine's death was orchestrated by someone who knew a hell of a lot about how shifters think. They shot her in her cougar form. They knew to aim for the heart to make her weak after she transformed back into her human form. They also knew that a single bullet wouldn't kill her; that's why they bled her out in the tub. That takes time and skill. They had to be calm enough, and good enough to get the shot right the first time, as she was attacking."

"After the coroner's report showed the bullet, I thought it had to be a shifter with a military background."

"Not necessarily. They just had to understand how a shifter behaves when under attack. The twins don't have it in them to be that cold, even if they possessed the knowledge and the skills." Lugos's explanation seemed to satisfy Talon. "If you want to get to know your daughters, you can find them through the Sacred Grove Coven. I don't know if Seraphine realized she was taking in her own girls, or if she even suspected it. My guess is that she was starting to figure it out."

Talon sagged a bit in his chair as if the girls were a new burden for the bear to carry. "That's a lot to absorb at one time. Two, you say?"

Lugos nodded. Then something else occurred to him. "There was an attack last night at the coven. One young witchlet was killed. It was a shifter, I have no doubt. At the time, I suspected a Pratt. Seems a good bit of bed-hopping has been going on there. I figured it was a jealousy thing. But if I'm wrong, and someone else knows about the girl's parentage, then they're going to need protection."

Talon sat up straighter. "That would mean that someone here, someone who read those emails, made the same connection you did."

"They would have to question a few general assumptions and see the girls to recognize their likeness to you."

"They look like me? That proves nothing. You'd need a DNA test."

Lugos nodded. Talon was already thinking several steps ahead.

"But you still don't have a motive for Seraphine's murder."

"Not a clue," Lugos said, lying through his teeth. The problem was that he had too many ideas right now. "How secure is your hold over the USL?"

Talon smirked. "It's secure."

"No undercurrents of discontent? No challenges on the horizon?"

Talon rose from behind his desk. "No. At least none I can't handle. We're having a celebration tonight. You should come and judge for yourself just how loyal my people are. It's Fight Night, quite the spectacle."

"That can get kind of loud," Lugos observed.

Talon shook his head. "Nah. The packs can get as loud as they want. We hold it in the basement, two levels below the lobby here. Huge area. Like I said, you should come. Bring Rhiannon's little pet. Either it'll be exciting for her, or it'll scare the heebie-jeebies out of her and the little bird will take flight back to Rhiannon." Talon seemed to like his pun. "Why would Rhiannon take on a human acolyte?"

Lugos didn't answer, just shrugged like it was none of his business.

"Well, who knows why the gods do what they do?"

Lugos grinned. "Preachin' to the choir here." That made Talon laugh again. The bear was easily amused, Lugos thought.

"There's going to be a big surprise tonight for the ones who come." Talon grinned. Then the grin abruptly disappeared. "It will also give you a chance to discover if any of my people killed my sister. If any of them did, they're going to wish they'd died that night instead of her."

Lugos had no intention of taking Keely anywhere near Talon's Fight Night. "I'll come if I can, but I have a few stops to make today."

"Good. It starts at nine. I'll have someone waiting at the door for you." Talon walked around the desk. "Let me walk you over to Larkin's office. Seraphine's journals are there. I know you asked for them."

As they entered the long white hallway, Lugos asked, "Have you seen her familiar, Alex?"

"No. Last I heard, Larkin said she was with Rhiannon."

"Larkin last saw Alex yesterday with me at Seraphine's house. So, no, she wasn't with Rhiannon."

Talon's brow furled. "Hadn't heard that. What happened? Did you misplace her, too?" The bear looked at him and cocked his head like a dog who hears a sound he doesn't understand.

Lugos stared down the length of the hallway. "Not exactly."

***

Larkin unlocked the desk's left bottom drawer and withdrew a stack of books.

"What are those?"

"Seraphine's journals and Book of Shadows. Llew—I mean, Mr. Hart—asked for them. Guess he hopes to find a clue to who killed her, but I didn't see anything useful in them. Maybe he will. I doubt it." He laid them on the desktop and sat back in his chair.

After a moment, Keely picked them up and stepped back again.

A light knock sounded at the door.

"Just a minute," Larkin bellowed. Not in any particular hurry, he studied her for a moment more before rising from his chair to cross the floor. He paused and aimed his index finger at one of the empty chairs.

Her chin jutted forward, but she sat, figuring she wouldn't have much chance squeezing past him, especially with somebody on the other side of the door.

"Good girl."

Keely's nostrils flared, but otherwise she remained in the chair, satisfied to simply glower at him when he turned his back to her. When Larkin wrenched the door open, he found the confident and capable Shea on the other side.

"Talon sent me to inform you that he's speaking with Mr. Hart at the moment."

Though Keely could only read a portion of Larkin's profile, it was clear that Shea's errand had been in vain.

"Thank you, Shea."

A curt nod was her only reply. She met Keely's eye briefly before turning on her heel to leave.

Larkin closed the door once again, more slowly this time. He didn't bother to relock it.

"She doesn't like you much." The observation popped out of Keely's mouth before she could think better of it.

For a few seconds, Larkin's thoughtful expression didn't change. Then he raised an eyebrow. "Why do you say that?"

Keely gave him her best bartender smile. "A girl can just tell."

He studied her once again, pushing out a long and loud breath through his nose as he did so. "You are not at all what I expected, Miss Lee."

His observation sounded like a compliment, not at all what Keely had expected.

"I'm unique." It was a smart-ass reply, a ready response she'd used often enough at the Witch's Whistle when some drunk had made a similar comment, like "You're too nice to work in a place like this," or "What's a pretty girl like you still doin' in a town like this?" But what the hell, if Larkin was one of those demon-shifting freaks Lugh had warned her about, then Keely was beginning to think she'd feel a sight better if he'd just show his true colors instead of pussyfooting around. She was terrified enough without her imagination making her think all kinds of scary stuff.

"Has Rhiannon truly taken an interest in you, or is that just something Llew has Rhiannon telling people?" Larkin was still eyeing her like he'd never seen her before.

Keely didn't answer, mainly because he didn't really seem to need or want her to answer. With a shaky hand, she absently reached up and touched the intricate braid gathered at the nape of her neck. The pins were still holding. If she was going to die today, then it seemed she'd die looking her best, thanks to Lugh's careful work.

"So, did you kill the cougar lady?" Her voice trembled a bit, but she couldn't help that. She'd bluff her way past that mistake. Keely held his gaze.

This time, both of Larkin's brows rose skyward. "How much has he told you?"

Keely smiled her bartender smile and lowered her hand demurely to the top of the books and broken tablet. "Oh, everythin', I suspect. We're partners in this. Thick as thieves, we are." Now her mouth was just running away with her. She needed to shut up. "So, did ya?"

"Is this how you plan to interrogate persons of interest, Miss Lee? Go around asking them outright if they killed Seraphine and hope they tell you the truth?"

"I believe that's exactly what I'm gonna do after Lugh—I mean, Mr. Hart—makes a lot of people uncomfortable with his questions."

Larkin chuckled to himself. "Good luck with that strategy. And why are you still calling him Mr. Hart? I thought we'd dropped that pretense."

"You didn't answer me," she said, ignoring his question.

Larkin had started to head back to his chair, but her persistence brought him up short. He was eyeing her again. But it was not a pleasant stare; more like she was a giant palmetto bug strolling across his porch. He appeared repelled and yet dumbfounded by the sheer audacity of her.

Keely hung on to her false bartender smile for all she was worth. "My question. You didn't give me an answer," she pressed. Surely by now he thought she was completely daft, too many cards missing from her deck.

"You see, I have a talent, Mr. Larkin." If he could be formal with her, Keely decided she could talk just as properly. "People tell me the truth, Mr. Larkin. They can't help themselves." Keely knew she was tossing a bit of bullshit his way. Men lied to her all the time, and she fell for those lies. It was only Lugh who couldn't manage fibbing to her.

"Is that what Rhiannon thinks she sees in you?" Larkin sneered. "No, Miss Lee," he said, shaking his head to shed the silly idea, "I didn't shoot Seraphine. She was like a sister to me. She and I and Talon grew up together, took care of one another. So, no. It wasn't me."

Keely gave him a nod that might have passed for satisfaction. "Thank you. See, wasn't that simple?"

Larkin's pupils shrank to pinpoints, but before he could say anything else, there was another knock at the door.

Without looking behind him, Larkin reached out and turned the door handle for the new arrival. Keely started breathing again when she saw Lugh step through the opening. He kind of filled up the room just by standing there.

Larkin mumbled a greeting as he retreated to his desk chair.

Without acknowledging Larkin's presence, Lugh's blue eyes settled on Keely. He gave the subtlest of nods in Larkin's direction, both a hello and a goodbye. "Miss Lee, time to go." He seemed to take everything in: her terror, her manufactured bravado, her utter relief that he'd come for her.

Keely rose from her chair on shaky legs and answered with a subdued, "Yes, Mr. Hart." She had just brushed past him when Larkin said, "I'm sure Talon invited you to the fight tonight."

"He did," Lugh replied, his arm bringing her under the protection of his body.

The silence expanded, then Larkin added, "Don't bring her with you."

Lugh turned his back on Larkin, moving them both toward the hallway. "Wasn't planning on it."

Then Lugh's arms encircled her in an unbreakable hold. "Close your eyes."

The command had been given quietly but with every confidence that she would obey him. And obey him she did, without a moment's hesitation.

Chapter 27

"Open your eyes, Keely, and get in the damn car before I lose my temper."

The second Keely's eyes snapped open, he released her. They were back in the parking lot. Lugh had bypassed the whole departure process: the elevator ride, the security guards, returning their tags, the walk down the concrete sidewalk like normal people. And he was seething. She could see the gathering storm clouds in those blue eyes of his. They had gone dark, with lightning flashing across the churning gray. It was startling to see. Keely didn't want to push him any further than she had already. She was grateful to get the hell away from Larkin, away from all of them, so she scurried to the other side of the Audi and slid into the passenger seat without a single protest.

Lugh got in as well, turned the motor over, and depressed the gas pedal a couple of times simply to hear the engine roar. He then abruptly cut the engine.

"Why did you leave my side?" His large hands still gripped the steering wheel, the knuckles white. "I told you to stay close, to not draw attention to yourself," he said, his voice low and carefully controlled. "Instead you go off exploring by yourself when I told you that bringing you was dangerous. But you promised to do as I instructed."

"I—"

"Shifters are unpredictable. I told you that," he went on, his voice never rising.

Keely squirmed in her seat anyway. "Yes, you did. I—"

"Keely, you can't do that kind of thing and stay alive in my world. It's as if you don't—"

She knew he was beyond angry with her, but she didn't think he'd ever hit her, no matter how mad he got at her. "I had to go to the bathroom." She threw the bold lie out there like a Hail Mary pass.

Lugh stared at her.

She started to say something else but then wisely shut her mouth. She was not going to confess to being jealous of Shea, to having had another panic attack, or to knowing she was completely out of her depth with him. Instead, she just said the only thing that might make him feel better, her eyes going watery.

"I'm sorry, Lugh." She meant every syllable of it. She didn't want to be the cause of his worry. Those doubt lines over his brows and the faint crinkling at the edges of his eyes were back. They had disappeared for a time while the two of them were inside Triton, but Lugh was wearing them again, and it bothered her that she was the cause.

The silence stretched between them, and she searched for something else to say that would make it better. But her mind was empty except for the self-doubts she didn't want to confess.

Lugh broke the stalemate first. "What am I?"

Keely's brow wrinkled.

"What am I, Keely? What have you decided I am?" Lugh asked the questions in that same cool and quiet voice he'd used with Larkin, but now he didn't sound nearly as frosty. He sounded weary.

"Well," she began, her heart in her throat, "I figure you're my angel, since you're always there when I need you." A blush rose to her cheeks. The idea sounded idiotic even to her own ears.

Lugh collapsed back into his seat like all the wind had been knocked out of him. "Keely, I'm not an angel. I'm not a devil. I'm not a demon, and I'm not anything taught in that religion of yours."

Keely bit down on the inside of her cheek. The storm clouds swirling inside his eyes were slowly fading, the startling blue reasserting itself. Even so, her mind couldn't accept his explanation. "You want me to believe that you are actually a pagan god, like, oh, I don't know, Zeus?" She couldn't hide her disbelief. The idea was preposterous. There was only the one true God, and he was in Heaven. Not sitting in a car with her.

Lugh's tight jaw twitched. "I'm a better person than Zeus ever thought of being, but, yes, let's start there. I am a god, Keely. Those shifters were behaving themselves because in the hierarchy of the Pale, the gods, no matter how minor, no matter how human they seem, still occupy the very top of the supernatural food chain. The shifters may not admit it, but those *people* inside *that* building are afraid of me," he said, stabbing a finger toward the brick building. "They are afraid of Rhiannon. Tying your name to hers is what kept you safe when you disappeared from my side to take your little bathroom break."

Keely took a deep breath, and then she dropped her gaze and looked down at the broken tablet. She felt like that screen. She was lost in all this weirdness. The only place she felt safe was with Lugh, and now he was upset with her. What if he decided she was too much trouble? "Why say I'm Rhiannon's whatever, and not yours?"

"Because she doesn't have the enemies that I do. She's the Pale's chosen leader, Keely. They respect her and those who belong to her."

"I don't belong to her, Lugh!"

"Rhiannon and I know that, but they don't."

"I'm not giving up my God, Lugh. You can't ask that of me."

Lugh covered her hands with his larger one. "I'm not asking you to, Keely." He paused a moment. "I just need you to accept that there's more out there."

Keely wasn't sure she could do more, but she heard herself say, "I need to see it. I wish I could just accept it all, but without seeing it, Lugh…" She let the statement trail off, not sure what more she was asking to see or why. He'd shown her witches who'd done nothing witch-like and shifters who just looked like military guys too full of testosterone. Rhiannon and Lugh's jumping through space was like something in a science fiction television show. And then there were the clothes he'd conjured for her. That had been both terrifying and wonderful. But none of it made Lugh a pagan god. Angels could surely do the same, even give off that angelic glow of his.

Chapter 28

Lugh took a deep breath and let it out slowly. He knew he'd been lucky so far. Dealing with the coven members had been relatively easy. He'd unearthed Seraphine's blackmailer, and Cassie had deferred to his judgment where the human authorities were concerned. Talon's people had all behaved—no snarling, no lost tempers, no physical transformations. So Keely had absolutely no reason to believe him. Despite the attack she'd endured at the Witch's Whistle, and the coven farm murder, which had happened under the cover of darkness, Keely had yet to witness a supernatural act. The sole exception to all of this apparent normalcy had been Lugh himself. And Rhiannon. For Keely to accept the truths that were his daily life, Lugos was going to have to go out of his way to show her. He'd have to introduce her to Murmur, a demon. But first he needed to take them to Salem.

"Okay, Keely." He squeezed the smaller hand in his and waited to see if she'd pull away. She didn't. That gave him hope. "Let me take you someplace safe where I can play show and tell. With luck, I won't scare the hell out of you."

Though her eyes were still watery, she replied with a resolute nod.

"So be it," he acknowledged.

For his kind, drawing power from others was as easy and natural as breathing. And even though he couldn't exactly suppress the euphoria that came with the gathering of power, he had disciplined his mind over the centuries to avoid reveling in the emotion. To successfully live among humans, one needed to appear and behave as a human. Studying his Keely, Lugos had to wonder if perhaps he'd gotten too good at it. If he was going to get through to her, he'd have to set aside his reluctance and embrace his god-ness and all that might come with it.

The little bit of excess glow he'd recently acquired because of Keely's belief and proximity was going to make his daily life somewhat more complicated. But her faith also enabled him to move them from place to place more readily. With a mixture of joy and trepidation, Lugos gathered and focused his will to teleport them, car and all, from the USL's parking lot into the interior of his cabin's garage.

"Jesus!" Keely's hand clutched at her chest. "How about warning me before you do that, Lugh?"

Lugos regretfully let go of the sudden rush of energy. Deep down, he was still upset with her for subjecting him to the old fear of losing her. His heart had nearly stopped when he'd realized she was no longer within arm's reach. And then there had been the gut-wrenching relief that had left him feeling both weak and vulnerable when he'd finally walked into Larkin's office and his eyes had found hers. The barely hidden terror reflecting back at him had nearly snapped his control.

Lugos gave Keely's hand a final squeeze before climbing out of the Audi to retrieve his bag and cane. By the time he'd slammed the trunk closed, Keely had emerged from the passenger side and was waiting in silence. He let her into the cabin, disarmed the alarm, and without a word stalked to the living room. Unlike the last time, Lugos used a wave of his hand to move the heavy iron coffee table out of his way. He knew Keely was watching him as he pulled the throw rug back to reveal the trapdoor beneath. With another wave of his hand, the door opened. Only then did he look up to meet her eyes. There was a glimmer of a smile on her lips.

"Handy."

Lugos grunted to hide his sudden amusement. Slowly he descended the stairs and turned on the lights. He didn't invite her to follow, nor did he order her to remain. If seeing his world was what it was going to take for her to understand that he was a god and not some biblical angel, then she should see all of it.

Lugos depressed the recessed node on the silver-capped cane. The ends extended, revealing the spear hidden inside. No longer compressed, it joyously sang up his arm. Deliberately he placed it back on the wall hooks. "Not today," he told the sultry voice in his head. The reply was a sigh followed by Balor's screams. Both faded slowly into silence as soon as he let go of the spear's shaft.

Lugos was aware of Keely's every move as he knelt in front of the safe. She'd crept halfway down the stairs and was watching him. "Come down, if you want, but don't touch anything." He punched in the code and pressed his thumb to the pad. There was an audible click of the locking mechanism. He put away items he wasn't likely to need.

"What is all this?"

Lugos closed the safe, shouldered the bag, and rose to his feet. "It's parts of my life. The weapons," he said, gesturing first toward them, then toward the crates, "the mementos, and a few things that are just too dangerous to let out into the world." He remained silent as Keely perused the contents of his secret hoard.

She didn't spend a lot of time studying the weapons on the walls. She didn't know their history, what battles they'd won, what wars they'd ended. She seemed more interested in the few portraits he'd kept of her. It was easy to read her dismay.

"The eyes are always the same," he told her.

"You think this was me?"

Lugos hid the smile he felt. "I know it."

She raised one eyebrow at him and then did that flick of her hair he'd seen so many times, in so many lives, when she was not quite sure of herself. After taking a turn around the room, she finally stopped again. "An old bicycle? Is it magical or something?"

The item in question was stored under a clear tarp behind a stack of crates. Its polished wooden frame and wheels were covered to protect the antiquity from dust. "Yes; at the time, it was quite magical."

"And what time would that be?" she asked with a laugh.

"Roughly?" Lugos shrugged. "The 1500s," he replied vaguely.

"Really?"

Lugos nodded. The answer had startled her. "I was working with a student at the time and sketched out the idea for him."

Keely blinked. "You have students?"

"No, though I do spend much of my time mentoring humans. I was once a teacher of sorts in Ireland, Scotland, and Italy." Then he added, almost as an afterthought, "During the Renaissance, of course. I can't do that kind of direct work again. Not in modern times."

"You know when you say 'humans,' it sounds odd, right?"

"It's precise."

Keely's eyes briefly narrowed before she plunged on. "And so now you solve murders for Rhiannon?"

Lugos headed toward the stairs. "And other things," he replied. "We need to get going." He started climbing.

"Why? Where are we going?" She scrambled up the stairs after him.

Lugos returned the rug and coffee table to their original positions with another wave of his hand. He then pulled out his cell phone and dialed.

"You'd make a good moving man."

He found himself trying to hide his smile again. "I'm pleased you think I have useful skills," he replied before returning his attention to the task at hand.

"I'm bringing in a package for you to babysit," he said into the phone.

"Really?" Griffin sounded both startled and excited by the prospect.

Lugos strode back toward the garage, confident that Keely would follow him. "I have something I need to do alone tonight, and I need a place to put her," he told Griffin. He guessed he'd have to bring the car along as well, for appearance's sake.

"Her? The same her from yesterday?"

Instead of answering, Lugos changed the subject. "Did you dig up anything else on Carson Pratt?" He'd reached the garage door and waved Keely through, pausing only long enough to punch in the code for the alarm.

"Yes. There were two domestic abuse charges back in 2013. Both were dropped. He's also been brought up on charges for excessive use of force, but again the charges were dropped. He might have gotten a slap on the wrist, but ultimately that's all. I'll email you the details."

"Don't bother. You can just show me when I get there." Lugos stopped Keely from climbing into the car, his arm slipping easily around her small waist. "Anything else on Talon Dunbar or Ken Larkin?"

"Some. I'm still working on it, but..."

"But what?" Lugos asked, bringing Keely's body close to his. She didn't pull away. He needed to hold her, just for a moment.

"It's stupid, but if I didn't know any better, I'd say someone was deleting the information as soon as I dig it up. It's like they're messing with me."

"It's a security firm. They probably are messing with you, Griffin. Just make sure they can't follow your code back to us." Lugos pressed his lips to her forehead before resting his chin on the top of her head.

"Ha! I'd like to see them try. I've bounced us through too many countries and IP addresses for anyone to do that."

Lugos could feel her body go soft against his. "Let's hope you're right, or we'll find out if all that security you've installed has been worth the effort."

Lugos ended the call with Griffin and held her, simply because he could do nothing else. Keely had no idea what she meant to him. He'd tried to tell her earlier, but her mind wasn't ready to accept the truth of what he was, or of what they were together.

"Lugh?"

Lugos smiled over the top of her head. "Yes, Keely."

"I really am sorry for upsetting you."

He pulled back just far enough to capture her chin with his hand. He wanted her to know that he was speaking the truth. "I know you are. But none of it was your fault. I should have been watching over you. Instead, I was busy trying to get information for Rhiannon. The fault lies with me, not you." He couldn't let her assume the blame when her safety clearly rested in his hands.

"But—"

"No, Keely, I need you to understand. As soon as I realized you were no longer next to me, it terrified me." Lugos could see the confusion, the denial swimming in her eyes, but he pressed on. He knew she wasn't ready to accept what he was telling her, but he had to share what he feared most. "I cannot lose you again. I would not survive the loss this time."

When she began to deny the truth of it, he pressed a finger to her lips. "I know you don't understand now. If you believe nothing else, then believe me when I tell you that I will not let anyone or anything take you from me again." Before she could protest further, Lugos leaned down and captured her lips with his own. In that one kiss, he tried to tell her everything he could not: the things that she could not yet understand, and what they could be together if only she would surrender to his keeping. When she began to kiss him back with the same desperation and longing, the knot in his chest eased. He knew that the fear of losing her would never leave him entirely, but for now he could breathe again.

By the time their lips parted, she was clinging to him, her body molded to his, her beautiful eyes soft with wonder and longing, her lips bruised red and slightly parted, wearing that same dazed yet trusting expression he lived to see. She blinked once, twice. His own body was so hard that it bordered on pain. As tightly as he held her, Keely could have no doubts where his desires lay.

"Keely." He uttered her name, his voice thick with need.

She pressed her fingertips against her lips, the look of dazed wonder slowly fading. "You can't do that again." She had not retreated from his embrace, but she had begun to tremble.

"Why not?" Lugos let his warmth and power seep into her. It was a sharing and a confirmation, a way to comfort her as well as himself. His Keely was beginning to accept what it was between them, and it frightened her.

"I don't think I'll ever be me anymore if you do that again."

He brushed his lips against her forehead. How many times before had he stood on the precipice of her total surrender? "You will always be you—strong, courageous, compassionate, giving. But when I hold you and we come together, it's not just our bodies uniting as one but also our spirits, our souls."

"I can feel you inside me."

"My power flows into you when our souls brush against one another. I gave my heart into your keeping so long ago. I have waited centuries for you to return to me. Trust me again as you once did. I cannot lie to you, Keely. Believe in me. You are my life, my other half. I will care for you as no other can. I will love you as no other can. I need you like no other."

He felt a sigh leave her lungs as she struggled to absorb all that he was confessing. It was too much, he knew, but he'd almost lost hope in the waiting this time. And then, after finding her again, he'd made the hardest choice of his long life. This time, he'd protect what was most precious to him by *not* claiming her. For five long years, he'd suffered by denying himself, all so she could live. And yet the dangers of the Pale had still found her.

"I don't want to see whatever the more was you had in store for me. I'm not even sure I can deal with this."

Lugos placed the lightest of kisses at the corner of her downturned mouth. "Tell me what you need. If I can give it to you, I will," he promised. Because he couldn't help himself, Lugos continued his feather-light kisses across her cheek, her jaw, the sensitive hollow of her neck, and then leisurely followed the same path back to her tempting lips. When he paused, she was clinging to him, and his groin was so full and hard that he found his control slipping.

In the subdued lighting of the enclosed garage, Lugo could clearly see that Keely's aura matched his own golden hue; his power moved effortlessly between them, an ebb and flow binding them together.

"I need you." Her eyes swam with desperation, with wanting. "Please," she breathed.

He softly grazed her swollen lips with his own. He had run out of time. Her plea now brought him to the very edge of his control. Lugos had wanted to give her more time to adjust to his world.

"Do you give yourself into my keeping?" He had wanted her to come to him willingly, embrace all that they could be together. He needed to hear her say the words in this lifetime as she had done in others. She nodded, but it wasn't enough for him. "Say it. Say it and know that there's no going back." He was barely hanging on. He needed her to say the words now. "You will be forever in my care. You will be a part of me always and for all time. I will have nothing less than all of you, Keely. It is a total surrender that I require." His body was on fire for her. But if she wasn't yet ready, he'd somehow find a way to pull them back from the brink. At least, he hoped he would.

"I need you in me," she whimpered in his arms.

"And you give yourself to me, all of you," he pressed, his control now crumbling at an alarming rate. Lugos wanted her more than he could say, but she had to make the choice for them.

"Yes. Yes. I give myself into your keeping."

"For all time," he insisted.

"Yes, forever. I am yours, forever."

Chapter 29

Keely had no idea how Lugh got them from the garage to his bedroom. All she could think of was him—the heat of him, his strength, his hands molding her body to his. She was melting into him, becoming one with him, whole. It was possession she was giving into, a total surrender of who she was. His desperation was her desperation. His hunger was her hunger. She wanted nothing more than to merge completely with him. He was the very air she breathed. His arms were her sanctuary, his body a fortress against all the craziness and dangers of his world. In his embrace she was safe, untouchable, complete.

His power moved through her bloodstream, a tingling, a warmth, unlike anything she'd ever experienced. It was addictive. She craved it, reached for it, soaked it in, absorbed it into her body and mind. Memories that weren't her own swamped her. There was recognition and pain. But there was also love. A part of her mind accepted that he had loved her before and would love her again. This felt like a first claiming and yet not; he'd claimed her before, and always with this same desperation.

Lugh was thoughtful in removing her clothes. He did it slowly and carefully because she loved them. His clothes, however, seemed to disappear with only a thought. As soon as they were skin to skin, he lowered her with infinite care onto his bed. He hovered over her, drank her in. She felt like a pagan offering, completely open to his view, a sunbather welcoming the sun's fire. And then he began to touch her, to scorch her with the heat of his hands and mouth.

"You are always so beautiful." His splayed hands moved across her abdomen and up her rib cage to cup her breasts.

His mouth lowered to hers, his hands were everywhere at once, trailing fire in their wake. Keely gave herself up to the sensations of him moving over her and through her. His power burned across her and into her like lava shaping the land. Her first orgasm began the moment his fingers found her slick entrance.

His hot mouth and hands suckled and kneaded, making her body whimper until she could not take any more. "Please," she heard herself beg into the hollow of his neck. He was consuming her. His name was forever the same, yet forever changing inside her mind. She clung to him now, to the heat and strength of him while he made her body sing. He'd been given lifetimes to learn how to please her, and he used all of that knowledge now, so that there could be no room for doubt as to who he was.

"Look at me."

Keely was mindlessly writhing under him, a puddle of need trying desperately to impale herself on his hard shaft so they could finally be one as they were meant to be. She understood now. She had always belonged to him, only him.

"Look at me, my love."

Her eyes snapped open to meet his incredibly blue ones.

"I claim you as my own. You are my other half, my love."

She could feel the hot head of his cock poised at her slick entrance. He had pushed her legs wide so that she was completely open to his invasion. She'd never wanted anything more in her life than to have him plunge into her, to fill her until she screamed with the joy of it.

"Now," she whimpered. The desperation Keely felt was beyond anything she had ever imagined. If he didn't take her soon, she thought she'd die. Somewhere in the house, a light bulb exploded.

He smiled down at her. He tilted her hips, his hands burning, branding her, holding her still. "You are mine for all time, the keeper of my heart."

He moved, then, a slow invasion. Impossibly large, stretching her, filling her. Keely clung to him. He was unrelenting in his assault. She tried to relax under the building pressure, but it was too much.

"Surrender, my love," he whispered against her neck as he continued to drive forward. A crack of lightning lit the sky.

"It's too much," she pleaded, suddenly afraid that he was so large that he might split her in two. She needed him to stop, only for a moment, so she could adjust.

"I will have all of you. Give yourself to me." The earth shook, and the air around them crackled with electricity. "You belong to me, as I belong to you."

Still the pressure built. Thunder rocked a clear blue sky. The ground heaved and rolled underneath her, and still he moved into her.

"I can't!"

But he did not slow down. He was taking all of her. She clung to him, afraid she'd shatter.

"Relax, my love. You were made for me." When at last he was lodged against her womb, Lugos paused for her to adjust to his size. "Breathe, my love."

Keely tried to do as he instructed. He was her world. Had always been her world. She knew that now. How could she have forgotten? He filled her completely, filled her body, her mind, her heart.

With infinite care, he kissed her, gently at first. Then, as her hunger grew, he deepened his kiss until she was writhing underneath him once again. Only when she was crying his name and begging him to move did he begin to teach her what it was to be cherished by a god. He was everywhere, his hands, his mouth.

She cried out his name, the one she knew in this lifetime and others that came to her from lives she'd lived before with him. How could there be anyone other than he? He was her sun, her moon, her world. Without warning, Keely's world fragmented, and he held her as a second orgasm overtook her.

Lightning arced between them, danced between her fingertips and his skin where her hands touched, caressed, and clung. "You are so beautiful, my love." And still he drove into her, unyielding in his quest to meld their souls together.

Keely surrendered to his hunger, to his body's apparent unquenchable desire. She would give him all and hope that he'd stop before he killed her. Another lightning bolt struck the ground just outside the bedroom window. The thunder that followed was deafening. And yet none of it mattered. For Keely, there was only him, his driving need, his desperation to unite them. Keely gasped into the heat of his mouth, heart shattering the moment his soul merged completely with hers. And then they were both flying, erupting into a million pieces, floating together as one, as they were meant to be.

***

Lugos was careful not to crush her with his heavier frame. He'd been as gentle as he could. She was mortal, and he needed always to remember to hold back a little when he made love to her. Keely's eyes were drowsy, content, and so beautiful. Still buried deep inside her, Lugos felt complete for the first time in centuries. Their souls weren't just brushing up against one another; they were united again, their spirits woven together as they were always meant to be. Her skin glowed. His power flowed in her as easily as it did in his own body. He had often marveled at that phenomenon, not ever sure why she could handle what no other mortal could.

He rolled onto his back and took her with him so that the glorious length of her languid body was splayed across him. Her silken hair tickled his shoulder and chest as her heart beat in rhythm with his own. Even in the sunlit room, they glowed, a pulsing of his god-power. It danced between them, a tango of give and take that never failed to astound him.

Keely mewed sweetly, sleepily. The sound of it vibrated through him and lodged itself in his heart.

"Are you still with me?" he asked, his hands caressing skin where he could reach. And he could reach a good deal of it.

Keely managed to prop her chin on his chest. Lugos found the bemused look on her face far too tempting to pass up. He gently slid her up toward him. With one arm he locked her to him; with the other he clutched a fistful of her tangled dark locks so that she could not pull away while he kissed her again. She didn't struggle but gave herself to him without reservation. When he relented, she was breathless and dazed anew.

"I have to be careful with you," he told her, more for his own hearing than hers. He was already hard and ready to bury himself in her again.

"Lugh."

There was that plea again. He knew he'd never tire of hearing it. She wouldn't deny him if he wanted to take her again. He could feel the wetness between her legs seeping onto him, a mixture of her own need and his seed trickling down her thighs. He sighed heavily and turned them both so that she rested on her side and he could spoon his body protectively around her smaller frame. "Rest, my love," he whispered into her hair. "Rest and dream of me. We are one, and we have all the time in the world."

Lugos felt the moment she gave into his command to sleep. He smiled, content just to hold her. Never again would anyone hold her but him. She was his once more, and he intended to be diligent in her care. She would be sore from his lovemaking; he would insist that she take a long, restorative bath when she awoke. He'd also make sure she ate again, and soon. She'd only nibbled at her breakfast at the hotel, had not eaten at all the day before. He would not lose her to something so trivial as her own neglect of her body's need for proper nourishment. And he would spoil her with whatever she desired, because it was in his power to do so. She would no longer worry about money; no more limitations except the ones she placed on herself and those he would demand of her to keep her safe.

Lugos nuzzled that sweet spot between her shoulder and neck as the feeling of utter peace stole over him. "I will hold you too tightly for fear of losing you again," he breathed against her skin. "Be patient with me, my love." He then brushed his lips one final time against the sensitive skin of her neck before allowing himself to float in the sea of contentment she'd given him.

Chapter 30

"You're still in the garage, and you're in drive," Keely warned. She felt different in an elemental way. She was still Keely, yet she wasn't *just* Keely anymore. She felt Lugh draw on his powers again.

"I'm taking you to Atlanta. To Griffin. Are you ready?"

Realizing it was the only warning he was going to give, Keely nodded and closed her eyes. She trusted him completely now. The Audi's engine revved, and then the tires squealed on the hard surface. Keely was thrown back into her seat with their sudden forward momentum. Just as abruptly, the car screeched to a halt.

"We're here."

"Yes, but where the hell is here?" she asked, daring to open her eyes. He was apprehensive, she could feel it flowing off him. Keely realized that this was new, this ability to feel his emotions inside her even when his expression said otherwise.

"You'll see soon enough."

Lugh abandoned the Audi in the warehouse's below-ground parking deck and led her up into the building's interior. She stood mutely behind him as he knocked on 3B's door and waited. After a moment or two of muffled noise on the other side, the knock was answered. Through the merest of cracks, Lugh said, "Murmur, let me in."

There was a hesitation, as if the person on the other side might be debating his choices, but then the door eased back just enough for Lugh to squeeze past. With a hand and a grunt, Lugh prevented the door from closing on Keely. As soon as she was clear, he let the door slam home.

"Why are we here, Lugh?" Keely asked.

***

"Who's she?" Even agitated, Murmur's voice was every bit as rich and warm as chocolate poured over honey. "You know I don't like strangers. Why have you brought a human here?"

Lugos had always thought that Murmur was quite handsome, as demons went. He was dressed today in one of his many suits, this one a gray pinstripe, with a fedora worn low over his forehead. The demon's apartment was the height of fashion as well—that is, if one were a child of the twenties and an ardent fan of art deco. Heavy velvet drapes shielded the interior from the sun's rays, leaving the crystal wall sconces and various ornate chandeliers—because why have just one, when you could have three?—to illuminate the apartment.

"Behave yourself," Lugos reprimanded the demon.

Murmur's square chin jutted forward. "When have I not?"

Lugos chuckled and nodded toward Keely. "I need to show her."

Murmur's eyebrow rose to disappear under the brim of his hat. "Her? You found her again?"

"She needs to see to believe."

Murmur snorted. "Oh, guess she doesn't change all that much." Chuckling to himself, he bent at the waist and bowed to Keely, sweeping his hat dramatically from his head.

"Who in blazes are you talkin' to, Lugh?" Keely asked, her eyes drawn away from the loft's décor to him.

Murmur straightened. "She can't see me yet?"

"Or hear you," Lugos replied.

"Lugh, if you're trying to scare me by acting all crazy, then—"

Lugos pulled Keely into his arms, fitting her back to his chest. "You can't see Murmur, but he's standing right in front of us."

"I can't hear him either, just a kind of buzzing in my ears."

Keely leaned back into him, seeking comfort. Lugos gave it, once again letting his power slowly seep into her. "I'm going to make it so you can see him. He's a demon, so don't scream." The moment he said the word *demon,* Keely tried to bolt, but Lugos held her fast, his arms a protective cage around her waist and shoulders.

Slowly the figure of a man manifested before her. He was very large and a little too handsome. And scary; Lugos felt the tremor run down her spine. There was nothing feminine about Murmur's features. He was over six feet tall, a warrior despite the suit. There was a touch of cruelty about his mouth. But it was Murmur's black-as-flint eyes that even Lugos sometimes found unnerving.

"My dear, a pleasure to see you again."

Keely's intake of breath was immediate. Her hands snaked upward to seize Lugos's forearm in a death grip.

Lugos tightened his hold for encouragement. "Murmur is a third-level demon of the Abraxas clan. He's immortal, like me, but on the whole, demons are very, very different from what your Bible portrays them to be." Through his bond with Murmur, Lugos thought, *Do not frighten her with the whole truth.*

Murmur chuckled again as he straightened from his second bow, his hat clasped before him in his large hands like a man waiting for his date. *As you wish,* he thought obediently back. To Keely, he said, "We're messengers now, mainly. I travel between the realms, you see." There was a rippling effect across his skin as the faint caramel color lightened to the palest of whites. "We can alter our coloring, much like this world's chameleon or cuttlefish—not that it does much good. Only other demons and the gods can see or hear us. Well, them and the occasional Mad Hatter."

The ripple seemed to travel once again over the surface of the alabaster skin, darkening slowly until it was the deepest mahogany. Noticing Keely's seeming fascination with his lack of horns, Murmur bowed his head and said, "Go on, miss, you can check. We have neither horns nor tails. Though I think Llew, here, would take exception to my disrobing in your presence." He glanced up at Lugos, a smirk tugging at the corner of his mouth. *She is the same.*

Even with Lugos holding her, Keely's complexion had paled considerably. "No," he said, "I'm fairly sure I'd never be comfortable with that." Lugos swung her around in his arms. "You're not going to faint, are you?" After a moment, she shook her head but still looked shaky. Satisfied that she wasn't going to pass out on him or start screaming, Lugos went on with his explanation. "Shifters are different from Murmur, here. His basic form will always remain the same, but a shifter's appearance alters drastically when they take on an animal form. Some manage the transformation smoothly, others do not."

Behind him, Murmur grunted in agreement. "Sounds none too pleasant, either. Cracking bones and whatnot. Plus, they have an odor."

"Are you sure you're not going to faint?" Lugos asked her again.

"Maybe you should make her sit before she falls down," Murmur suggested, his coloring now back to its usual neutral caramel. He'd replaced his hat and looked ready to leave the apartment. Lugos knew Murmur couldn't set a toe outside the confines of the building without his express permission. It was simply too dangerous.

"I...I...I'm fine," Keely stammered. "He's really a demon?"

Lugos stopped the flow of power to her. Without it, Murmur would start to fade from her sight. He gently pushed her down into a velvet-covered chair as a precaution. "Yes. And he will protect you while I am gone. You won't see him, but he'll be close should anyone breach this building. Think of him as your own personal security detail."

"Can you trust a demon, Lugh? I mean, he's a *demon*."

Lugos smiled at her and then kissed first one palm and then the other. "He is completely loyal to me and has watched over you before, centuries ago. I think at some point you even grew kind of fond of him."

Keely gave him a halfhearted laugh. "Well, that changes everythin', now, doesn't it?"

Lugos breathed a sigh of relief. She'd handled it well.

"The buzzing sound is back. Is he laughin' at me?"

Lugos glared at Murmur, who was indeed chuckling to himself. Turning back to Keely, he grinned. "Yes, a little. He's fond of you, too."

***

"I'll be back later tonight. Griffin is just outside, if you need anything." Lugh pointed at the wall instead of the locked door, as if he could see Griffin's exact location through the plaster and steel. His imposing frame came closer, filling her line of vision. Leaning forward, he frowned. "You still look pale. Are you sure I can't get you something before I leave? Crackers, perhaps?"

His concern for her was palpable even without this strange new connection to him. But the last thing she wanted was something in her stomach. He'd made her eat before they left his cabin, and Keely wasn't sure that meal wouldn't make a reappearance all over the carpeted floor. She shook her head, and he straightened. He'd hustled her out of Murmur's apartment and into this one, the door behind them closing seemingly on its own, though she suspected Murmur had done that.

Lugh had then carried her into this apartment past its only occupant, Griffin, with nothing but a nod and a grunt. Compared to the glittering opulence of the demon's apartment, the bedroom he'd brought her into seemed slightly depressing in its simplicity. There was the rock-hard bed on which she now sat and a dresser that appeared unused. No pictures hung on the wall. No mirror, no throw pillows or rugs, nothing had been done for this room but the most basic of linens on the bed, and they were an uninspired navy and gray houndstooth, likely from Walmart.

"You stay here much?" Keely asked, wanting to distract him from his concern for her.

"No," he replied, stepping into the adjacent bathroom and then back out.

"Everything accounted for?" she teased. Ever since they'd had sex, he'd been fussing over her.

There was the briefest flicker of confusion and then an upturn of his lips. "You're in luck. The cleaning lady came yesterday."

"Oh, good." She gave him her bartender grin. She knew he needed to get on with his investigation, and she was the reason he was still here. "Go, Lugh. I'll be fine." Then she hastily added, "He's not in here now, is he?"

"No, he's just out there. By the way, Griffin has no clue what Murmur is or what I really am. You understand what that means? These are secrets we must keep. At least for now. I'll eventually tell Griffin about the Pale, but not now."

Keely nodded. She wasn't about to go telling anyone that her new boyfriend was an ancient pagan god who'd claimed her body and soul with earth-shattering sex, or that Lugh kept a demon around just to guard her when he was out. "I got it."

Lugh reached into his pocket and pulled out the keys to the car they'd left below in the parking deck. He put them in her hand. "I don't think anything will happen, but if something does, and you and Griffin have to get out, I want you to drive straight to the cabin. When you get there, type your name into the security pad. It will turn the alarm off and allow you to enter. The system will notify me that you've gone there, and I'll come. Do you understand what I'm telling you?"

"You're worried something might happen?"

"Yes." Looking away, he immediately changed his answer. "No, not really."

"Yes, you are." She hadn't meant it to sound like an accusation, but it had.

"No, Keely I'm not," he replied, his gaze still averted. "But—"

"But someone, something could come after me here," Keely finished. She'd asked him a direct question while their gazes had been locked. He could lie to her while he was looking away, but that first answer, that yes, had been the truth.

"Zee is across the hall. And Murmur will keep anyone from...damn it, Keely," he hissed. "It's just a backup plan. I shouldn't have mentioned..." He turned back to her, his blue gaze alighting on her face ever so briefly, only to flit off elsewhere like a dragonfly afraid to land.

In that moment, Keely realized that her presence weakened him, handicapped him. Lugh couldn't lie to her, couldn't hide his secrets, his feelings from her, his most guarded thoughts. Worse, his enemies could hurt him through her. "Sorry. I'm sure everything will be fine. I'm just being a ninny." His sapphire gaze swung back to find her forced smile in place. Their eyes locked.

"It *is* just a precaution. One of many."

"I believe you." Keely managed to get a little closer to a genuine grin. "You're a planner, Lugh. I'm sure even your plans have plans."

He chuckled, and Keely could feel the tension he'd been carrying since leaving the cabin begin to drain away. She rose from the bed and stepped into his arms because he needed her. "I'm still getting used to the idea of all this. I'm just a little nervous to be apart from you. I don't mean to be clingy. You know I'm not really a clingy kind of girl." No matter how frightened or lost she felt, Keely needed Lugh not to worry so much about her. Somewhere deep inside, she knew he was as afraid as she was. Bad things had always happened when they were apart.

Lugh nuzzled her neck and then captured her lips with his. In that moment, Keely forgot to be afraid for herself or for him.

"I'll try not to be long," he promised.

"Just be careful."

Chapter 31

It was just past nine in the evening when Lugos put his cell phone away. "You're late."

"Hardly. No goddess in her right mind enters an empty room." Rhiannon was dressed in a crisp white pantsuit and strappy silver four-inch heels. She had left her red hair unbound to cascade wildly down her back and about her shoulders. The untamed tresses and the heels made the goddess a good four inches taller than Lugos's sometimes imposing six feet four.

"You always did know how to make an impression."

She winked at him. Then, as if just noticing his black jeans and T-shirt, she plucked at his cotton sleeve. A hint of distress wrinkled her nose. "Perhaps you'd like a few pointers, dear. Anticipating blood tonight, I assume?"

Lugos grunted. He'd been waiting for the goddess to arrive for a good thirty minutes in the Kentucky evening heat, and he was sweating. The sun had finally turned the sky red and orange, but the humidity had climbed. "It's a shifter Fight Night. No one gets out without a little blood on them."

Rhiannon's smile had always made him a little nervous, and now was no exception. "Shall we, then?"

Lugos offered her his arm. He wanted to get this over with and back to Keely. The golden glow of his aura wasn't yet noticeable in full daylight, but after dusk it definitely was. He was whole again, and Rhiannon would soon notice.

"This is going to be fun." Rhiannon's god-powers looked to be fully charged, her distinctly red glow only growing stronger as they approached the entrance to Triton Securities.

And why shouldn't it? Lugos thought. Everyone inside both loved and feared the goddess. "What a lovely distraction your god-powers will make."

"That is my role tonight, is it not?" she asked sweetly.

Lugos grinned. "How well you know me."

Chapter 32

Keely remained in the bedroom for what seemed like hours, trying to sort out her mind. Everything had happened so fast, and she'd not had time to come to terms with it all. Before Lugh had left to go investigating, he'd thoughtfully retrieved her things from the car downstairs. Griffin had knocked twice on the door to check on her, but otherwise he'd let her be. On the last knock, he'd announced that he was ordering Chinese food for dinner and there would be plenty if she wanted any. Keely had thanked him but declined.

Somewhere beyond the closed door, there was a demon she couldn't see. She didn't know what to think about that. Ostensibly Murmur was hanging out to protect her, but she couldn't shake a lifetime of her church's teachings in a day, not even with the absolute conviction that Lugh would never knowingly put her in a dangerous situation. Did demons eat Chinese food? Lugh had spent a good bit of time explaining who Griffin was, that he was human, and that she'd need to watch what she said because apparently he was crazy smart. Keely felt very protective of Lugh, even more so now that she had committed to him. She didn't want to slip up and give away any of

Lugh's secrets. That was her second good reason to stay put till Lugh returned.

But as more time passed, Keely got antsy. She had her things but no cell phone. It had been taken at some point after Mr. Red T-shirt's attack and Lugh's arrival to fetch her from Rhiannon. Keely hadn't noticed the phone missing until now, when she had nothing to do but worry about Lugh, what he was doing, and when he might be back. She missed him. It was crazy that she would miss him as much as she did. She'd spoken the truth to him, wanting to be as honest with him as he'd been with her. She had never been the clingy type. But the crazy idea kept circling in her head that she was running out of time.

Out of sheer desperation, Keely reached for him with her mind. It was a silly thing to do, but it made her feel better to just try. She built the image of him in her mind, slowly and as completely as she could. As she did so, that same warm tingling of his began to spread through her. It was faint, but it calmed her to think that maybe, just maybe, they were still somehow connected even though she knew he must be miles away.

Just as quickly, Keely became aware of someone singing. A baritone voice, Murmur's.

"What the hell?" Not sure what just happened, Keely abandoned the bed and moved toward the door for a better listen. The voice began to fade; more precisely, her ability to hear it faded.

The aroma of Chinese food hit her first as she wandered forth from her haven. Griffin's dinner had arrived and appeared half eaten. Keely could see no signs of Murmur, though she was almost sure he was still in the room. Griffin was glued to his computer screens and had not noticed her yet. Standing very still, Keely tried to will herself to see or hear Murmur. It didn't work. Why didn't it?

She closed her eyes and thought about Lugh again. That was easy. To her astonishment, the tingling sensation was back. It was faint but steady. And so was Murmur's voice.

"The little bird has left her nest," he chuckled. "But can she find me?"

Keely glanced over at Griffin. He was still concentrating on the various screens in front of him. "No, but I can hear you," she whispered, her voice but a thread of breath. Her eyes darted back and forth, searching for any hint of the demon's whereabouts. He'd sounded close. She wasn't sure if she was less afraid because she couldn't see him, or more afraid because she'd managed to find a way to hear him.

"Good for you! It took you nearly eight months last time."

For Keely, the connection wavered, just like her Rover's radio when it tried to hang on to a station, minus the annoying static. "Where are you?" she mouthed. "I want to sit down."

Griffin had turned just enough in his chair to catch sight of her. "Got hungry? There are plates in the kitchen, but I just eat out of the boxes. Hope you don't mind."

Keely jumped when an invisible Murmur touched her shoulder with what she hoped was his hand. "Thank you," Keely replied to Griffin. "I think I'll just sit over here for a while." She could hear Murmur's chuckle. It was a little too close to her ear, and she tried casually to swat at him. She connected with something, his jacket maybe.

"Ah, don't let that monstrosity scare you. Agent Hart put it here."

"What?" Keely squeaked as Murmur pushed on the small of her back to get her moving toward the couch.

Griffin's eyes narrowed. "That espresso machine of his. That was why you jumped, wasn't it?" As if on cue, the contraption in question hissed.

"Uh, yes. Guess I'm a little jumpy today," Keely replied, sinking down into the leather cushions and giving him a completely honest smile of relief.

"Don't upset the boy," Murmur advised. "Or smile too sweetly... him."

Griffin smiled indulgently back. "Well, no coffee for you, then. There's bottled water in the fridge."

"Llew... tell him... So don't give .... okay?"

"Okay. Thank you. I'm fine. Just go back to whatever you were doing." Her heart was pounding.

He shrugged and turned his attention back to his screens.

"Where are you?" she mouthed again. Carrying on two conversations at once was beyond her right now. It was difficult to maintain the concentration necessary to keep hearing Murmur. By way of answer, Keely felt the edge of his shoe gently tap her bare toes. She snatched her feet off the floor and onto the couch. "Sorry, this is so weird," she breathed, hoping that only Murmur would hear her.

There was that deep laughter. She'd amused him yet again. Keely rolled her eyes. She wasn't hungry. She missed Lugh way too much. She had a demon laughing at her, and she was strangely bored and yet antsy.

Time was running out. There wasn't a television in the room—only Griffin, the hissing espresso machine, the lingering aroma of Chinese takeout, and the hum of computers.

She wondered what Cutter was doing, back at the Witch's Whistle. Should she call him? Was he worried about her? She hadn't thought to call anyone since it had all started. On the tail end of that thought, she wondered what she was going to tell her mama about Lugh. Could he even go into a church? If he couldn't, that was going to be a problem with her mama. Thinking about Lugh, Keely began to feel that faint tingle under her skin. She also began to hear Murmur again.

He was talking to himself just to hear himself talk. Keely tried to imagine what it might be like to be neither seen nor heard. It might drive a person insane after a time. Despite the fact that he was a demon and everything she'd ever been taught since she was a baby screamed at her that he had to be evil, she took pity on him. He didn't feel evil. There was no smell of sulfur about him. "I can hear you again," she whispered.

"About bloody time. Concentrate, girl."

She smiled at the exasperation in his voice. He obviously craved the sensation of talking to someone, anyone. Keely darted a glance at Griffin. "Talk to me," she breathed. She'd try to keep picturing Lugh in her mind so Murmur could ramble. It would pass the time and give her something to do while she waited for Lugh to return. It might also keep her mind off whatever new weird thing tomorrow might bring, because she still couldn't shake the feeling that time was running out. Whatever new monster surfaced, she was counting on Lugh to stand between her and it.

Friday

Chapter 33

Lugos didn't return to Atlanta until two in the morning. He'd gotten Rhiannon the lead she needed on the Talon front, but he had been required to enter the fight ring to obtain that information. Talon had collared Shea early in the night. But the highlight for the USL members had been when Rhiannon declared that Llew the God-Killer would take on any and all challengers, with the stipulation that Lugos would not draw on his god-powers to defeat his opponents.

The first few fights had been easy for him. The last three had not. He'd gotten tired and had been a little slow in avoiding claws and teeth. Rhiannon had bet heavily on him. Lugos hoped she enjoyed her winnings at his expense. Right now, all he wanted was to get to Keely and fall into bed beside her.

Griffin looked up from his workstation when Lugos entered the loft, this time using his key. "What the hell happened to you?"

Lugos waved him off. Murmur was already moving toward him to give aid, but with a look he waved the demon off as well. Lugos already felt better than when he'd climbed out of the ring. In a few hours, most of his cuts would be healed, thanks to the shifters from whom he was able to draw energy. Beating the hell out of all comers had done his street cred some good in that community. By the end of the night, a good many had been cheering for him, chanting his name.

"I'm fine. Just do me a favor and go on and scrub Keely Ann Lee's Internet footprint. I want her to have ghost status."

Griffin nodded. "Sure. I'll get it done for you."

"Thank you. Use Stone for her new last name." Lugos moved toward where he knew Keely was. He could feel her just beyond the bedroom door. Murmur got there first and opened the door for him. "Follow me," he whispered for Murmur's ears only.

"You should never hang out with goddesses," the demon replied. "None of them have ever been good to you."

Lugos would have agreed with Murmur, but Keely got to him first. He opened his arms to catch her as she threw herself at him. Despite his injuries, he was happy to hold her. Home, he thought, his eyes closing.

"What happened to you?" The question was muffled against his shirt.

"You should be sleeping," he gently scolded. She was barefoot but still wearing the skirt and top he'd asked her to put on for him back at the cabin. He liked her in skirts; the way the fabric draped over her hips and round bottom appealed to him. He also liked the idea that he could reach out and touch that welcoming heat of hers without having to wait for her to wiggle out of a pair of pants. He realized it was an archaic, almost Neanderthal idea to Keely, but his preferences for what his woman should wear had been formed in another lifetime.

Murmur pushed the door shut so the three of them were alone. "Rhiannon happened," the demon supplied.

"I couldn't sleep," Keely explained, pulling back just a little. "Did she do this to you?"

Lugos had just managed to close his eyes again before she could capture his gaze. He didn't want to lie to her, but he also didn't know what she was going to ask. "No. I had a choice."

Murmur harrumphed. "Not likely. Owe a goddess a favor and she'll screw you every time. I hope Rhiannon got whatever she was after."

"Did she get what she wanted?" Keely asked.

Lugos had yet to open his eyes or release her completely. "You can hear him without my aid." He made it a statement. He pinned her with his blue gaze, his expression stern. Hers was full of concern, concern for him.

"Hell, yes, she can." Murmur slapped Lugos's shoulder hard.

Lugos grunted.

"A damn sight faster than last time, too. I'm proud of her." Murmur shoved at him again.

Lugos growled. "Stop it. I think I've taken enough of a beating tonight."

"I still can't see him unless you help me," Keely offered.

Murmur chuckled and crossed his arms. "Don't worry, Keely, he'll be good as new in a few hours."

Keely's eyebrows rose. "Is that true?"

Despite the cut to his lip, Lugos grinned down at her. "Yes, my little love, but first..." He turned to Murmur, the grin for his woman sliding away. "Go to Rhiannon. She wants you to do a bit of spying, and perhaps other things. We need to know their timeline. She's going to confront Talon in a few hours, so you won't have much time to confirm what we think we know. I'll stay in touch."

Murmur grimaced but didn't argue. He nodded once; then his form wavered, and the demon was gone.

Lugos turned his attention back to the woman in his arms. "Rhiannon will call only if Murmur gets in trouble. You have me for a few hours. Do you want to go back to the cabin, or stay here for the rest of the night?"

Keely ran her fingertips over his face. "Murmur's absolutely gone now? I didn't want to get undressed with him around."

Lugos felt no pain, no sting as the pads of her fingers touched where the cut to his lip had been just moments before. "He would not have intruded on your privacy. But, yes, we're alone."

"The gash on your lip is gone."

The expression of awe he loved was back on her face. "Remember, I told you that I heal quickly. There really is no need for you to worry about me."

She forced a smile. "I remember, but I just thought..." Keely paused, dropped whatever she was going to say, and instead said, "I'll have to work on that."

Lugos leaned down and kissed her. He had to. She was looking up at him as if he were her entire world, when in reality she was his. He'd have the rest of the night with her and maybe a few hours in the morning before the shit hit the fan and Rhiannon needed him.

There was no resistance from Keely, no asking him to slow down. She clung to him, ripped at his bloodied shirt and pants so that her hands could touch skin. Lugos winced when her hand moved over his two broken ribs. But he didn't stop her from reaching for him. He had to touch her, had to bury himself inside her body. Impatient, Lugos removed their clothes with a thought and lowered the two of them onto the bed, his body blanketing hers. She was burning up for him and he for her.

His hand moved between her legs to make sure she was ready, and then he surged into her in one hard stroke, opening the floodgates that held back his power so that it rushed into her as his body took hers. She gasped into his mouth as the force of his power and body slammed into her. She trembled in his arms, clung to him. Her nails raked his glowing skin. His breathing ragged, his heart pounding, Lugos paused for both of them. He needed this, but he also wanted it to last.

His power crashed into her, the sea hitting upon her shore. He could feel her now, drinking him in, drawing his power into her. She was welcoming, greedy for him. They were one. He was home. This was home. She would always be home for him. As soon as a portion of his power began to recede from Keely, he found her lips again and feasted on her until she moaned sweetly into his mouth. Lugos moved then, picking up the rhythm of the ebb and flow that was unique to them. "Hold tight, my love," he breathed across her golden skin. "I have such great need of you."

"Lugh." Her hands tunneled into his hair, frantic in their efforts to hold him to her.

He kept his pace slow and in perfect timing with the flow of energy between them. He needed always to be careful not to demand what her body could not take. He nuzzled her breast, suckling strongly to hear her cry out his name. Her hips rose to meet his, urging him to move harder, faster. But he refused. He needed this slow reaffirmation. Her skin was so soft, so sensitive to his touch. He needed to touch all of her, to know that she was truly his again, that she was safe even from him. He felt her first orgasm take her. It was so beautiful. To be able to surround her and also be inside her as she came apart in his arms amazed him. Her mewing and sighing were like the sweetest music. He craved the sound of them. Once would never be enough, and so he continued their dance as her body pulsed and pulled at his cock.

"Look at me, my love. Look at the one who loves you."

She complied with his command, tears leaking from her eyes. "You're so beautiful. This is so beautiful."

Lugos smiled down at her. "You are my woman. Why would I not love your body as you deserve?" He was already pushing her toward another climax, his hands commanding her body to give him what he craved most.

"I can't."

He heard a note of panic in her plea. He was forcing her to climb again quickly. "Trust me, my love. Let yourself fly. I will always catch you." He changed his angle so that his body rubbed against her clitoris. Two deep strokes later, she was trembling with the force of her orgasm as it roared through her and him. And still he did not stop.

***

Her body was no longer entirely hers. Keely was aware that in her mind she was no longer alone. There was more than just Keely, there was *her*—his woman, his other half. She was strong and giving, loyal and brave. She had many names, many lives, but she was forever the same when he found her, when he held her, loved her, cherished her. She was his, as he was hers. She felt the power of him flow into her and then back again. The beat of who they were rolled and crashed inside her. Back and forth. Retreat and return. Life and death. Joy and pain. Again he came, driving into her, sharing his power, sharing his body. And she received him, welcomed him, soaked him in, drank her fill before giving back. Giving herself, giving her body, giving her life, giving her love.

"Stay with me," he coaxed against her ear.

He breathed with her, across her skin, his body hot and hard, hers soft and melting. There was nothing more perfect than when he came to her, needing her. There was only Lugh, his heat, his body, his need, his power flowing through her. She was a part of him as he was a part of her.

She felt him swell inside her body. She was coiling again, racing for the edge with him. Her nails dug into his skin. He was her anchor. They would fly together this time, him cradling her, surrounding her always.

"Please," she cried.

The rhythm of their music changed, became faster, a driving beat. He was pushing them now, sweeping her toward the edge with him. He moved into her harder, the power of him crashing into her more quickly.

She responded in kind, giving all of herself to him, a complete surrender to him and to what she would become because of him.

And then they were exploding together, two stars burning with one light, beyond the bonds of time. They were perfect. They were eternal.

Keely kept her eyes closed. Her mind felt scattered, different, not entirely her own. She accepted the change because time was running out. Her time was running out.

Lugh rolled them over so that she lay on his chest. She smiled against his shoulder, her body pleasantly boneless. He was still buried deep inside her, filling her, stretching her. It felt right, all of it. The strength of him, the heat of him. The storm inside her body was subsiding, but the pulsing energy of him still throbbed in her bloodstream, a steady reminder of something Keely's mind reached for but could not yet grasp.

She sighed contentedly as his hands stroked and caressed her cooling skin. He didn't hurry her. He never would. Keely was as aware of him as she was of the other her, the one that rose up to meet his hunger. Keely was becoming more familiar with her, the her that was eternal. There were memories, now, crowded inside Keely's mind. Memories of her eternal self and him, always him. Lifetime after lifetime, Keely's eternal self had loved him. She needed to escape the pattern of death and separation that they seemed bound to repeat. Each lifetime, she'd failed. Desperation was growing. Time was running out. On some level, the current incarnation, the one known as Keely, understood this. She would have to allow it. Allow the other, the eternal self, to consume her. Time was running out. It was happening all too quickly this time.

"Did I hurt you?"

The concern in his voice amused her, both hers. He would never hurt her. It wasn't in him to cause her pain. "No," she managed to reply but gave him no more. Keely was still trying to sort her selves out. She needed more time. But soon there would be no more time. She would lose him again.

He shifted underneath her, gently rolling her onto her side as he slipped from her body. He cradled her close to his chest, the weight of his leg trapping her thigh. His hand still stroking, petting. "You should sleep."

She snuggled closer to the heat of him. "I don't want to."

"I will not let you neglect yourself. Did you eat tonight?"

"No." She sighed and then admitted, "I wasn't hungry."

"You need to eat, my love."

Again, she told him that she just wasn't hungry. "I've hardly seen you eat."

He reached down and lifted her chin so he could look at her. "My body makeup is different. I don't need as much nourishment as you."

"Don't look so worried. I'll eat when I'm hungry."

"You aren't smoking, either."

Keely blinked. He was right. She hadn't craved a cigarette for over twenty-four hours. "I'm told it's a bad habit."

His lips quirked. "It is," he agreed. "Why are you hearing Murmur without me?"

"Should I not be able to do that? He said I heard him before."

Lugh's eyes narrowed into slits of blue. "I was always there, before."

"I didn't know that," she lied. "So, did Talon kill your vic?" Keely asked, changing the subject quickly, knowing he had to answer her question honestly.

"No, he didn't, but it was a shifter. What aren't you telling me?"

Keely smiled sweetly up at him. She loved him, even this modern incarnation of her loved him. "What secret would I have?" she asked.

"I don't know…" His brow creased.

"So, who killed her?"

"Blye, most likely," he immediately answered.

"How do you know that?" she pressed, hoping he'd not ask her any more questions that hinted at what was going on inside her mind. She would not tell him, afraid to give him hope when she wasn't sure she wouldn't still fail him.

"I went to talk to Old Man Grady Pratt. Blye was there."

"Does Rhiannon know?'

"Yes, of course. Why are you distracting me?"

"Am I? I didn't mean to. I really will eat something in the morning if it makes you feel better." She bent her head and placed feather-light kisses along his chest. "If Murmur's gone, who will you leave me with?" she breathed the question against his skin as she moved downward.

"Zee."

He grabbed at her shoulders, but she wiggled free and continued her journey down his body. She scraped her teeth across his nipple and then kissed each rib. He growled at her when she swirled her tongue along this hipbone.

"Be careful, Keely, I don't have endless control."

She chuckled, her mouth against the top of his right thigh. He was already hard again. His cock jerked as her hair slid over the length of him. She moved further down and lightly bit the inside of his thigh. The golden hair on his leg was fine, and she rubbed her cheek against it like a cat.

A groan escaped his lips. "Keely, get back up here."

She would never deny him what he wanted, but she would take what she wanted along the way. With a mischievous grin, she technically did as he ordered but not before she licked him from the base of his shaft to that glistening velvet head. His body shuddered beneath her. Swirling her tongue around him a second time, Keely savored him, the feel of him in her mouth, the taste of him. His hand dug into her hair, and he began to guide her slowly, carefully, so that she didn't take too much of him. His hips bucked upward when she sucked hard, her tongue swirling again as her lips moved up to the sensitive tip. She engulfed him again with the heat of her mouth, flicking her tongue along the hard length of him, and again until he pulled her from him by her hair.

"Woman, you're killing me." Using his enormous strength, Lugh clasped Keely about the waist, lifted her into the air, and impaled her on his shaft. "You started this, now ride me," he ordered.

Keely smiled and did as she was told, his hands on her hips guiding her so that she could not go too fast or too deep. In this, their lovemaking, she would always obey him. As she took him into her, his power flowed more fully into her. With each long and delicious stroke, Keely and her eternal self drew on his power. Time was running short, and Keely knew instinctively that they would have need of it.

She curled down so that she lay cradled upon his chest, his hips still thrusting upward. She let him take complete control, knowing she was safe even as he moved them to the edge. Their time was short. She needed every precious moment with him, needed to draw as much of his power into her this time as she could stand. Store it, hide it away.

They were so close. His hands were back on her hips, a bruising grip. Harder. Longer, until he was slapping into her. She would have all of him. Take all that he was. She felt his release begin a moment before her own. She struck, then, claiming more of her current incarnation's mind. The self known as Keely understood and did not fight the change but gave way, embraced all that had come before, so that when they settled back to earth there was only one mind, one complete being still wrapped in his arms.

Chapter 34

The next morning Larkin was livid. During the chaos of Fight Night, Shea had found a way to smuggle information to Rhiannon. The goddess had appeared to Talon at dawn and dismantled all that Larkin had worked so hard to put in place. Talon had first blustered at her but then caved as soon as he realized that his life was on the line, as were the lives of his newly discovered daughters.

Rhiannon had also enlightened Talon as to who had shot Seraphine. It had been a love triangle of sorts. Not that Larkin had ever thought any of these animals capable of such feelings. But although he had never been the brightest one in the room, the bear had at least been smart enough not to confess to killing Seraphine's little kitten the night before. Not that Prideaux's deviant nature had left much for the bear to torture.

Luckily for Larkin, he'd realized that the pieces on the board were in motion by the time the sixth fight was over. He'd immediately retrieved the early rough cut of the promo from the production company before Rhiannon got a chance to destroy it. He now had a copy safely stashed away. He'd also sent Prideaux to ground, just in case Llew showed up with his sweet little indulgence in tow.

Knowing all this made it easier for Larkin to watch Rhiannon try to eradicate his vision. Her people were all over the building, going through every bit of data they had, erasing, destroying, obliterating Triton Securities bit by bit. Some hacker had gotten past their firewalls to their internal company system as well, managing to hack into their financial accounts and freeze them all. The USL assets were now in Rhiannon's hands. And she intended to make the bear dance to her tune before she gave any of it back.

Rhiannon's team had already rifled Larkin's office. But there was nothing for them to find. Larkin had never been that stupid. He had learned patience a long time ago. He also knew what it was to hold a grudge. Llew and Rhiannon would eventually pay for their interference on the eve of his great victory. Larkin would win in the end. The shifters would get the genocide they so richly deserved. But first he needed to make a call.

All the employees' cell phones had been confiscated. As a precaution, Larkin had not brought his own into the office that morning. The company land lines had been disconnected as well. With a sigh, he announced to no one in particular, "It doesn't look like I'm needed. If anyone wants me, I'll be at the McDonald's down the road getting a late breakfast."

No one stopped him from leaving; no car followed him from the lot. Larkin drove to McDonald's, ordered from the drive-through menu, collected and paid for his food and coffee, and then parked. He left the car running, the air conditioner on so he wouldn't have to sweat. He ate slowly, savoring every bite. The coffee was hot enough to burn his lips, so he waited for it to cool. He drank about half of it, then reached under the driver's seat and pulled out his personal cell phone. He typed a simple text, *Rook takes queen,* and hit send.

Larkin then went about the business of cracking open the device. When he had it in pieces, he dropped all of it into what was left of his coffee. Smiling, he replaced the lid, gathered his trash, got out of his car, and threw it all into the trash bin.

Then he returned to his office.

Chapter 35

In Atlanta Lugos was uneasy. Murmur wasn't back, and Rhiannon had yet to reach out to him. True, with the goddess no news was usually good news. And yet something was coming; he could feel it. He reached out to Murmur, mind to mind. Their bond was a strong one, and the demon answered immediately, a question in his mind.

Come back to me.

As you wish.

Lugos withdrew from Murmur's mind and turned his full attention back to Keely. She pushed away the plate of Danishes he'd put in front of her.

"Stop trying to feed me, Lugh. Give them to poor Griffin, over there."

She was sitting on the couch, the sun streaming in through the window behind her. As a precaution for him, she'd turned on every light in the loft. He'd forgotten what it was like to have someone worry over him.

"He won't notice. He's in too deep right now," Lugos told her. Griffin had hacked into Triton Securities on his orders and was now holding all the firm's files and financial assets hostage while agents on the ground searched the building. The kid was thrilled to be a part of such a big operation. He just didn't know it was for Rhiannon or that he was saving shifters all over the world by freezing the company's assets. Rhiannon had Talon by the balls this morning, and Lugos was sure the goddess was enjoying it as much as Griffin was enjoying showing off his talents.

"No, she's right. I want a Danish," he answered, eyes still glued to the array of screens.

Lugos obliged and took him the pastries, then quickly slid away. His god-power was more noticeable than he liked this morning.

The air wavered near Keely, and Murmur appeared. Keely didn't flinch. Lugos wondered how long it would take her to start seeing the demon. That she could hear Murmur without Lugos's aid worried him; he didn't know what it meant. "Griffin, I'm going to step outside with Keely. Holler if anything happens."

Griffin didn't bother to look up. "Sure," he mumbled around the mouthful of pastry.

Keely understood the cue and rose from the couch. As a precaution, Lugos checked the hallway before letting her step through the doorway. Murmur followed.

"What?"

Lugos put a finger to her lips and then pointed to Murmur's door. She didn't argue until the three of them were inside the demon's loft.

As soon as they shut the door, she asked, "What was that all about?"

"Cameras in the hallway," Lugos replied, pulling her next to his body. Her skin still retained a faint glow from their lovemaking again this morning. He hadn't noticed it until now. "Well," he said, turning his attention to Murmur.

"She's got Talon dead to rights. There was a production team; all involved were shifters, so there's no spillage to worry about in that area. He's capitulating as we speak. He'll fall in line. I think you and Rhiannon will have to worry about rogue elements in the coming days, true believer types that will try to make a public splash without Talon's backing."

Talon was charismatic, but if he really believed in taking the shifters public, he'd be fighting back, so his capitulation told Lugos that Talon was more concerned with hanging on to his power. "And Larkin. Tell me how he reacted." Lugos watched Keely locate the invisible demon by following the sound of his voice.

Murmur shook his head. "Honestly, I didn't take much notice of him."

Lugos grunted. "I think he wants to be overlooked."

"Can I ask a question?"

"Of course, Keely. What is it?"

"Why did you notice Larkin in the first place?"

He smiled down at her. She had always been quick. "Talon told me that between the two of them, they run Triton Securities. So Larkin is more in the thick of it than he wishes Rhiannon to know. I got the impression that he was something of a mover of people. At first, I thought it was at Talon's direction, but then I spoke with Talon."

Murmur crossed his arms over his chest. "Sounds like you should join Rhiannon."

"Probably." He turned Keely in his arms and kissed her decisively. "I'll be back shortly. Stay in the loft with Murmur and Griffin. Tell Griffin that I'll be back within the hour."

"You're leaving from here?" Murmur asked.

Lugos gave a nod. "No cameras in your loft."

Keely captured his chin so that he had to look at her. "Be careful, Lugh."

He kissed the tip of her nose. "Stay safe. When I get back, we can begin that date."

She beamed up at him. "I'd like that."

Lugos grinned. "You'll like it more when I have you sitting outside a little café in France." And then he was gone.

Chapter 36

Keely feigned distress as she watched Lugh disappear, but that was for Murmur's sake. She was no longer overwhelmed with the new world in which she found herself; she'd done all this before. The memories were clearer now, from who Murmur was to Llew, Lugh, Lugos. She remembered that Lugh had used the demon to protect her once before. She could hear Murmur clearly and see him as well. It had taken discipline not to give her secret away when he abruptly shimmered into solid form. She'd gotten used to all their comings and goings before, in another life, another time. Her current incarnation's memories were still at the forefront, the easiest for her to draw on. She liked Keely's memories; they showed her to be feisty, funny, and loyal. They were so alike, in fact, that their merging had been far easier than in other lifetimes. She was Keely and yet so much more.

"I'm going back to Lugh's place," she announced, her eyes searching blankly just over Murmur's right shoulder.

"I'm right behind you," he replied.

Disappointment softened the hard lines around his mouth. He really was quite handsome in a dark and deadly kind of way. Keely wanted to tell him that she could see him now, but she remembered that he could not keep a secret from Lugh—that was part of the vow that bound a demon to a god. "Okey-dokey," she replied, aiming her bright smile at the demon's shoulder.

Griffin glanced up when she re-entered the loft. "Lugh said he'd be back shortly. About an hour, he thought." Keely held the door open longer than she should have so Murmur could pass through. Murmur had the ability to move in the form of vapor, but Keely wouldn't know that yet.

"Kind of tired. I'm going to go lie down." She pushed the door closed and began to walk away.

"Until he's back, you're on lockdown; that includes that door," Griffin grumbled, stabbing a finger at the loft's door. "I can't leave this station, so lock it for me. Please."

Murmur was about to smack Griffin in the back of the head for the disrespectful tone, but his hand halted just inches from the kid's scalp at hearing the tacked-on *please*.

"Yes, of course." She walked back to the door and turned the two locks. Griffin glanced over again, and she gave him her best bartender smile.

"Stop that," Murmur grumbled. "There will be no smiling at the boy."

Keely pursed her lips to hide her amusement. She was never truly safe when Lugh wasn't with her. Despite knowing this, she was glad to be fully back in the world, even with all its dangers. Keely sashayed toward her assigned room.

Murmur shadowed her, his body between hers and the loft's large-paned window. Keely ignored him, even though everything in her wanted to hug him for his absolute loyalty to Lugh and his diligence in protecting her. Because he mustn't yet know she could see him, her searching gaze landed on his chest and stayed. "I would like to be alone, please, Murmur," she whispered.

"I'll be right outside."

Her gaze never wavered, but she gave him a small smile of gratitude, then slipped inside the bedroom and locked the door.

***

Lugos materialized inside Larkin's office. It was empty except for Rhiannon's people. He went in search of the goddess. She was on the premises still; he could feel her on the opposite side of the building. Talon was probably with her. But Lugos chose to walk down the hall and turn the corner to Talon's office, rather than transporting again, just in case. When he entered the office, he found a chastised bear. "I'm looking for Larkin," he announced when Rhiannon turned toward him.

She raised a single eyebrow at Talon.

"I don't know. I've been with you since your arrival," replied the bear.

Rhiannon gave Lugos a shrug. "He's probably downstairs with the rest of the employees by now. All the offices have been searched. We're almost done here. Talon's going to get his company back, as well as control of the USL. I'm not sure he can keep it after today, but that's his problem, not mine."

"Did you find Alex?" Lugos asked her.

"No."

He could tell by Rhiannon's tone that she didn't think they ever would. That was on him more than on Rhiannon. "If you run across Larkin before I do, I want him."

Rhiannon's eyebrow rose again, but she didn't ask him why. "As you wish." She then turned back to Talon, and Lugos abandoned the office to head toward the elevator, where he came upon a few Triton employees getting off on this floor. Rhiannon's people had cleared them, satisfied that they were no longer part of the threat to expose the Pale to the world.

Shea was among them. She still wore Talon's collar from the night before. With a hand to her arm, Lugos detained her. The elevator doors closed to return downstairs. He waited until the three other analysts had walked away.

"Is Larkin below?"

She shook her head. "He was cleared about thirty minutes ago."

Lugos swore. "Where does he live?"

She gave him the address.

"That's only a few doors down from Talon's house. The one he shared with his sister."

Shea nodded. "Yes. Is that important?"

"Thank you," he said, letting her go. Clearly, she didn't understand the significance of the information she'd given him. Larkin was in this mess right up to his neck. He was the unassuming right hand of power, the puppet master. How often had Lugos seen that play out over the course of human history? Larkin had grown up with Talon and Seraphine. Two of the three had reached for leadership roles, while Larkin had preferred to remain in the background, moving pieces around the board. Lugos swore again and teleported himself to Seraphine and Talon's address.

He materialized in the backyard, slipped through the gap in the bushes, and hurried down the drive. As luck would have it, Larkin was just letting himself in through his front door. As Larkin put one foot across the threshold, Lugos teleported again and materialized right behind him. He then shoved Larkin forward, entered the house, and slammed the door behind him. The single push sent Larkin tumbling forward onto the carpeted floor.

"Start talking. I warn you, I'm not in any mood to hear a bunch of lies."

Larkin took his time climbing back to his feet, time Lugos was sure he used to school his features into something nonthreatening.

"What would you like to know?" Larkin asked, turning to face him. "Rhiannon's people are satisfied I'm no threat. Clearly you think otherwise."

"Where's the shifter you sent after Keely? I would like a word with him."

Larkin nodded. "By 'a word,' I assume you mean you'd like to kill him." He paused to mull the idea over. "I don't know precisely. He didn't show up at work today. And my phone is gone. I have no way of contacting him."

Lugos's hard expression didn't waver. He was surprised that Larkin had just admitted his involvement in the attack on Keely. He thought the puppet master would stonewall him. "Give me a name."

"Bo Prideaux. You should have an easy time accessing his employee file, home address, and whatnot." Larkin paused. "Is that all you wanted to know? The name of the wolf that scared your neighbor?"

"What do you think would happen if I told Talon that it was you who actually bled his sister out?"

Larkin appeared surprised. "I thought Blye did it. Some love triangle, I was told."

Lugos grunted. "She all but admitted to shooting Seraphine, but she didn't finish it. You were here. Seraphine wasn't on board anymore with the USL going public. She was now a problem, and you saw an opportunity to eliminate that problem. I read Seraphine's journal, what was left of it."

"That's one theory. Do you plan to tell Rhiannon that story?"

"No, but I won't hesitate to inform Talon that his right-hand man, the brains behind all his success, was the one who killed his beloved sister and the mother of his only two daughters. That is, if I have any suspicion that you've sent anyone after Keely again." Bo Prideaux was already a dead man as far as Lugos was concerned. He just didn't know it yet.

"Interesting that one human would mean so much to you."

Lugos ignored Larkin's remark. "The bear will tear you limb from limb for such a betrayal."

Larkin nodded. "Yes. Yes, he would."

"And that's not the worst of what I'd do to you. Do we understand one another?"

Larkin bowed his head, nodding. "Yes, I think we do."

Lugos turned to leave. Removing Larkin from the board wouldn't stop whatever was already in play. Better to know whose hand moved the chess pieces than to wonder.

Larkin's voice followed him. "If you don't mind my saying, I hope you have someone watching her now. Rhiannon may have the bear in line, but I fear there are others who'll search for ways to retaliate."

Lugos stopped in his tracks, his heart suddenly slamming hard against his chest. "To attack those under my protection is to seek death," he replied, his voice not quite human. Deep inside him, lightning arced; somewhere in the distant sky, the thunder answered. Lugos glared over his shoulder at Larkin. "Be sure to tell your underlings that," he said. And then he disappeared.

Chapter 37

Lugos materialized inside Murmur's loft and dialed Rhiannon. The phone rang twice before she picked up.

"I'm a little busy at the moment."

"Did Larkin have any time to contact anyone this morning?"

"I doubt it. We confiscated all the cell phones and cut the land lines. Why?"

Lugos wasn't sure how much to tell her, how much of his assumptions might prove themselves to be true. Larkin would be foolish to retaliate at this point. But regardless, the goddess needed to be warned. "He's the brains to Talon's brawn. We need to keep an eye on him. I have a bad feeling that the game is not over."

Rhiannon was silent for a moment. "Alright. Thanks for the heads up."

"You're welcome." Lugos then ended the call. He'd done what he could, what he was obligated to do for her. Now it was time to protect his own interests. He'd take Keely away for a while, away from any threat to her life. A remote island for a short time, he thought as he made his way back to her, to home. Rhiannon was aware of Griffin's talents and would take him under her protection for the foreseeable future. Educate the young man, bring him into the fold, explain the world of the Pale and the important role he'd played in protecting humanity.

Lugos had turned the second lock, his thoughts centered on the future, their future. He would marry her...again. He'd show her the world and then an extended honeymoon. Rhiannon would understand his need to have Keely all to himself for the next several years. Lugos was opening the door when he heard the sound of glass being pierced and the whine of a projectile as it moved through the air.

Time slowed.

He saw the joy on Keely's face turn to sudden horror, her eyes growing wide. Griffin was just rising from his chair. Murmur stood solidly between the window and Keely, a hole in his chest. And then Lugos was a blur of motion, inserting himself between her and Murmur. Two more bullets hit their target as he dove with Keely toward the floor. Lugos felt them knife through his body, hardly slowing. Keely jerked in his arms, and then they were landing heavily, his body wrapped around hers.

"No!" he screamed. It couldn't be happening again. He pulled back to see two circles of red begin to expand. The sky outside darkened. "No. no... no... No! You cannot leave me!" She still wore an expression of shock but it was changing quickly to one of abject grief. His hands came away bloody as he searched her body for a third wound.

Pain. He could see it in her eyes. Feel it in his own body. Tears leaked down her cheek. "You will not leave me again," he ordered, his voice no longer human. He ripped off his shirt and pressed it hard against the entry wound at her side. The other hand he pressed against the more lethal hole near her heart. Lightning slammed into the sidewalk outside, rattling what remained of the window.

"Send me," Murmur growled.

Lugos was only vaguely aware of Murmur and Griffin, his thoughts were solely for her. He began to pour himself into her. If only he could stop the bleeding this time... His golden glow moved down his arms into her wounds.

"I will not fail you. Send me now!"

Griffin was scrambling for a phone and the medical bag.

"GO! Bring him to me!" Lugos roared at Murmur.

"Put that damn phone away and go get Zee!" he commanded, sparing Griffin a token glance.

Griffin skidded to a halt, a look of sheer terror on his face.

"Go now!" Lugos bellowed. Another bolt shook the building. Outside the wind howled as the sky boiled in sympathy with Lugos's fear and fury. She could not die now. Not now.

Keely's hand rose to caress his cheek, a feather-light touch, her hand as bloody as his own and glowing with the same pronounced light. Instantly his gaze sought hers.

"I thought we'd have more time." Her voice was but a whisper.

Lugos's heart lurched as hers stumbled. "And we will, my love. I will not lose you again." She was slipping away too fast. She was bleeding out. He could feel the beginnings of her soul pulling away.

"Move. Let me see the damage," Zee demanded.

He did not know when the demigoddess had arrived, but he shifted the bulk of his body out of her way so she could begin to work to staunch the flow of blood. As she worked so did he. Lugos opened up the floodgates of his power saturating Keely's damaged body. This was his gift to her. This time he would not remain behind. He had kept his promise to her. She could not expect him to live any more lifetimes without her.

"You need to call 911," Griffin said.

Lugos didn't have time to explain. His entire world had narrowed to the whole of her, each strangled breath she took, each labored beat of her heart. Her struggle was his struggle, her pain his pain. Her eyes didn't waver from his. If he could keep her here by sheer will he would. He'd command her to live.

"She will die before they get here. Shut up and stay out of the way," Zee snapped. "I've patched up more wounds than you can ever imagine."

Lugos cradled Keely to him as best he could while giving Zee room to work. "You will not go alone this time. I will not be left behind to exist without you." His power flowed only one way, into her. On some level, Lugos was aware of it. He would not hold anything back this time. He would give her all, and if that wasn't enough, he'd cease to be. Their souls would not be parted, not ever again. Some part of him, perhaps his best part would go with her if she chose to leave.

"Ease up. One bullet went through, the other is lodged inside her. I've got to extract it and the wound is trying to close around it. I don't want to cause any more damage than she has already sustained."

Lugos tried to rein in the flow, but it was a struggle. Keely seemed to be drawing from him as much as he was pushing into her. With difficulty, he narrowed the current and gave Zee a nod. "Just a moment, my love. The bullet has to come out. Stay with me. Breathe with me."

Fear and desperation stared back at him. He knew it mirrored his own. She knew. *I thought we'd have more time.* She was remembering other lifetimes. She knew what was happening now had happened before. She had known what was coming. She must have also known that he'd failed her before.

Lugos panicked the moment Keely started to drift away from him. Her eyelid's drooped. A fresh tear leaked down the side of her face. "No! Fight, damn it. Fight for us!" He would bully her, coax her, tease her, rail at her if it would keep her from leaving.

Without looking up he snapped at Zee, "Call her!" When Zee didn't immediately obey him, Lugos growled, "She has always come for you."

Zee groaned but fished out her phone. With bloody hands, she dialed her mother. "I need you. Lugh needs you. She's been shot."

The storm outside and inside Lugos was growing. He had held back before, before when he'd possessed a tremendous amount of power. He no longer had that kind of power. And it would take an enormous amount to heal her. He had tried too long and too hard to be what he wasn't. What power he did have was draining from him fast. He was giving all of it to her, none of it was returning. The ground shook and the building rolled underneath them. He was failing her again.

"Don't bring the building down on us," Zee admonished next to his ear.

Lugos had no way of stopping the weather outside. It was merely a reflection of the storm raging inside him. Both would continue until Keely rallied or he departed with her.

Lugos felt Rhiannon's arrival, punctuated by Griffin's squeal of alarm. He was aware of Zee working hard to dig out the bullet. The moment the demigoddess was done he was going to give Keely the last of his power. Not because it would save her, but because it would free him to go with her. He was conserving, giving Zee time, breathing for Keely, taking on as much of her pain as he could, but they were losing her. He'd done this too many times not to acknowledge that they were fighting a battle that was already lost. Rhiannon was his last desperate hope.

"If she goes, I go," he told Rhiannon. Keely's eyes were closed now. She felt weightless in his arms, insubstantial despite all he'd given to heal the damage done to her mortal body.

"And what happens when she comes back and you aren't here?" Rhiannon asked.

There would be no coming back for either of them. There would be no reason to come back if his soul remained with her. "If she leaves, I'm going with her. Twin stars cannot revolve around each other forever." His gaze lifted from Keely's broken body to Rhiannon knelling next to him. "I am nearly done. I have very little power left to give. What I do have is not enough to heal her. Will you help us remain?"

"We don't know what it will do to her, how it may change her."

"It is a risk I'm willing to take."

Zee pulled the bullet from Keely's body. "Well, whatever you two are planning, you need to do it soon. I can start stitching but I don't have enough time to save her by myself. We're losing her."

Lugos could feel Keely's spirit unwinding from his. He dropped Rhiannon's gaze and turned to the only woman he'd ever loved. "So be it," he whispered and laid a kiss on each closed eyelid. He'd step into whatever lay beyond this existence with his soul surrounded by hers. Lugos gently brushed his lips to her cool ones and sent the last of his god powers, that which made him immortal into the woman cradled in his arms.

Her damaged body greedily drank all he could give, and still it wasn't enough. Lugos began to drift away from the pain with her, holding tight to the one whose soul he shared. He was only remotely aware of the chaos he was leaving behind; of Rhiannon cursing him, of Griffin sliding down the wall to the floor. And then there was another presence floating in the nothing with him and Keely. He sensed the thread of power wrapping itself around their joined but dying golden light. And then the two of them were being pulled back from the horizon.

Abruptly Lugos was back in his body, a bloody Keely locked in his embrace. Rhiannon's red glow encircled them. Strength steadily flowed into him, and through him into Keely's healing body.

"This still may kill her," Rhiannon cautioned.

Lugos allowed himself to feel hope where a moment ago there was none. "Not if it comes from me."

"What you ask has not been done."

"I ask it nonetheless."

Rhiannon sighed. "So mote it be."

After...

Chapter 38

It was the wrenching of one state of being into another by forces greater than herself that made her birth feel like death. She could not fight it, so she accepted it. He was with her. She could feel him pulsing through her and around her, a steady flow of power.

Slowly Keely became aware of another, one who burned hotly, one whom he shielded from her. Keely took her first breath, and he breathed with her. She felt the first moment her heart moved, beat, paused, and then beat again. His did the same.

Another breath. Another beat, perfectly in sync with his.

"I've got you, my love. Rest and heal. Dream only of me."

Keely could not respond. She could not move, could not reassure him. He was her world. She wasn't sure what had happened to cause him so much fear, so much pain, but she had shared it with him. She no longer needed all the power he sent to her, and so she gave back. It began to move between them, an ebb and flow. Back and forth, in rhythm with their heartbeats, as sure as breathing, as sure as the tide. She felt his lips brush across her own, and then he moved on to lay a kiss on each closed eyelid. She struggled to open them, to see him, the beauty of him, the strength of him, but her body refused to obey.

And then he was lifting her, holding her close to his chest, the heat of him sinking into her icy limbs.

She became aware again sometime later. He was still close. She could hear him moving about in the room. She lay in a bed. The sheets were cool and clean. It was easier to breathe now. Her heartbeat was stronger. Keely tried again to lift her eyelids, to call to him. But all she could manage was a moan. It was enough to bring him to her side.

"You are still very weak, my love. Rest. I will not leave you alone. We are safe here. Rest."

His fingers traced the contours of her face, the line of her jaw, the length of her neck. Keely sighed and let herself drift, content in knowing that he watched over her.

When Keely woke again, she knew something was fundamentally different. Power hummed between them. He lay facing her, his head on the opposite pillow. How would she know that?

"I'm waiting to see you, my love."

This time, Keely managed to open her eyes and find his blue ones. Whatever he saw in her gaze startled him. When he read the panic in her mind, Lugh raised his hand and ran his thumb over her bottom lip.

"I have missed those eyes of yours."

She felt weak. It was difficult not to close her eyes again, but his concerned expression worried her. "Lugh?"

"Shhh," he hushed. "I will love this color, too," he said, a small smile tugging at the corner of his lips. His so kissable lips, she thought.

"Color?" she asked, her eyelids drooping. She was so tired. Why was she so tired?

"They're the color of the night sky, with all the stars shining brightly, like diamonds catching the light. They're absolutely beautiful, like you."

Keely sighed under the combination of his compliment and his fingertips moving along her skin. "I love your eyes," she mumbled.

He carefully gathered her into his arms. She snuggled close, melted against the heat of him, and gave in to her exhaustion.

Keely didn't know how long she'd slept, but it had been long enough that he'd abandoned the bed. She could still feel him in the room. But there was another. One she'd felt before.

"If I have been remiss in saying so, let me say it now. Thank you for letting her heal here. But I intend to leave as soon as she is able. Any of our kin could return, and then it wouldn't be safe for anyone."

"Where will you take her?"

"Away."

"That's vague. You will need to find followers if you want her to flourish."

"No."

"Lugos."

"No, Rhiannon. She doesn't know what's happened. Not yet. She needs...normalcy."

Rhiannon snorted. "No one knows. What we did hasn't been attempted since the beginning."

"Shhh! She's waking."

"He's still waiting for your judgment. Murmur insists on keeping watch. And don't hush me. I'm practically her mother."

Lugh didn't respond. A moment later, he was moving toward the bed. Keely felt Rhiannon leave, heard the door gently close. Keely still didn't move, not until he came to her, touched her. His power flowed into her and back again, a reaffirmation of all that was between them.

"My love. Do you have the strength to look at me this day?"

Keely groaned, even though there was no more pain in her body. She knew she was different, no longer herself, no longer locked in the cycle of death and rebirth, but she didn't know what that meant, what lay ahead for them. And that scared her.

"Keely."

Her eyelids fluttered. The way he said her name felt like a caress, sounded like a prayer. "I'm afraid you will love me less now that I am changed," she confessed, her gaze unable to meet his. She remembered that her eyes were different.

"That is an impossibility."

"I am no longer entirely Keely, or any of them."

Lugh ran his hand through the fall of her hair. She watched as he let the strands of it slip from his fingertips like dark water to rest against her bare shoulder. "That is not true. They were part of you and you of them. They are the history of your beginning."

Finding the courage to meet his impossibly blue gaze, she asked what worried her most. "What am I now?"

He smiled gently at her. "You are like me."

Keely stared at him. She knew he spoke the truth to her. She didn't know how to be like him. Keely only knew that she never wanted to be ripped from him again.

"Don't look so worried, my love. I will teach you and protect you. But most of all, I will love you until you decide it is time for us to move on."

"Move on to what?"

"Whatever comes next for an immortal."

She reached for him then because she needed to feel the strength of him surrounding her, holding her, loving her. "I need you," she confessed.

He chuckled. "And I will always need you. But first I must be sure you are healed." He pulled back the sheet that was covering her. "It's only been two days. Rhiannon and I are both surprised at how quickly you are mending."

A web of ugly scars marred her left breast. The skin was newly knitted together and angry. Down low on her right side was another scar. That one looked as if it had been there for some time; the lines of the starburst were white and no longer raised like the wound near her heart. Lugh traced both areas with his fingertips before laying a kiss on each.

"This one at your breast will continue to heal. There will be no scars," he told her, his warm breath teasing her taut nipple.

Her body reacted to his gentleness and the reverence with which he touched her. Her womb clenched, sending a welcoming surge of wetness between her thighs.

Lugh smiled her. It was a wicked smile, full of promise of what he would do with her. He then moved down her body, slowly kissing as he went. The sight was erotic, he still fully clothed and she completely naked. He parted her thighs with kisses, his tongue swirling and then nipping until her legs were splayed as wide as he wanted. Lugh took a moment to gaze down at her, stark possession stamped in every line of his beautiful face. Whatever he read in her own expression must have pleased him, because that same slow smile returned, and he dipped his head down between her thighs to take what she offered.

Chapter 39

Keely studied her reflection in the full-length mirror. Lugh stood behind her, one hand splayed wide across her midsection so that he could press her firmly against his harder frame. He'd deemed her well enough to be released from her sickbed, though to be honest, she had healed quite sufficiently for him to do all kinds of wonderful things to her. She was now deliciously sore from his lovemaking.

Her skin had the same warm golden glow as his, yet here and there she spied areas that were almost red. Rhiannon's influence, he'd told her. Between the two of them and the multiple lifetimes in which she had absorbed his god-powers, Keely was now a goddess—but a goddess of what, no one could say.

"That knowledge will come in time," Lugh whispered near her ear.

"My eyes will scare people. What of Keely's mother? And Cutter and all the other mortals that made up her life? What are we going to tell them?" How do you extract a person from a life half lived without causing disruption in the lives left behind?

Lugh's hand wandered up to cup her scarred breast, distracting her from her worries. Whenever they touched each other, they shared power. It was as intimate as it was natural. The redness of her marred breast had decreased, just as Lugh had promised it would. Eventually there would be no scar except the one in her mind from the trauma of the event. She closed her eyes, gave up her worrying, and centered her mind on the way his power moved through her bloodstream, as hers moved through his.

"We will call your mortal mother from our exotic honeymoon destination. She will be upset that I didn't marry you in her church, but I will make a sizable donation in her name to ease her disappointment."

"But the eyes." They were like looking at pictures of the Milky Way that Keely had seen. The eyes were dizzying and entrancing but in no way human. Even she had a hard time looking at them. When half shut, they looked almost demonic.

Lugh turned her in his arms. "Look at me, Keely."

She let him capture her gaze.

"Beautiful."

His fingers glided down the length of her back to her hips, where he cupped her bottom, his hands hot and possessive. "They are the eyes of a powerful goddess newly born. You will learn to change them at will. But when your power rises, like when you are angry with me, or when you are giving your body to me and surrendering to the passion between us, these are the eyes that will dominate."

"Like when yours turn stormy, and I see the lightning flash inside the pupils."

"Yes. Exactly." He frowned. "You look disappointed."

She smiled up at him, her arms encircling his neck. "I thought the blue was their natural color, and the stormy ones were only when you were mad. I love how incredibly blue they are."

He kissed the tip of her nose. "I know you do. That's why they're blue most of the time." He then smacked her bottom to make her jump.

"Ouch!"

He stepped away from her, his power going with him. "First lesson."

She raised an eyebrow.

"Dressing yourself, 'cause if you don't, you're going to spend an eternity on your backside with me buried inside you."

Keely laughed and flicked her hair over her shoulder. "That doesn't sound entirely awful," she teased.

He gave her a lopsided grin, his own body's arousal apparent for her inspection. "Stop tempting me, Keely," Lugh said with a groan of frustration. "Rhiannon's hospitality is not without its dangers. I intend for us to leave here soon." With a wave of his hand, he clothed himself in jeans and a black t-shirt, though the bulge in the denim did little to hide his desire for her. "Now you try. Think of what you want to wear, and it will just be there for you."

Keely was skeptical, but she closed her eyes and pictured a simple white sundress she'd seen in a catalog, with halter-style top, mid-calf skirt, and belted at the waist. "Abracadabra," she added. But when she opened her eyes, she was still naked. "Damn it."

Lugh laughed.

"Stop it!" She had wanted to be good at this.

"Don't fret. It will take practice. But since you are so gloriously naked—" He started to move toward her.

Keely held up her hand and giggled. "Stop. I want to get this."

He immediately did as she had bidden, standing just out of reach.

"Do I need to wave my hand to make this work?"

"No, my love." He took a step closer and caressed her cheek with his thumb and fingertips. At once his power jumped to her. It tingled just under the skin, making her feel worthy and cherished. "All it requires is that you believe in yourself, in your ability to manifest what you want. You were human only a few days ago. There will be boundaries within your own mind that only you can overcome." His hand dropped to his side so that he was no longer sharing his power with her.

Keely nodded. That made sense. She closed her eyes because it was easier to concentrate that way. She felt the steady pulse of her power deep within. It was all her own, unique to her, its own notes, its own song. Again, she thought of what she wished to wear, of the feel of the fabric against her skin, of how perfectly it would fit. She opened her eyes to find him smiling at her, tremendous pride shining in his eyes.

"I did it."

"Yes. But you forgot your shoes." He held up a pair of sandals. "And this." In his other hand lay a ring in the center of his palm.

"You gave that ring to me before," she said, recognizing the band. She glided forward into his arms.

"Will you wear it again?"

It was a simple thing, a band of silver woven with a Celtic design, a never-ending knot. She had loved it then. She loved it even more now. "Of course, but it seems to me we have entirely skipped over the part where we date," she teased. Keely held out her hand so he could slip the ring on her finger.

Lugh's lips turned downward. "I wish that weren't so, but at least I still have the ability to spoil you rotten." The ring slid into place. He then lifted her hand and laid a kiss in the center of her palm. "Thank you," he whispered, his breath warm against her skin.

She cupped the side of his cheek with her hand, the stubble of his two-day beard coarse but real. "Whatever for?"

"For coming back time and time again."

Her eyes filled with tears. "Always. I love you."

He kissed her palm again and hugged her close to his chest.

***

Lugos had no words at that moment. His heart was too full and too sore from almost losing her again. If Rhiannon had not agreed to help, he would have traveled with Keely past that horizon. But now she was here, alive, and in his arms declaring her love for him, for the one who had failed her time and time again. Despite all the evidence, Lugos wasn't sure he was ready to believe that she wouldn't be torn from him still. There were his kin to worry about, his mother's wrath, Blodeuwedd's disdain. Lugos stiffened. He had never had reason to tell her about the bloody spring goddess. He would deal with that problem later, he decided. Right now, Murmur had Larkin's underling caged and waiting for him.

Lugos had refrained from unleashing his wrath on those who had thought themselves able to take what was his because Keely had needed him. Three days had now passed, and she was healed. Lugos needed to make good on his threat to Larkin.

"My love," he began, pulling away from her. "Murmur has tracked down the one who shot you. You will stay here while I go speak with him."

Keely laughed at him. "You aren't going to talk. I know you. He's a dead man."

Lugos didn't try to deny his intentions. "You're right. I will even admit that I am looking forward to it." He let her see the rage he'd been holding back from her while she healed. He had no doubt that his eyes had changed to reflect his anger. "That brings me to your all-important second lesson," he said, his voice still gentle for her sake, even as lightning streaked across his pupils. "Beware of what you promise or to whom you offer protection. Once your word is given, it can never be taken back."

Keely smiled up at him. "So, for example, if I were to promise to—"

Lugos put a finger to her lips. "There are no hypothetical promises. Once said, it must be seen through to the end. You are now like me, like Rhiannon, part of a larger universal order. There are real consequences to what I tell you."

Keely nodded, her expression suitably sober. "Lugh?"

Lugos raised an eyebrow. "Yes, my love?"

"I promise to love *you*."

He smiled down at her. "I will hold you to that promise, as will the Fates," he warned. "Even when you are spitting mad at me, I will hold you to it as you held me to mine." He then kissed her because he could do nothing else.

Chapter 40

Lugos had not wanted to bring Keely with him, but she would not be denied the right to lay eyes on the one who had tried to take her life. Rhiannon was there as well, once again declaring that it was her domain and within her rights to come and go as she pleased. They were in a subterranean building well away from the house, the pool area, and the barns. It was dank and very much like the dungeon in Lugos's Irish castle, but for the fact that this one still had an array of period torture devices. And a few not-so-old BDSM additions.

"Murmur!" Keely shrieked, just before she threw herself into the demon's arms. "I'm so glad you're okay!"

"Stop that!" Lugos snapped.

Murmur dropped his arms from Keely as if he'd been burned.

"I should be the only one you throw yourself at," Lugos declared.

Keely stepped back from Murmur and grinned at Lugos over her shoulder. "But I can see him now." She batted her eyes at Lugos and blew him an air kiss.

"Did I tell you I liked her?" Rhiannon teased.

"Yes, you have said that on many occasions. None, to my knowledge, was meant as a compliment," Lugos grumbled.

Rhiannon laughed. "I don't know why you try so hard to keep her in check. She was never obedient, even when she was mortal. Now, she's going to lead you on a merry chase."

"You're right. She's not all that nice," Keely complained, indicating Rhiannon. She then glided into the shelter of Lugos's body, just in case the redheaded goddess took exception to her observation.

"I like a challenge," Lugos told Rhiannon. He then tilted Keely's chin up so that he had her full attention. "Rhiannon saved us both, my love, and is as close to a mother as you will ever have in this new life. She deserves your respect."

Rhiannon raised an eyebrow at him. "Well, I'm not sure I want to claim her as my own. She has poor manners and goes all dewy-eyed when she looks at you."

"I think you're jealous," Lugos teased.

"Hardly. But she makes you happy. Perhaps that's reason enough to claim kinship with her."

Lugos stared at the redheaded goddess. Why would she do such a thing? "To claim kinship is to offer your protection," he reminded her.

Rhiannon rolled her green eyes. "Zee will have nothing to do with me. Keely is as close to a daughter as I am likely ever to have. And so, yes, despite her faults—and there are many—I claim kinship."

"Thank you. I think," replied Keely.

Murmur chuckled at the befuddled expression on Lugos's face. Then he bowed to Rhiannon, a goddess and the Pale's chosen leader. "Rhiannon, he is inside, in accordance with your instructions. I have not left my post for three days or nights. He awaits the gods' punishment."

With that ominous statement, Murmur stepped aside so the three gods could pass through the doorway. It was not locked, as there had been no need. Larkin's underling could not have hoped to get past the demon guarding the door.

"Shall we?" Rhiannon asked.

Lugos nodded, pushed Keely toward Rhiannon, and entered the cell first. It was very dark, the only light filtering through a small opening near the very top of the circular stone cell. The shifter rose from a sitting position on the bare floor. Lugos had no problem seeing him, nor the prisoner him.

"Oh, it smells in here," Keely declared, her hand rising to cover her nose. By the time all three gods were assembled in the small enclosure, the cell was illuminated by the telltale glow given off by each of them.

"Bo Prideaux." Lugos's voice had already lost all traces of humanity and sounded more like the roll of thunder.

The man Prideaux was as white as a sheet. His fear was palpable. He knew he was dead. His knees buckled and he knelt before Lugos.

"That's Mr. Red T-shirt," Keely informed them.

"Yes," Rhiannon replied. "I thought it was. Cutter gave me a good description."

Lugos did not move. He would not do so until Rhiannon took Keely from this place. She didn't need to see what he would do to this man, this shifter. Nor did she need to stand by and watch as information was extracted from him. "Rhiannon, it's time. Take Keely back to the house. I will be along shortly."

He felt Keely's hand on his arm, not a request to stay or to grant a reprieve for her attacker, but a show of solidarity. He gave her a nod, his eyes never leaving the condemned man. Without a word, Keely departed with Rhiannon.

Murmur then entered, closing the cell door behind him.

"I'm going to give you an opportunity to tip the scales of justice, Bo Prideaux. The only question I have for you is, what else does Larkin intend? He doesn't strike me as someone who would share his plans, but perhaps he slipped up. Give me something, and I will end your life quickly, regardless of the harm you've caused to those under my protection. Give me nothing, and I will make sure that you suffer fully for the crimes against me and those I hold dear. These are your only two choices." At no point did Lugos raise his voice, although to Bo's hearing it sounded like distant thunder. Lugos couldn't help that. He wasn't human, and he'd been pushed far beyond his limits.

"I...I...I can't...can't...give...wha...what I don't know."

Lugos had no sympathy for the mortal shifter. "So be it." He jerked his head at Murmur. The demon smiled grimly in return, then strode forward to begin.

Chapter 41

Lugos did not return to Keely immediately. He stalked across the estate to clear his mind and then showered at the pool house before searching out Rhiannon.

"Learn anything?" she asked.

He'd found her overseeing the repairs to one of her barns. Just before Keely was shot, someone had tried to set fire to the buildings. The culprit had been stopped and the fire quickly extinguished, but the damaged had remained until now.

"Larkin was behind it. I suspect behind this as well."

"Seems I need to pay a visit to Larkin."

Lugos shook his head. "No. I struck a deal with him. In the end, though, I think he'd wish you had."

"Using past tense already?" she asked, her pink lips pulled back into a tight smile.

Lugos mirrored that smile. "Seems appropriate."

Rhiannon grunted. "Well, get it done, then. And hurry back. I don't like babysitting."

Lugos laughed. "It's not babysitting if it's your own child."

Rhiannon grinned. "Just go."

Lugos gave her a mock bow and vanished, materializing a moment later in Talon's office. The god's sudden appearance nearly caused the blond bear to fall out of his chair.

"Talon."

When Talon had recovered somewhat, he muttered, "Lugos...Llew...what a pleasure. What can I do for you?" His face had turned ashen, and his sausage-like fingers fumbled among the papers on his desk.

"Actually, it's what *I* can do for *you* today."

The bear's head snapped up. "And that would be what?" Talon had no reason to trust Lugos, but he was ambitious and had learned to pounce on an opportunity when one presented itself.

Lugos sighed. "I made a deal of sorts with Larkin. He was not to come after those under my protection, and I would refrain from telling you who actually killed Seraphine. He failed to uphold his end of the bargain. I'm here to uphold mine."

"Blye killed her."

"No. Blye only shot her. Someone else dragged the wounded Seraphine upstairs to the master tub, ran the warm water, slit her wrists, and watched her bleed out before draining the tub and hiding the evidence of his involvement."

"And you know who that was?" A growl had entered Talon's voice, the beast in him rising.

"I do. I also suspect that Seraphine would have told you about your daughters herself if she had lived, because she loved you. She was training them, earning their loyalty, perhaps even eventually their love. Now, all that is gone. All because of him." Lugos knew he was laying it on a bit thick, but Talon liked drama. He lapped it up like honey.

Talon rose from his chair, his fists at his side. His bearish eyes were already changing. "Who."

It was no longer a question but a demand. Lugos smiled. "The man you trusted with everything. Larkin followed up on what Blye had started. Seraphine was a roadblock to his desire for you to take the shifters public. He used you. He slaughtered the mother of your children because she got in his way. I just thought you ought to know."

With that, Lugos vanished. He'd baited the bear, and now he had other things on his mind. He centered his thoughts on her, on the only home he had ever wanted.

He materialized to find her practicing clothing herself. She had added the hand wave and abandoned the abracadabra. Lugos said nothing, just watched as she cycled through three outfits with only one mistake.

"I think I'm getting the hang of this." She turned to him and raised a single eyebrow. "Do you like this one?" It was a leather catsuit with four-inch pumps.

"I think you know I'd prefer you without any clothes. Next to that, I like skirts on you."

"Without underwear," she added.

He laughed. "Yes, without underwear."

"Even the lacy ones?"

He went to her. "Yes, even the lacy ones." With a wave of his hand, he changed her outfit to a bikini with a sheer wrap around her hips.

"You forgot the shoes," she giggled.

He grinned down at her. "You don't wear shoes on a virgin beach. It's sacrilege." He then leaned down and captured her lips with his own. When she moaned in his mouth, he reluctantly pulled back. "It's time to start our honeymoon, my love. Trust me?"

His Keely nodded happily, still a little dazed from his kiss. "Always," she sighed, the soft curves of her body melting against him.

Lugos smiled down at her. He was home.

**The Legends of the Pale Series, Book 2
Coming soon…**

The Fate of Wolves

Chapter 1

Bigger, stronger, and faster than any natural wolf, the werewolf is thought to be the stuff of nightmares, of myth. It is not.

When still in control of itself and not blinded by madness, the werewolf is the perfect killing machine. But this…this was the work of one of their own, one who had surrendered all traces of his humanity.

It was not yet dawn, but Deegan's enhanced eyesight took in every detail. The trunks of the bare hemlocks, white pines, and balsam firs that circled this once damp and sleepy campsite were now splattered like a Jackson Pollock painting with blood, bits of intestine, and ripped flesh. Two tents lay in tatters on the still-frozen ground, their green and orange coloring barely discernible amid the blood-slick leaves and gore. No one had grabbed a rifle; no defense had been made. The attack had been too sudden, too unimaginable. Deegan stepped carefully through the kill zone, his boots as silent as the dead.

Deegan Volkov counted two dismembered campers. No, three bodies, he decided after a hasty assessment, and one boy, who had been badly bitten and was still bleeding profusely. This lone survivor had lost control of his bowels. Deegan's heightened senses easily detected the foul stench of shit mixed with the prevalent scent of death.

When Jerrod ran up to stand beside him, Deegan aimed a finger at the boy. "Do it. And then sedate Dax so Roland can change back into his human form. Waverly and Lorenzo will be here in a moment to help us."

The boy was all but catatonic, crouched in a ball and shivering at the base of a red-soaked maple tree. He was half covered in dirt and leaves. Earbuds still hung from his ears although their cord was no longer attached to anything. This group of humans had made the fatal mistake of setting up camp on pack lands. It was too early for the beginning of turkey season here in northern Vermont, but even poachers, if that was who they were, hadn't deserved such a gruesome end.

Obeying his alpha's command, Jerrod approached the survivor. He looked very young. Though as Deegan, too, moved closer, he realized that he'd misjudged; the boy was closer to eighteen. Deegan didn't want to add to the boy's terror, so he remained a short distance away but close enough to aid Jerrod should he need it.

Jerrod eased into a crouch beside the teen. The boy flinched defensively, but he was in no condition to flee. He'd lost too much blood and looked on the verge of passing out. Deegan listened as Jerrod muttered assurances that they were the good guys and that the boy was now safe. Out of Jerrod's pocket came the needle; the dose was delivered, and the boy was allowed to escape into unconsciousness. Jerrod then wasted no time field-dressing the worst of the wounds.

Roland was in his wolf form and had Dax subdued, but his struggle to hold the young werewolf was not without effort. Deegan had been aware of this from the moment of his arrival; he'd heard the muffled growling but had needed those few precious moments to watch Jerrod's healing work before confronting the inevitable. With a sigh, Deegan now turned toward the sounds of defiance. It took only one look at Dax for Deegan's heart to break.

The wolf's black eyes were rolled back in his head. Saliva and blood dripped from the long muzzle and razor-sharp teeth to mix with the leaves and mud. Though pinned by the neck against the ground by the larger Roland, Dax continued to fight. Roland's massive jaws tightened into the younger wolf's blood-matted coat, but the mad snapping and snarls did not abate. Roland had managed to save one out of four campers, for which Deegan was grateful, but this fact did little to balance the scales. Dax was out of chances. The pack knew it. Deegan knew it; he'd just hadn't wanted to face it.

Deegan silently approached and laid a hand on Roland's coarse fur. "Thank you, old friend." Roland didn't move, but Deegan felt Roland's heartbreak through the link they all shared. As he'd fought with Dax, Roland had managed to force the younger wolf past the ring of trees and into a natural depression that was not quite a creek bed but damp with mud from earlier rain.

"Hurry up, Jerrod. I need you down here," Deegan barked, his eyes not leaving Dax. Dawn was coming. They didn't have much time. Confident that Roland's grip would not slacken, Deegan took a few steps back up the slope, pausing in partial view of the campsite. He tore his eyes away from the black wolf and scanned the area. A few crows had gathered, but the rest of nature remained still, as if shocked at the violence done in this place.

Deegan had felt Waverly and Lorenzo's arrival even before he'd seen them. Lorenzo had dropped the bundle of clothes he held near the boy, and then ran back toward the truck. Jerrod had abandoned his patient and now came to Roland's aid. Sliding on the wet leaves the last few feet, Jerrod brutally jabbed the tranquilizer's needle into Dax's haunches, then scrambled back, his boots heavy with mud. Deegan watched and waited, as helpless as the others. He could no longer reach Dax's broken mind. He had tried. His son was beyond him now.

"It looks like it might be a family group," Waverly called out. He held aloft a set of drivers' licenses. His job had been to search the campsite for personal effects.

The pack would dispose of the bodies, clear the site, and then deal with the campers' vehicle. Later in the day, Lorenzo would lay a false trail in the event a search party was formed. The trail would lead away from the Volkov lands to eventually peter out, leaving those who might follow it no clear understanding of what had happened. These dead campers would be just another unsolved disappearance. The authorities would never find any remains—Deegan's pack would make sure of it. His job as alpha was to protect them all, no matter the cost to others or himself. Maintaining the safety of the pack always came first.

By the time Lorenzo returned with the tarps, Dax's wolf body had stilled. Deegan realized that they were becoming far too good at this. There were three humans to dispose of, one more than last time. It would be more complicated this time, for there was a survivor to consider. Through no fault of his own, the boy was now one of them.

Roland's position had not wavered as the tranquilizer took effect; his teeth remained buried deep in Dax's fur. Only his eyes moved, asking the silent question of Deegan.

"The boy's been laid in the bed of the truck. Lorenzo has started the transfusion," reported Andre, Deegan's second, who had just arrived at the godawful scene.

The sound of bones cracking, so familiar to all of them, filled the silence as the pinned wolf's bones began to reshape themselves into something more human. Dax's unconscious body was beginning the transformation process. Eventually, a boy not much older than the surviving camper would be lying at Roland's feet. The jaws of the larger werewolf remained in place, his eyes once again asking the question of his alpha.

"It has to be done," Andre said. His tone was as grim as his expression.

He was right, of course. The expedient solution would be to allow Roland to break Dax's neck, to bite clean through the fragile, emerging human flesh, but Deegan didn't want his son to die that way. He didn't want the last memory of Dax to be as the bloody monster lying at Roland's feet. With a wave of his hand, Deegan motioned his old friend to release his hold.

The order was immediately obeyed. The werewolf gave Deegan a sorrowful glance and limped off toward the bundle of clothes that had been brought for him.

"I will not ask it of Roland, Andre. I'll do it. It's my responsibility." There was no argument from the others. Deegan knew there wouldn't be. He held out his hand to Jerrod. "Give it to me."

Jerrod swallowed, the only sign of his unease, but then the syringe of morphine was produced and given over. "His heart might stop before we get him home," Jerrod warned.

Deegan knelt beside his naked son and nodded. Then, just as the sun kissed the horizon, he inserted the needle into the smooth pink flesh and depressed the plunger.

Other Books and Short Stories by Tarrant Smith

Enchanted Darkly
Bound Darkly
Kept Darkly
Surrendered Darkly
Resurrected Darkly

Dark Craving
Blood & Fire
Forbidden

About the Author

Tarrant Smith graduated from Queens College in North Carolina with a degree in English literature. She currently lives in the beautiful town of Madison, Georgia with her husband, son, dogs, and the odd assortment of stray cats. As a self-described kitchen witch, she has always sought out and nurtured the magick that can be found in the mundane trappings of everyday life. For more information about the author and her other series please go to www.tarrantsmith.com

Made in the USA
Columbia, SC
09 April 2019